IYRIS
Disaster Kingdom
The Dark Sea
Metal Kingdom
N
W
E
S

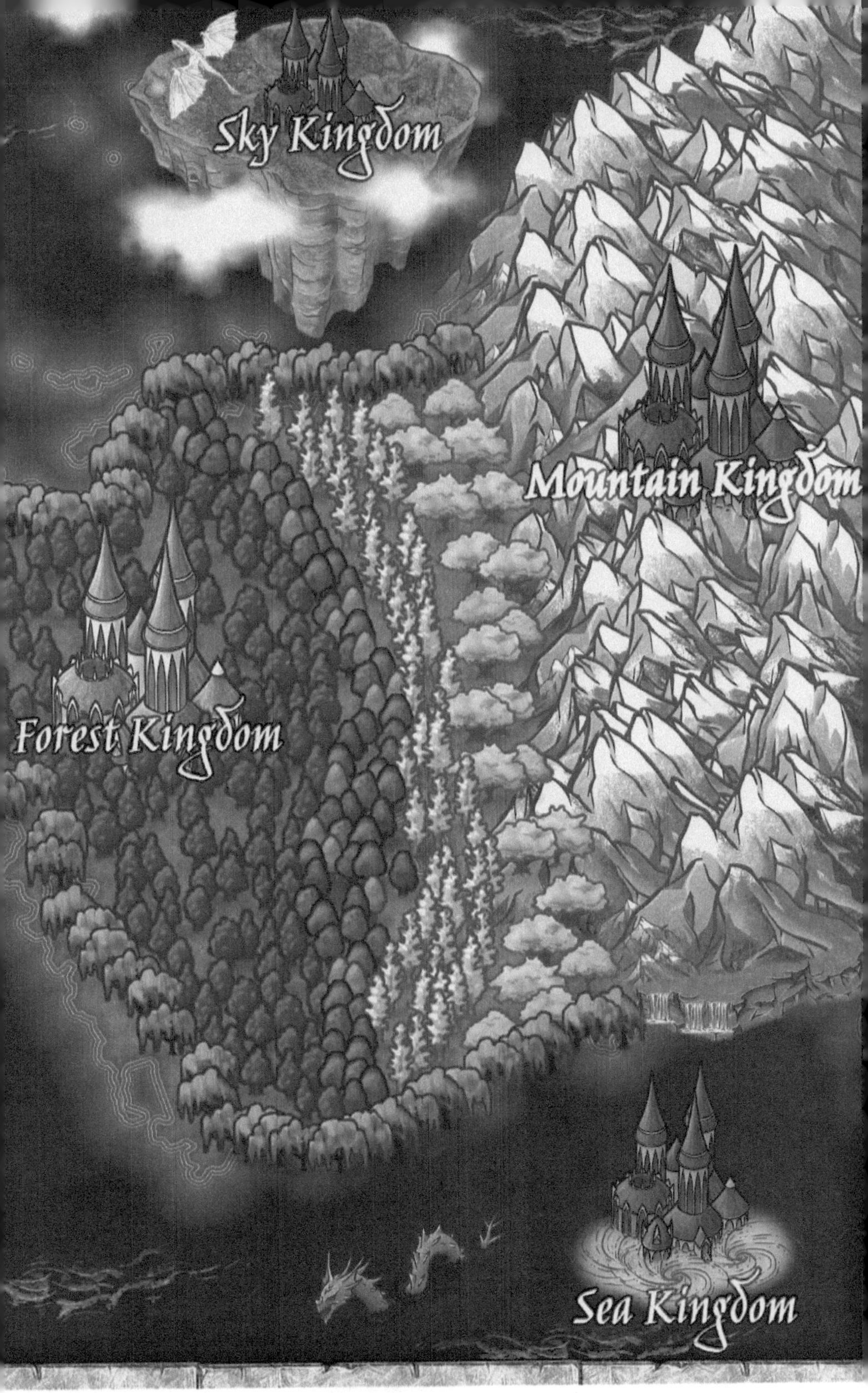

Sky Kingdom
Mountain Kingdom
Forest Kingdom
Sea Kingdom

Also by Shaquilla Lunsford

<u>Fall of the Dragon King Trilogy:</u>
After the Fall of the Dragon King
Rise of the Phoenix Queen
Downfall of the Blood King

<u>The Forces of Nature Series</u>
Heart of the Forest

Author's Note

The Forces of Nature is a New Adult Romantasy series of interconnected standalones that touch on some topics such as torture, abuse, rape, and sexual assault (not by MMCs) that may be triggering for some readers. Due to this, and other adult content, all books in The Forces of Nature Series, including Heart of the Forest, is intended for readers 18+.

Please contact the author if you have any questions.
shaquilla.lunsford@gmail.com

Nature is about balance.

Destruction is necessary for resurrection.

Contents

Pronunciation Guide

The Nature Kingdoms

Akabe – uh-kah-bay   **Alyvia** – pronounced Olivia

Amethyst – am-uh-thist   **Anore** – uh-nor-ray

Forest Kingdom Cities

Boric – boar-ick   **Dirk** – durk

Corr – core   **Gris** – grease

Hoark – hork   **Iyris** – pronounced iris

Laark – lark   **Siris** – sigh-ris

Sorlic – sir-lick   **Sorren** – sore-ren

Terc – tur   **Verdis** – ver-dis

The Princes of Nature

Thatch – that-ch   **Therek** – there-ek

Theseus – thee-see-us   **Torm** – torm

Other Characters

Lurk Sempris – lurk sem-priss

Zyran – zur-rye-an

Silent.
That is what I'm encouraged to be.
Don't speak too loudly.
Don't think too boldly.
Don't assume your life has worth.

I am left alone in this darkness.
You turn a blind eye at my bruises.
You smile despite my tears.
You say you love me
But refuse to acknowledge my cries.

But there's this heat rising
With every punch
Every sneer
Every derogatory term.

There's this flame flaring.
This inner power that says
I don't have to take this.
That I don't deserve his spite.
His cruelty.
Your blatant disregard.

And when it grows...
When it becomes greater than his power over me,
When my body cries out no more,
And my soul begs for fight instead of flight,

I will be the one smiling
But I won't turn away.

No, I will watch with glee
As I burn his kingdom to the ground.

The Four Princes of Nature are cursed with the power over life and death, but one being was never meant to carry both. As the princes succumb to the darkness flowing through their veins, the kingdoms reflect their changing hearts. A flicker of hope still remains, but only the Princesses of Disaster can reverse the curse and restore balance to the forces of nature.

- The Forces of Nature Series

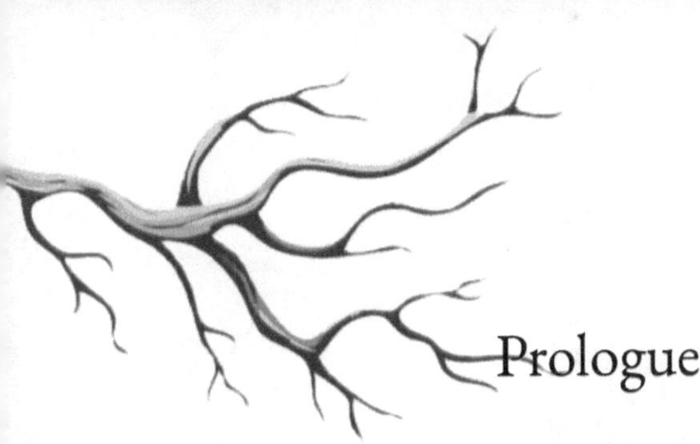

Prologue

Prince of Forest

The forest moaned as if in pain, the trees crumbling in on themselves with branches almost dragging the ground. Leaves crackled on too weary arms and fell. Plants big and small wilted and molded to the earth, their once lively green now a resigned brown or deadly black.

A dyrewolf howled forlornly somewhere in the distant. An owl cried out its woes. Even the insects' once lively calls turned to melancholy twitters. Then they all went silent under the stars' watchful gaze. Waiting. Hoping. Fearing.

His normally silent footsteps were resounding in the cold night, even as his black attire blended into the shadows. The breeze ruffled his dark hair, beseeching him to save that which he once lived to protect. But the moonlight reflected off eyes so dark, they were almost black – eyes that had once been as lively a green as the forest itself – as he stood inert in the middle of the destruction.

Piece by devastating piece the forest was fading away, like the light snuffed out from a candle. Like the light in the once spirited Prince of Forest. In the absence of light, no hope remains...only death.

Chapter 1

Ember

I squinted at the early spring light from my perch on the old sycamore tree. Night time was falling but the light still stung my swollen right eye. Another black eye. You would think I would be used to them by now. You would think I would have learned to avoid his wrath. I snorted, then winced from the still healing bruising along my ribs. As if that had saved my mother in the past.

A shot of pain flooded my chest at the thought of my mother. She'd been gone over eleven years now, leaving little nine-year-old me to bear the brunt of his drunken rage. I never understood why she didn't take me with her. Could I not fit in her suitcase? I would have willingly twisted myself into a pretzel to do so. Anything to escape this prison as my mother...and then my brother had. As soon as he turned eighteen he snuck out of the house, a quick hug and promise to rescue me someday on his lips. That was six years ago.

Sighing, I looked out over the two hundred acres of apple orchard to my right and the infinite forest to my left where the giant peaks of Blue Mountain could be seen. In the center, the laborers' cabins sat, all in nice little clustered rows. The forest was my escape, but the orchards were my family's pride and joy. The Lanxter apples. The best apples in the state – or at least they used to be.

A large stream split the orchard and forest in half even as it branched and disappeared into both. A family of deer carefully slipped from the forest to take a drink as I watched, their ears twitching every which way. A pair of cardinals called as they swooped past my tree to the ones below. The old sycamore sat tall on a hill looking down at the forest and orchard. Its branches stretched wide as if it could keep the disease of the decrepit ranch house behind it from spreading to the life below.

I glanced back at said house. It felt small despite its two stories, five bedrooms, and industrial sized kitchen. The blue paint on it was peeling and the wooden, wraparound porch groaned in strong winds. The barn that sat to the right of it used to be a rich red. Now it was rundown and the color of long dried blood – a color I was well acquainted with. When I was a kid it used to hold a couple of horses and the chickens, back when my father was still pretending to love my mother. The horses were the first to go, but a few chickens remained.

The house was quiet at the moment, but then, the old pickup that usually sat in the driveway had rode into town, most likely to replenish the gin, beer, or whiskey.

Plus, there was no one else left, but me.

I turned back to the deer who were now grazing along the stream, one making sure to serve as lookout. A gentle breeze danced by, pushing my long, curly hair into my eyes, and swaying the grass around the deer's long legs. Oh, to be as free as the wind. To bound through the trees as carefree as the deer. To sing as cheerfully as the birds. Yet, despite the knowledge of my mother and brother's freedom, and my twenty-first birthday next month, I was still trapped.

The truth of the matter was, I had nowhere to go. I was not like my few friends at school who went off to college. I'd made good enough grades to get by, but with the number of days I had to stay out due to my father, my grades weren't college worthy. When graduation came, I found myself void of friends and the excuse to avoid home. Now I worked full time taking care of the orchard and household.

I sighed. I would have to avoid the orchard for a few days until the swelling in my eye went down. Dad didn't often hit me in such a noticeable place, but with it being the anniversary of my mother leaving...

The laborers stayed out of it. Needing the money more than they needed to save me. I had no doubt they could hear my father's rants from the cabins some days, or when we used to have weekly breakfast up at the house back when my mother still lived here. But besides an occasional pity infused stare, they stayed silent. Especially after the last one to stick up for me ended up in the hospital with broken ribs and a shot to the leg. Cops didn't even bother getting involved. Sheriff was old army buds with Dad and said, on his land, my father's word was law. In other words, "Mind your own damn business or face the consequences". So, yeah, I was on my own. At least until I found the courage to get away from here.

I jerked as I heard the tell-tale sound of tires on gravel and turned to see said father pulling in. Any second now he'd start calling for me. Just as soon as the alcohol kicked in. He'd likely already started on it on the way back from the store. Luckily, I had left dinner on the stove so I could remain hidden until his drink finally lulled him to sleep.

I flinched at the sound of the door slamming and watched him stumble slightly, bottle already at his lips. My face twisted in disgust, and I shivered as I turned away. I tucked my knees close to my chest, tears slipping from my swollen eyes. The wind caressed me sadly as I implored it to take me far away. Anywhere. God, please *anywhere* but here.

Chapter 2

Ember

Today was peaceful for once. I'd woken early, prepared breakfast, eaten, and slipped out to do chores all before Dad had managed to slip out of bed with his latest hangover. I snorted. As if that ever stopped him.

"The best cure for a hangover is to drink, Em," he'd told me once. He'd flinched at the morning sunlight, chugged some Jack Daniels, and then smacked his lips. "See, magic."

I'd laughed it off then. Still too young to realize that Dad's good days were the true miracle. A miracle that occurred further and further apart as I grew older. It was best that I just stayed out of his way.

Shaking my head in resignation, I lifted my hand to wave to George, the leader of the laborers, who was high up in one of the apple trees pruning branches. He waved back with a grin, but I could see the underlying concern in his eyes. My black eye had only just healed enough for me to be back out and about, and although I knew he wanted to ask about my absence, he, like everyone else, kept his mouth shut.

"Well, hello there little missy," Frank greeted me as he finished the grafting on one tree that had already been pruned. Others were raking, laying down new wood chips, planting new trees, or other various tasks.

Yet, it seemed like there was less and less work getting done. I tried not to dwell on the fact that despite being two hundred acres, only about fifty of it was being maintained. The number had dropped over the years as my father fell deeper into the bottle and fewer laborers returned each season. I tried not to think about what would happen to me the day they didn't come back at all. When there were no more profits to supply the liquid love of my father's life.

"Hi Uncle Frank," I replied, smiling sweetly despite the foreboding I could feel pressing down on me as of late. We weren't related of course, but everyone addressed the older male with the peppered beard and hair this way. He had those rooster feet around his eyes that reminded you he liked to smile often. He always complained about how I didn't smile enough, so I always tried to wear one just for him.

"Where you been missy? These grafts aren't going to finish themselves," he teased. His grin, like George's, held concern, but he still preceded to show me where to place the new grafts. For once I wished he would do more than show concern. That he would ask questions. That he would do something to help me, but how could I ask him or George to risk their livelihood? Maybe they would if they understood the extent of what I suffered. Maybe if I ever found the courage to show them the scars they couldn't see.

The day went by quickly, and before I knew it, I was helping clean up for the day: collecting gardening tools, and raking up the trimmed branches. As I did, I frowned as I noticed that a few men and women were missing. Maybe they were sick? Although, I found the idea unlikely this early in the season.

"Hey Uncle Frank, George. Are some people not here today?" I turned to see them sharing a look, and my frown deepened as my gut twisted with trepidation. Please no. I couldn't take more bad news. I wasn't even sure if my father was aware of just how little acreage remained of the Lanxter Orchard.

"Um, yeah. Nothing to worry about little one," George assured me, but he wrung his hands as he threw glances at the other man. "Some just found better places to work for the season." I lifted a brow. It was unusual for the laborers to just up and leave during the harvest. They tended to travel to the same farms every year once they started and remained there for the entirety of the season.

"Really? Right now?" The two men shared another look and the dread in my stomach flared higher. "I thought the pay was pretty good." At least it used to be. To be honest, I wasn't sure how Dad managed the financials when he spent so much time doing other more "interesting" activities. His drunken laughter mixed in with the screams of his latest conquest ricocheted through my head, and I hid my shiver of disgust.

"Well." Uncle Frank scratched his scruffy beard. "The pay has gone down considerably over the years." George shot him a look that said he wasn't supposed to reveal this, and Uncle Frank winced. "Like we said. Nothing to worry about."

But I didn't believe them. My father's reputation plus the lack of pay was not conducive to keeping staff, and I worried that someday, sooner than I realized, I would have to break it to him that they'd all quit. Worse. Then I'd really be all alone.

I don't generally stick around for meals, except for dinner where I was required to sit across my father at the dining table and pretend we were still a family. On his good days, he'll ask me how my day went, or tell me dinner was delicious. On his bad ones.... well those were more typical and usually consisted of him complaining about how much of a wasted space I was, and how I should have left with his "good for nothing" wife and loser son. If only he knew how much I wished it was so. But I'd learned very young that wishes weren't made for girls like me.

After the already bad news about the laborers, the last thing I wanted was for the sheriff to stay for dinner. He came over for a chat and beer or two occasionally, but the fact that he let my dad get away with basically murder always put me on edge around him. A person who allowed evil so openly, couldn't be further from it themselves. Oh, how I longed to be wrong.

Dinner started off fine. Dad and the off duty sheriff chatted about the good old days as they chugged beer. I mostly tuned them out, waiting for it to be acceptable for me to excuse myself to my room.

"I'm telling you, women aren't loyal." I frowned at the disgusted tone of the sheriff and lifted my head slightly to peer at him across the dinner table. "They're only good for two things. Bedding and cooking." I crinkled my nose in revulsion and lowered my eyes again. What was this, the 1800s?

"You ain't never told a lie," my father agreed with a snort.

"Luckily you have one already around to do just that," the sheriff continued. I stilled. Surely, he didn't mean me. It was silent for so long, I risked a glance up. The sheriff was hungrily staring at my chest as he took a swig of his beer. After a few seconds, he lifted his eyes to mine and winked.

"Have you broken her in yet?"

I almost choked on my nausea as I waited for Dad's response. I glanced over to him to find him considering me as if he'd never realized I'd grown into a woman. My stomach rolled with horror. The look on his face was anything but fatherly. He'd never done that to me. Physical and mental abuse, yes, but never sexual. God, please don't let this turn sexual. I knew that it hadn't always been consensual with my mother, but my god, I was his *daughter*. Her screams for him to stop still haunted my dreams some nights. In my mind, I was still that little girl curled in the closet with my brother, hands pressed to my ears as I cried.

I gulped and stayed still, hoping if I didn't move that they'd forget I was here.

"No, not yet," Dad said finally, chugging his beer.

"Should let me have a go at her. Wouldn't want her to go uneducated or anything." I was going to puke. They were drunk, talking about raping me in front of me, and I was going to vomit all over the dining room table.

Dad squinted as if he was actually considering it, but then shook his head. "No, not yet. Maybe another time." Yup, I was definitely going to throw up.

"Can I be excused?" I whispered, barely managing to keep the bile down. Dad tilted his head, and the sheriff gave me a knowing glance, but finally I was dismissed with a hand wave. I darted from the table, making it to my bedroom – where I locked the door – and further to the bathroom just in time. There went dinner.

I sat on the cold bathroom floor wondering what I had done in my life to deserve this. To deserve my father *thinking* of letting his best friend rape me. I lay with my head propped against the cold tub, my stomach still rolling.

I need to escape, I thought sullenly, hopelessly. But where would I go? It was the same question I asked myself whenever I thought about leaving. I had no money. No real family. And no idea how to live in the real world. I was trapped. Tears welled and ran over. Trapped in a never ending nightmare. Where was my superman? Hell, I would have called CPS a long time ago if I thought they'd actually help. But I was alone. So painfully, painfully alone.

Chapter 3

Ember

I walked between the apple trees trying to understand what I was facing. The late summer heat was dwindling and we were well into the harvest season, but the trees were overburdened with fruit. Equipment lay discarded and abandoned. And when I did an actual count of the acreage we had left, it was much less than the fifty I'd been told by George and Frank at the end of last season. Mind you, I rarely had time to walk the full orchard myself, and I'd never had a reason to doubt them before, but when I'd peeked at the profit brought in last month versus last year, it hadn't added up.

We should be looking at bringing in at least $125,000 for the year if we still had fifty acres up and running, but based on what I saw, we were nowhere close to reaching that goal. As I continued to examine the trees around me I realized we wouldn't. There wasn't enough acreage...and there weren't enough laborers.

I felt nauseated and dizzy, and I leaned against a tree fighting to catch my breath. I inhaled deeply, trying to tame my rolling stomach, to stop the tears blocking my view of the rotting apples at my feet. I had to do something. Maybe I just needed to work extra hours to pick up the slack.

Maybe see if George and Uncle Frank could convince the other laborers to do an extra shift for the next few weeks. I could fix this. I had to fix this. My life depended on it. I glanced up at the quickly receding sunlight. And I needed to get home and make dinner before the crash of the great Lanxter dynasty wasn't my only problem.

Maybe God hadn't forsaken me fully because somehow, despite my utter exhaustion and barely restrained sanity, I beat my father home. I quickly whipped up some barbecue pork chops, green beans, and mashed potatoes before warming up leftover apple cobbler for dessert. I was hoping the cobbler would be enough to distract him from asking about the business.

Just as I was placing the food on the table, I heard the front door slam and male laughter down the hall. My blood ran cold. Dad had brought the sheriff again tonight. He'd been coming over more and more lately since that last dinner where they discussed "breaking me in". Both of their gazes had become more lingering, and I found myself wearing the baggiest clothes I owned in hopes they wouldn't follow through with the threat. I swallowed past the bile in my throat as I glanced down at my outfit. I hadn't had time to change when I came back from the orchard so I wore a tank top and jean shorts. Way too revealing for comfort, and too late to do anything about it.

"Ember!" Dad called, and I flinched as he and the sheriff strolled in. "Good, you finished dinner. We're starved." He already had a beer in his hand as he settled at the head of the table and started making his plate.

"Ember," came the rough voice from beside me.

I swallowed and turned to face the burly man. "Sheriff," I managed. "I'll grab you a plate." The sheriff's eyes raked down my body, making me feel like I was coated in filth before he gave me a lopsided smile and took a seat.

"You do that sweetheart."

I spun and went back to the kitchen, already heaving before I even reached the sink. I quickly ran water to wash away the evidence. I gritted my teeth as I took deep breaths.

"You can do this Ember," I whispered. "Just eat as fast as you can and you'll be fine." Even if the thought of food made me want to hurl all over again. "You can do this," I whispered again and turned to return to the dining room. I froze in place when I saw who stood before me.

"You were taking a long time. I got worried," the sheriff said. I swallowed, but my mouth was dry.

"I…" I swallowed again, my heart trying to escape from my chest. "I was checking on the cobbler." I gestured at the oven where it still sat. "I was just headed back." I hurried past him, but that was where my mistake lay. You never turn your back on the enemy, and I didn't see the hit coming. He smacked my butt so hard I gritted my teeth against the sting, and the too tight squeeze afterwards. I froze and felt his hot, alcohol breath down my neck. I fought my revulsion as I saw his cruel smile in my peripheral.

"One day soon," he whispered, "I will come collect what has been promised to me." Then he strolled from the kitchen again. I stood there hyperventilating, knowing I just dodged a bullet, but eventually what little luck I had would fail. And then I would lose what little I had left to give.

Chapter 4

Ember

When I woke in the morning, I had a feeling of such overwhelming apprehension I cringed. It was the same feeling that had haunted me for weeks now, ever since I learned about the diminished acreage. My talk with George and Uncle Frank had confirmed what I feared. We had less than thirty acres remaining and the laborers continued to disappear. Something told me this was going to be another very bad day.

I wasn't wrong. From the start, I burned breakfast, so caught up in my anxiety that I was jumpy and too absent-minded to notice the sausage I'd left to cook had turned to smoke. Then I spilled his favorite coffee – the last bit we had in fact – all over the floor in my mad dash to take the pan off the stove. In my haste, I grabbed the skillet with my bare hand only to release it with a hiss and dodge the spitting grease that went flying. My elbow then decided to overturn the flour bowl on the counter. And that's how he found me. Flour, grease, and coffee all over the counter and floor with smoke billowing through the kitchen.

I could hear his teeth grinding together from the doorway.

"I'm sorry Daddy," I begged quickly. "I'll clean it up. I swear." I didn't meet his gaze and scrambled to do just that, only stopping to peek over when he'd said nothing for several moments. He still stood in the door, his arms crossed, an unreadable expression on his face. It sent a cold chill down my spine.

"Be sure you do. I expect this kitchen to be cleaned and breakfast on the table in twenty." His voice was heavy with reproach and warning. I nodded vigorously, relieved to find I'd supposedly received his mercy this morning. Breakfast went smoothly after that. The rest of the day did not.

His old truck broke down again, and he spent most of the day shouting and tinkling with it. I'd gone to the orchards to find that not only had more than half of our remaining laborers left overnight, but that they'd stolen a chunk of the harvested apples as well. I spent the majority of the day making up for the missing workers so I was late making dinner. By the time I remembered, the sun was low in the sky, and Dad had already started on the gin. Who was I kidding? That had started at some point during the truck repair rant.

"I'm dead," I muttered to myself, my body sore all over. "I'm so dead. And I haven't even told him about the workers and apples yet." Fear. Unadulterated fear squeezed my gut as I raced to get back to the house. I didn't want to think about who would be invited over again if I stepped out of line. Disgust and shame flashed through me, and I bit it back desperately.

I ran in already spewing apologies as I quickly whipped up a dinner of Salisbury steaks with potatoes and greens. His dark gaze followed me as I did, but he said nothing. Somehow, that was scarier than his rants. We ate dinner in silence and as I picked up the plates to wash the dishes, his fingers started tapping on the old, wooden table.

"Is there something you need to tell me Ember," he said quietly. Too quietly. A slight slur to his words. *Oh gods.* He knew. I swallowed past the lump in my throat.

"Um...well.... I," I sputtered.

"Spit it out child," he sneered, and I flinched.

"Most of the laborers left, and they stole some of the apples." I froze and waited, not daring to take my eyes off the dishwater in front of me.

"And how could you let this happen?" Me? How was I responsible for employee displeasure in a business I didn't even own?

"Are you incapable of doing anything right?"

I said nothing, still frozen by the sink. Suddenly, awareness shot through me and I ducked, just missing getting a gin bottle to the head. The glass shattered against the wall, and I barely had time to spin around before pain shot through the left side of my face. I fought to stay upright as blood flooded my mouth.

"You good for nothing piece of shit! I have been patient." Backhand to the face. "I have raised you to the best of my ability." Gripping of the hair in a tight fist. "And all you've given me is pain! Is it not bad enough that I have to look at your face and be reminded of that betraying whore of a mother of yours?"

My eyes widened in horror and before I had a chance to fight back, he was shoving me face first into the dishwater. I struggled fiercely, trying to loosen his grip. Panic rushed through my veins as bubbles escaped from the corners of my mouth.

"I should have gotten rid of you when I had the chance," he sneered above me. "You have always been a worthless waste of air and you always will be. You couldn't even give the sheriff a decent lay."

I screamed, taking in water as I did so. He was going to kill me this time. Like really kill me. My hands reached franticly around me, one touching the handle of a small knife. Not stopping to think, I swung it back. He swore fiercely and released me. I yanked my head from the water, choking and sobbing uncontrollably. I staggered away from him, taking in the knife protruding from his arm and the blood pouring onto the floor.

"You bitch," he snarled. And then he was coming for me. I screamed and dodged, but he caught me by my hair and yanked me to the floor. I fell so hard the air was knocked out of me, but I never got a chance to get it back because then he was kicking me. In the stomach. In the chest. In the head. Agony shot down every nerve ending as I curled into a ball. Then he was squatting over me and pummeling me with his fists. All of his rage amplified and concentrated on me.

Reaching out blindly for the alcohol bottle next to his chair, I turned and smashed it into his face. He roared, hands going to his eyes as I darted from under him, going for the only thing that could save me now. The lighter on the table. I grabbed it just as he spun me around.

The devil looked down at me in all his evil glory. So, I sent him right back to hell. Flames whooshed as his clothes ignited and not stopping to take in his screams, I bolted, the lighter still in hand. I ran out the front door, down the porch, and before I could think about it, out to the orchard. Then I stopped, glancing at the trees around me with such loathing. They represented the shackles that still tied me to this nightmare of a house. To a father who was anything but fatherly. To the idea that *they* would finally come back and save me. There was no one coming. I needed to unlock these chains on my own.

I glanced at the ground. We were overdue for rain and the leaves beneath the trees were crunchy and dry. I didn't think any further than that. I just started lighting different patches until flames began engulfing the trees. Until I could barely breathe from the smoke. Then with one more glance at the house that also burned, I sprinted for the forest.

I ran so long and so far, I no longer recognized where I was. I mean being blinded by smoke and tears didn't help. I ran until I couldn't breathe. Until the adrenaline wore off, and the pain radiating through my entire body had me tripping over the next tree root and crashing to the ground. There I lay. Too exhausted and defeated to move. I wished for salvation. I wished for death. But most of all, I wished for my mother. I closed my eyes and sobbed.

I don't know how long I lay there, the darkness waiting on the edges of my consciousness, but suddenly, I could smell a soothing woodsy and spicy scent that enveloped me in warmth and hugged me tight. Maybe this was heaven come to take me at last. At the thought, I smiled and let the darkness carry me away.

Chapter 5

Thatch

"What have you done Thatch?" Her worry was evident. Her fear concealed right under the surface. Fear of me? Or the curse?

"I'm not sure," I told her, holding my hands out in a placating gesture. "It rarely happens, and I fix the damage when it does." My betrothed glanced around us at the clearing now healed. She'd found me here, lying in a bed of blackened grass. My heart had clenched in horror, but it had been easy to coax the grass to grow again. Now you couldn't tell that I had destroyed it in my sleep. Even if I couldn't tell you how I'd even come to be here. Last I remembered, I was still in bed next to Briar.

She raised worried silver eyes to mine. "It's getting worse Thatch. This sleepwalking." She gestured at the clearing. "The destruction. What happens when the curse takes full control of your power?" I could almost taste her fear, and I frowned.

"We have no proof that this is the curse," I told her, not even believing my own lie. Briar gave me an incredulous look.

"Since when does your power destroy?" Since my parents had us cursed by some seer. But I had it under control. As long as I healed the damage, it couldn't spread. My gut churned, but I ignored it. Repairing the destruc-

tion was the only option I had currently. If I let myself believe otherwise, then the curse would truly win.

I wrapped my arms around my betrothed and hugged her close. "Don't worry my love. The forest will not fall. I will not allow it." She stiffened and pulled away to look me in the eye.

"You're too late." I frowned. A shiver went down my spine and suddenly my hands felt sticky. I looked down to find them painted with blood. Panicked, my eyes shot to Briar's. She was bleeding onto the ground, each drop of blood causing a ripple of death until the grass around us was once again dead.

"Briar?" I pleaded, not even sure what I was asking for. The darkness spread, and I was helpless to stop it.

"You are too late," she said again. "The Forest Kingdom will fall, and you will become the Prince of Death."

I jerked awake, my heart beating out of my chest. I could still feel her blood on my hands, still see her clouded eyes as her life force returned to nature. I sucked in breath after breath as I gripped the dead grass under my nails. Wait. Dead grass.

"No," I whispered. "Not again." I was in another clearing and there was death all around me. The trees leaned away from me as if terrified to be too close less they too withered to nothing. The curse curled triumphantly through my veins as I surveyed the damage, my eyes stopping on several small lumps on the ground.

I frowned as I stood shakily to my feet. When I reached them, I fell to my knees again, guilt and regret choking me. Three young fawns who'd been hiding in the grass lay staring into the nothingness. Their devastated mothers watched me from the forest, but when my gaze fell upon them, they startled and leapt away.

Once nature welcomed me. Once I could be trusted to make it flourish. Now...now all I did was destroy. I hung my head, letting the cold death of the land around me seep into my blood. I didn't bother to heal it again. I'd given up on that centuries ago.

It was several minutes before I could find the energy to move again. Rising to my feet, I turned to head back toward the city, but a flash of orange and blue had me stopping and staring into the trees. Something flickered and danced in the distance, right on the edge of the boundary that separated the human realm from this one. And then it flickered out before flaring right as it broke through the barrier. Shocked, I watched in wonder as a figure ran several more steps before collapsing.

Racing towards the disturbance, I stomped out the spreading flames as I went. Then I was looking down at the unconscious, broken figure curled in the grass, flickering flames all around her. She was wounded all over, so much so, I could barely make out her features besides the shredded clothing clinging to her, and the countless bruises and cuts marring her from head to toe. None were caused by the fire that appeared to hover over her skin as if in a loving embrace before they extinguished. The more my eyes trailed over the damage of her and the ground around her, the greater an unexpectant wave of rage grew, until its force was so strong it almost sent me to my knees.

Gasping, I shook my head to clear it. I didn't know who this female was, but if she could cross the boundary, she needed to be questioned. No human should be able to do that. And she'd burned my forest while doing so. I didn't dare let my thoughts linger on why she would need to run so desperately in the first place.

Growling, I knelt and lifted her into my arms. For a second all I could do was stare down at her in confused wonder as she rested against my chest, but then a burning sensation started as flames sprouted anew along her body.

I gritted my teeth against the sharp pain, but they dowsed as quickly as they'd appeared, leaving patches of my clothes burned through, including a patch right over my heart. I froze as I noticed what had appeared on my skin right underneath the cheek resting upon me. A tattoo of a sapling with a single tendril of fire in the center. A soft hum deep within my core pulsed through my entire being, sending an unknown wave of power through the forest. The residual flames on the ground around us flared before extinguishing with a sigh.

Chapter 6

Ember

I was burning up. At least, I thought I was. It felt as if both the external and internal parts of my body were on fire. Gods, I'd really taken a beating this time. My lungs ached from the ingested water and the rest of me felt like a swollen piece of meat. But I needed to get up. I needed to get away from here before Dad came back. He was going to be so furious, and I wouldn't survive his wrath this time.

I could still hear his roars of pain and fury. What would he say...*what would he do*...when he saw the orchard? I shouldn't have done it. I hadn't been thinking straight. I'd wanted him to feel just a sliver of the pain I felt every day. I'd wanted to burn away the place that continued to thrive despite the constant filth I felt coating my skin every second of the day.

Now I needed to get out of here before he ended my life for good. But I couldn't move. It felt like someone had buried me in concrete. I could barely breathe. Panic rose as I thrashed internally, trying to get my body to respond. I was screaming, but they did not make a sound except for in my head. At least I thought it was in my head.

"Shhh child. Rest. You are safe here," a soft voice told me. Safe? I will never be safe. Safety was nothing but a dream that ended once you woke.

I could feel tears streaking down my face as the screams continued. My skin felt like it was crawling along my body. It wasn't supposed to do that. It wasn't supposed to feel like that.

"Stop! Please stop!" I begged silently.

"Come closer Prince. Only you can calm her." Prince? What prince? What dream was I having? Better yet, what nightmare, for I never dreamed anymore. But then, I could smell sandalwood mixed with spice. Something about it smelled right...like coming home. But I had no home. I frowned, even as I took in a deeper breath. I could feel my body calming with each inhale.

"That's it child. Sing for her my Prince as your mother used to do you." Sing? What an odd request to make of a prince. Apparently, he agreed because there was a disgusted snort and then a few words spoken harshly back and forth that I couldn't make out. And then.... a lyrical sway of the wind. A lullaby. It with the scent seeped deep into me until my body settled and mind calmed. Suddenly, I felt safer than I'd ever felt in my life. It was light. It was life itself. It was home.

As I drifted away on that warm scent and lyrical wind to a land where nightmares did not surface and dreams used to abound, the pain fell away.

Chapter 7

Ember

Everything should hurt. That was my first thought as I slowly became aware of the world around me. The air smelled sweet. Like fresh alyssum. And a cool, gentle breeze seemed to sway around me. Whatever I laid on was definitely not my lumpy bed from home. It felt like sleeping on memory foam and the sheets slid through my questing fingers like silk. Unable to quell my curiosity any longer, I opened my eyes.

I was in a room twice the size of my bedroom. The canopy bed I was in was queen sized with lavender colored sheets and shimmery curtains pulled back. The windows to my left were both open to allow for the breeze and flower scent that had awoken me. The floor had a long lavender rug that extended the full length of the room. There was a single loveseat between the window and fireplace. The door in front of me obviously led out of the room, so I gingerly slipped from the bed to wander to the door to my right.

It opened up to the largest bathroom I'd ever seen. The tub was more of a pool and sat in the ground with twin sinks and giant mirrors to the side. On the other side was a walk-in closet with more clothes than I'd ever owned in various colors and designs. There were dresses and what looked like blouses, tunics, and pants, but none were the kind you would find in a normal closet. All were feminine and forest-themed. Many had intricate leaf designs, while others were made of thin, almost sheer fabric with tree bark textures as accents.

Frowning now, I returned to the bedroom just as the door opened. A petite girl in a flowing periwinkle dress with dark caramel skin, long white hair, and...were those pointed ears?...walked in.

"My Lady, it's so good to see that you are finally awake. The king and queen await." I blinked. My lady? King and queen? Where in the world was I?

"Come. Come. We must get you dressed." She herded me back into the bathroom where she quickly filled the tub and encouraged me to enter and bathe. She added something that smelled of lavender and honey into the water and then handed me a soap that smelled the same.

"I'm Periwinkle. Wink for short. I'm your handmaiden while you stay with us in the Forest Kingdom." I blinked again as I washed in a daze. Was I still dreaming? That was the only thing that could make sense because surely that wasn't an elf pulling out a lovely, hunter green dress. It was short in the front and long in the back with lace sleeves, and a belt of thin, elegant leaves. And surely this same elf didn't just do my auburn hair into a beautiful half up-do and give me hunter green wings along my hazel eyes.

"Beautiful," Wink breathed, clapping her hands. "There. Now you're all ready to meet the king and queen."

"Um," I mumbled, finally untangling my tongue. "Where am I? Who's this king and queen you keep mentioning? And are your ears really pointed?" Wink giggled.

"Why the Forest Kingdom, Alyvia, at the capital city Verdis of course. King Hyperion and Queen Sequoia rule it until Prince Thatch is deemed ready to do so. You know the King, Queen, and Prince of Nature? And I'm Fae silly. Surely even you know that."

She giggled again, taking my questions in stride. I blinked again. Disbelief must have shown on my face because Wink took my hand and led me out of the room. I had a brief second to notice there was also a sitting area before she was leading me out the door and two guards in brown armor – that looked suspiciously like tree bark – were following behind us.

"Don't worry. It'll all become clear once you talk to the king and queen," she assured me. "Your arrival has caused such an uproar, especially when you arrived in Prince Thatch's arms." She sighed dreamily and I lifted a brow. *I'm sorry, what? And who was this prince she kept mentioning?*

I didn't have time for additional questions before I was dragged into what could only be a throne room. People – no Fae – stood along the sides allowing us space to walk up to two thrones that sat center stage with two smaller thrones spanning out on either side of them like the head of an arrow.

While the main throne chairs were shaped like trees with the grooves and roughness of one, the other four depicted different aspects of nature. One was shaped like a cresting wave with sea creatures etched into it. One was shaped like a mountain with three peaks. Another depicted the sky and had wings. The last was similar to the tree shaped chairs but was etched with thorns and various plant and animal life.

"Curtsy," Wink whispered, and I quickly followed her as I tried not to stare at the beautiful Fae dressed in flowing gold and her male match adorned in ebony and gold accents.

I could feel the power radiating off them as I took in their pointed ears and overall beauty. To say the king was as handsome as he was terrifying was an understatement. He looked like he could crush me with one hand but only sat imposingly as he studied me with narrowed bronze-colored eyes. The queen was no less intimidating with her more subtle power insinuated by the hand on his.

"So, this is the human our son found in the woods." The queen said as the king gave me an unimpressed glance over. "Tell me, my dear. How did one such as yourself slip past the veil?" I frowned.

"The veil, Your Majesty?" I asked softly. She waved a hand.

"That which separates Iyris, a world of Fae, from that of the human world." She considered me closely with forest green eyes that saw more than I liked. "One does not simply walk in. They must hold some type of power of this world, be invited, or be drawn here. So tell me child. Which are thee?" I shifted uncomfortably.

"I do not know, Your Majesty," I answered honestly. "It was not my intention to travel here. Honestly, I'm still trying to wrap my head around the concept myself." The queen lifted a brow.

"You did not intend to escape whatever left you barely conscious and beaten almost unrecognizably when my son found you?" I winced and she gave me a knowing, sad smile.

"You may have not directly intended to travel to the Forest Kingdom per se, but you did intend to pass through the veil. The only question I would like answered now is how." Queen Sequoia turned to King Hyperion. "Maybe our son can be of assistance to her memory." The king considered me again, his face carefully indifferent now.

"Perhaps." He gestured to someone behind us. "Summon the prince." Wink shuffled excitedly at my side but kept her eyes lowered.

It wasn't long before a booming voice was proclaiming, "His Royal Highness, Thatch Redwood, Prince of Forest." I fought to keep my mouth from dropping as I took in the tall warrior – for with the rippling muscles he bore and grace in which he strode, there was no doubt – who stopped just slightly in front of me. He wasn't as big as the king who was built like a mountain, but that didn't stop me from fighting to retreat from his presence.

Prince Thatch wore a green so dark it was almost black and with his likely shoulder length black hair pulled back in a messy bun and equally dark eyes, he looked like a wreath. A longbow and quiver full of hunter green arrows were draped on his back, and the holster attached to his thigh bore a dagger etched with plant life. It was as beautiful as it was deadly.

As he bowed to his parents, all I could do was try not to stare, or cringe away from the power radiating off him. It felt like life, but with such a dark tinge I wasn't sure if he was supposed to be the Grim Reaper or Father Nature.

The prince didn't spare me a glance and instead stood to address his parents. "Mother. Father." His deep voice was like velvet trailing a dark caress across my senses. I could also smell a familiar scent...sandalwood and spice. When was the last time a man triggered a *positive* response in me? I fought a shiver, and Wink giggled softly beside me.

"Thatch, my son," The Queen said fondly. "The girl you found has finally awakened, and I must say, she has healed into quite the beautiful female. And yet, she tells us she has no idea how she came to be here."

Beautiful? I fought the flush overtaking my cheeks. Had I looked that bad after what happened in the kitchen? I fought a wince. I had no doubt that I had, but why was the queen making it a point to tell Thatch so?

"The girl is obviously lying Mother," he answered smoothly. "The forest was aflame when I found her." I stared at him, shocked. Why would the forest be burning? I had only set fire to the orchard, and it wasn't close enough to spread to the forest. I stiffened as memories of that night came flooding back again. I suddenly felt nauseated, and a cold sweat broke out along my entire body. Distantly, I could feel Wink's concerning gaze on me. I fought to refocus on the royals' conversation.

"What is your name child?" The king suddenly asked. I froze, lifting startled eyes to his hard ones. Should I tell him? Why did they suddenly want to know it?

"Ember…. Ember Lanxter, Your Majesty." The king and queen shared a look. What was that about?

"And you say she burned a section of the forest?" King Hyperion asked Thatch. I got the impression this wasn't the first time the prince was saying this if his barely concealed annoyance was anything to go by.

"There were small fires around her that were slowly fading when I approached. She'd left a trail of them in her wake." *Impossible*, I thought, but the royals shared another knowing look that I didn't like before turning back to me.

"Is your father your true father, child?" I blinked. What kind of question was that?

"I…I believe so," I stuttered, frowning.

"And your mother?" Queen Sequoia prompted.

"Gone, Your Majesty. Left over eleven years ago." I glanced between them, tiring of the knowing looks. "Forgive me, but what does that have to do with anything? I can't create fire on a whim. And I really need to get going."

"We believe you can," King Hyperion said in a deep, gruff voice, ignoring my last comment. "Same as we believe that your actual biological father is not the one you know, but the King of Disasters, King Zeus, himself."

"I'm sorry, what?" I glanced between them, blinking rapidly in disbelief. "This is crazy. I'm just a normal girl. My father isn't some god with lightning powers." Queen Sequoia snorted in amusement, her eyes twinkling with mirth.

"Humans. They always twist the story. Zeus is not a god, but a powerful Fae king, and if you embody the element of fire, you are his daughter. Princess of Fire to be exact."

I took a step back. These people were crazy, and this dream had gotten out of hand. To make matters worse, my supposed savior still hadn't even bothered to glance my way. Prince Thatch just stood with his hands in his pockets, an expression of boredom on his face as if he simply waited to be dismissed. Yet, I could feel the undercurrent of fury radiating off him, just waiting to be released.

"I have to go," I muttered again. The queen lifted a brow.

"Is this not what you wanted? To escape the world you found yourself in? Is it too much to believe that you not only entered a parallel world, but that you also contain power over fire?"

Yes. Yes, it was. Because where had that power been when I needed it most?

"I only want to go home Your Majesties," I insisted, pleading with them to let me go.

"That won't be possible," King Hyperion stated resolutely. I stiffened, the shivers and nausea increasing. Why was it so hot in here?

"Why not?" I choked out. The queen smiled meaningfully.

"Because you're our son's mate."

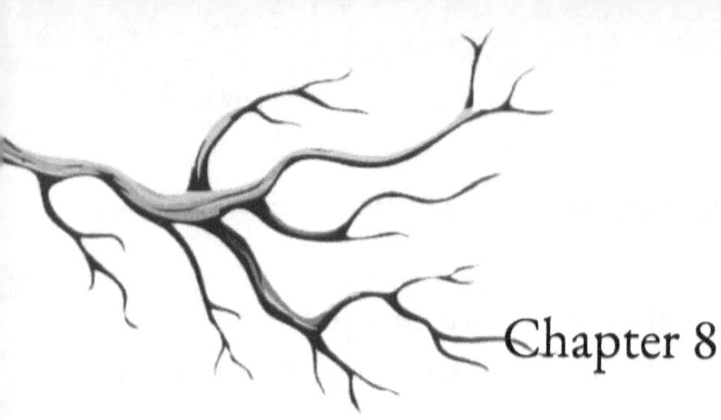

Chapter 8

Thatch

"What in the forces of nature was that?" I snapped in disbelief. "I told you I was likely mistaken." My mother simply plucked invisible particles off her long dress. A beautiful, flowing gold that did nothing to hide her growing displeasure at my refusal to acknowledge the scarred female as anything more than an intruder. She'd been the talk of the castle for days now and frankly, I was over it.

"Don't be so dramatic dear," she admonished. "Having a mate is a blessing."

"Blessing for who?" I growled. "She's human and has no regard for the forest."

"Apparently, not entirely human if she can burn parts of the forest by herself," My father pointed out, a hand on his chin as he considered. "If this is the first time she has shown such power, can we blame her for a few flames here and there? A natural disaster will be a natural disaster after all."

"What you're implying cannot be," I insisted, bristling. "The curse will not be broken by some human girl." My stomach twisted at the mention of the curse, its dark tendrils spreading through my veins as we spoke.

"You speak as if you do not wish the curse to be broken." Both of my parents stared at me disapprovingly as I said nothing. It was not a matter of what I wanted. Ever since the curse began eating away at my power, I'd realized I was fighting a battle I had no hope of winning. As its grip became stronger over the decades, my desire to fight it weakened. One did not fight a hurricane, you simply withstood it. Or so my elder brother, Theseus, Prince of Sea, once told me.

"The fate of the forest – the sheer balance of nature – is dependent on you defeating this curse. Same as the land, sea, and sky are dependent upon your brothers," My father said sternly. "It is a prince's duty – as well as a king's – to do that which he may not desire for the good of the kingdom." I gritted my teeth as my nails surely drew blood in my tightly fisted palms.

"The seer said only your match bred from the line of the King of Disasters could break the curse and bring balance back to the forest."

"What if she's simply human?" I growled, determined to fight this.

"What if she's not? What if she is actually your fated mate?" my mother said softly, but not meekly. No one could ever accuse the Queen of Nature of being weak no matter the compassion she wore on her sleeves.

"We do not ask you to immediately accept her, but to keep an open mind and see if she may be."

"The mark does not lie," my father declared, and I stiffened. I avoided looking down at my chest where underneath my tunic the tattoo had slowly begun to unravel across my heart. Last I checked, it still depicted a sapling with a flame within.

I still didn't understand the fit of rage I'd felt at the sight of her bruised and broken body. For a moment, it had gone beyond the burning forest. But she was just a human girl.

Except...she'd relaxed in my arms when I'd held her close, and again later from my scent and voice as she screamed in agony during the healer's work. As if I was the sun to her darkness. Something I could not and would not ever be. Any hope of that disappeared once the darkness leaked through my veins.

I turned away from my parents. "You will be disappointed," I told them. "She is not the one." As I stormed out of the throne room, I could hear my mother's quiet voice on the wind.

"We shall see."

I ducked and spun to parry my brother as he slashed his rapier at my head. I returned his strike for strike as we danced around the training field. It wasn't often all four of us were in the Forest Kingdom together – not since our nature specific abilities manifested and encouraged us to be in our element – but they'd all arrived today at the request of our parents. Apparently, the wonder at the girl's arrival hadn't waned as I'd hoped.

"Come little brother. Is that all you have?" Therek teased as I ducked a vicious swipe from Theseus. The Prince of Mountains was huge with bulging muscles and an even bigger mouth and temper. His light brown eyes, skin, and spiky brown hair made him look like a giant mountain cat. Despite his teasing, I could feel the undercurrent of wrath he always held and was thankful I did not fight him. I didn't feel like experiencing the full force of his twin axes today.

"He's too busy moping over his new mate, "Theseus replied, his blue eyes twinkling. I sneered at him, tempted to cut the long white locs he loved so much as they spun with him. Closer to my build, the Prince of Sea was a formidable warrior despite his playful banter.

"She's not my mate," I gritted out, hardening my attacks. Surprised, Theseus went on the defensive, only barely keeping up with my aggressive strikes. We went on for several moments, my hits a little too close for comfort, before he finally signaled a time out.

"Woah," he huffed, stepping away for water. "For someone who doesn't believe she's your mate, you sure are worked up." I growled, pulses of energy radiating from me, causing the forest around us to shudder in pain, and the animals to scurry away in fear.

"*Easy.*" Our eldest brother's commanding voice cut through the darkness in my head. "Calm little brother."

"Not little," I gritted out, but I closed my eyes and focused on taking deep breaths, until the waves of power ceased, and the forest calmed. Then, I opened my eyes to meet the worried lavender eyes of the Prince of Sky. As the oldest of us, Torm had been dealing with the curse the longest, and somehow still hadn't succumbed to the darkness seeping through his veins. At least not in the same way the rest of us had.

He was tallest, and not as muscular as Therek, but his twin blades strapped down his back between massive black wings warned you to never underestimate him. His skin was a dark tan compared to ours due to his regular exposure to the sun.

"Better?" He inquired. I inclined my head, and he nodded. "Tell us about this female then." I stiffened. Torm held out his hands. "Just to have all the facts."

"She's not my mate," I snapped. "She's just some human I found past the veil who happened to light fires as she ran." All three of my brothers blinked.

"Pause. She ran through the veil? Just like that?" Theseus gaped. I shrugged.

"And she can light fires naturally?" Therek asked skeptically. I folded my arms across my chest with a scowl.

"And you just so happened to develop a new tattoo overnight?" Torm added, indicating my chest. I glanced down at the tree with a heart of flame that had grown slightly in the last week. There were more branches and roots spanning from it now. If I wasn't so angry at what its appearance implied, I could admit that the artwork was impressive and went well with my other pieces.

I growled, making the forest tremble again. My brothers shared a look. "Don't," I snapped. "You're starting to act like Mother and Father. You know this curse is bull. We all agreed."

"Aye, we all agreed," Torm admitted. "But that was before all the signs we just pointed out." I glared at him.

"There is no magic fix. Same as there is no way to go back in time and prevent the curse in the first place."

"I never said it was a magic fix." His brows furrowed as he studied me. "Our parents will have you test it regardless. There's too much at state to assume this is a coincidence."

"There is no such thing as coincidences," we all mumbled as one. I shook my head incredulously.

"Forcing us together is supposed to do what exactly? She doesn't believe she's who the signs say she is either. You should have seen her expression when they proclaimed us mates. The poor girl almost fainted, and I could taste her terror tinted confusion long before she had that mountain dropped on her."

I snorted in annoyance. "She likely thought this was all a fever dream until Mother and Father refused to let her return to the human side." Theseus grimaced, and Torm frowned, likely just as unsure of what to make of the situation as I was.

"Okay fine," Therek cut in. "Let's say you go through this test together and she's not this mythical Princess of Fire. What have you lost besides time? We are immortal and if you don't believe the curse is going to be broken, you have nothing to lose in traveling across the forest with this girl."

"It's a means to an end," Theseus added. "Just do enough to keep Mother and Father happy." He gave me a knowing wink. "There's plenty of other things to get up to on the way."

I sighed. It made sense and it wasn't like I really had a choice in the matter. I glared out into the forest again, wishing for the solace it once brought me. My brothers were right. I knew none of us were convinced that our fated mates were the answer to our problems – if they existed at all – but there *was* no such thing as coincidences. Even if she wasn't some fated mate, there was a reason she was here. It was my duty as Prince of Forest to discover that reason.

"So we leave it up to nature," I muttered, already dreading the journey across the vast kingdom.

"To the forces of nature," my brothers muttered in agreement.

Chapter 9

Ember

You're my son's mate. I hadn't been able to say anything after that declaration. I'd just stared at them, waiting for the punch line. Instead, those words had played over and over in my head for the last week after I'd been dismissed to *rest up*. More like come to terms with the fact that I'd jumped from the frying pan into the fire.

Mate. Wink had squealed with excitement once we'd returned to my rooms. Saying how lucky I was to be mated to one of the four Princes of Nature. How now the forest was saved – whatever that meant – and that she couldn't wait for me to meet the other princes. Apparently, Thatch was her favorite of the four brothers.

Meanwhile, I felt like the walls were closing in on me despite the open windows. I had no desire to meet three more imposing males who would also likely loathe me like a certain Forest Prince.

I'd been told I would be leaving soon to go on some trip with him. What this trip entailed I didn't know. What was I expected to do exactly? Travel through a world I knew nothing about with a prince who thought I was here to make his life miserable? I couldn't even blame him for his animosity. If someone came into my home and convinced my family that they had this magical control over me, I would be pissed too.

I swallowed uneasily as I stared at myself in the mirror. The newer scars were gone as if that night hadn't even happened. But nothing could erase the ghost of them or the ones that marred my skin long before I crossed into this world. It seemed even Fae abilities were limited.

I shivered involuntarily. Fae. Magic. Any other girl would be ecstatic about the prospect of fantasy books coming to life, but I'd never had that privilege. I'd grown up with too large a villain to believe in fairy tales, and all I heard with the word Fae was a group of males I had no defenses against. And now I was being forced to travel with one who likely wished me dead. What if I'd escaped one demeaning situation just to enter another? Maybe I would feel better if I really could yield the fire they so insistently believed I could. But I was not some mythical princess, and although escaping into the forest hadn't held the results I'd hoped, I could not remain here.

I startled as the door slammed and the hurried footsteps of Wink echoed through the room.

"Oh good," she exclaimed, racing into the bathing room. Was periwinkle the only color this girl...female...wore? "You've already bathed. Now we just have to get you ready for the ball." I blinked as she hurried to collect supplies to do my hair.

"I'm sorry. Did you just say a ball?" Wink nodded excitedly as she gestured for me to have a seat on a stool. I moved hesitantly to do so and stared at her in confusion as she began fussing over my hair.

"Yes! All four of the Princes of Nature were summoned to court and when they are, we usually hold a ball to celebrate. Prince Torm, Theseus, and Therek finally arrived early this morning." I frowned, confusion growing.

"Are they not the king and queen's children?"

"Of course."

"So then, why do you have a ball every time they come home?" It didn't make sense. It was like the equivalent of hosting a party every time you returned home from work or school.

"Well you see, the princes aren't home all at once as often any-more," Wink explained as she brushed my curls until they shone. "As they grew older, they began to spend more time in the parts of the kingdom related to their element. Although, they won't be kings until their parents step down."

Meeting my bewildered gaze, Wink gasped. "I'm so sorry. I keep forgetting that you aren't from Iyris. And here you are, in the world for two weeks and we've yet to fully explain anything."

Understatement of the century, but I decided to not hold it against her. To be fair, I was unconscious for the first week, and in shock the second. I'd barely been able to absorb anything during the time spent in various parts of the castle and Verdis itself, still trying to wrap my mind around the fact that this wasn't some elaborate waking dream.

"There are four additional thrones," I said thoughtfully, remem-bering the chairs that had sat to either side of the king and queen. "I'm guessing that means four kingdoms for the four princes?"

Wink nodded enthusiastically. "Exactly! The Forest Kingdom Alyvia sits in the center, the Mountain Kingdom Amethyst to the east, the Sea Kingdom Akabe wraps around from the south, and the Sky Kingdom Anore sits over the north."

"Of course, there are other kingdoms besides the Nature ones, but they are separated by the Dark Sea on the west side of the Forest King-dom, and we don't generally interact." Wink shifted uneasily, her smile faltering slightly. I frowned, but she smiled broadly before returning to our previous discussion. "Plus, the ball holds another purpose."

When she didn't continue, I lifted a brow. "Which is?" I prompted. Wink hesitated and pinned my hair in a half up-do. My frown deepened, a headache forming. What wasn't she saying?

"Come, come! We must get you dressed. We're late as it is." Wink prompted. There wasn't time for me to push her for more answers as she became a whirlwind of makeup, jewelry, and finally a dress. By the time I stood before the floor length mirror, I no longer recognized myself.

She'd kept the makeup to a minimum but had painted my eyes with a gorgeous, deep green. It matched the emerald dress that hugged my chest and gently fanned out at my hips in more material than I'd ever worn in my life. Yet, somehow it lacked the poofiness of what I'd seen of Cinderella dresses. I felt like I was dressed in clouds, it was so light. The forest theme continued with delicate, glittering veins stretching down the bodice to my waist, and the golden shoes, necklace, and bracelets she added had me gaping at the woman before me.

I had never looked more beautiful.... but it was a waste placed on a broken soul such as mine.

"Oh! One more thing." Wink opened a box and pulled out a golden diadem encrusted with rubies and a large emerald in the center. She placed it upon my head and held a hand to her heart.

"Now you are every inch the princess you represent," she said in awe.

"I'm no princess," I whispered, but even I couldn't deny the faint feeling of rightness at seeing my reflection. I felt a warming in my chest as I eyed the jewels likely meant to represent "fire" and "forest". Having them on one crown only meant one thing. But I was no Cinderella, and this prince had no interest in seeing if the shoe fit.

"Come. It's time to greet the court." I followed her as we made our way to a large ballroom. The dais was a mirror image of the throne room with the six, intricate chairs, but the rest was decked in shiny chandeliers and more finery than I'd ever seen. Along the walls on either side were hors d'oeuvres and seats for the guests. In one corner a string quartet played as the Fae danced in the center of the room.

I tried to keep my jaw off the ground as Wink led me to the thrones to greet the king and queen. Never had I seen such finery in one place. Add in the people of every shape and size and my headache grew.

"Welcome Ember, Princess of Fire," Queen Sequoia greeted me. She was in a lovely, blush pink gown with a slit down either leg. The king was in a deep ebony tunic and pants. King Hyperion ignored me as his wife scanned my dress. "My, you are lovely my dear. Green is most definitely your color." She gave me a secret smile that I struggled to return, especially when I knew what she implied.

"Thank you Your Majesty," I managed, feeling like I was going to explode with anxiety at any moment. There were too many people here. I could feel their gazes dragging along my skin. I had the sudden need for another bath just to remove the sensation.

"I hope you have been enjoying your time at court so far." She gestured at the ball. "Please, enjoy the festivities. Hopefully, my sons will be along shortly to make your acquaintance." I tensed and swallowed down my fear. Oh goodie.

"Thank you Your Majesty," I said again curtsying before Wink dragged me away.

For a while, I was able to forget all about the princes as Wink pointed out different creatures to me. There were fairies with opaque or translucent wings in neon colors. Males with horns who could transform into a bull, I was told were called toros. Fae with attributes from various animals, like the tail and ears of a fox called foxlings. And of course, there were elves. How I didn't have a coronary at the sight of so many unique people I didn't know. They acted similar to humans and yet weren't, and I wasn't sure how I was expected to interact with them.

There were a few humans sprinkled among them, but they ignored the girl trying to not draw attention in a very ostentatious gown. Luckily, Wink was amused enough at my side along the wall as she ate snacks and shared the tea on the drama around court.

Hours seemed to pass quickly while we sampled the food and fairy wine that sent tingles down every nerve ending in my body. I was actually starting to have fun laughing at Wink's sarcastic description of the snobby people present when suddenly a hush went through the crowd. I frowned in confusion as I scanned the ballroom. Then I saw them.

The crowd parted as they were announced and made their way to the king and queen. They were huge, powerful, and every inch the warrior princes I'd imagined them to be. Immediately, my eyes were drawn to the handsome male in a green so dark, it was almost black. His pants and jacket hugged every inch of his physique, and although his bow and dagger were absent, the deadly aura around him was not. But if I thought Thatch was intimidating, then every brother after him was just plain terrifying. The one to his right was huge, his biceps and legs the size of tree trunks. His spikey brown hair almost clashed with the deep mahogany outfit he wore, and yet it worked.

"That's Therek, Prince of Mountains," Wink whispered, noticing where I gazed. I jumped, forgetting she stood next to me. I recovered, nodded, and switched my gaze to the one in front of Therek. This male wasn't as massive, but he was taller with long white locs and was dressed in a deep azure.

"Theseus, Prince of Sea." I nodded and glanced at the last male to the Sea Prince's left. I could tell he was the oldest. He had this air of ancient pain that told me he'd been through some things, and a lot of it wasn't pleasant. He also had the oddest lavender colored eyes. They were cold though as if the pain he carried had frozen every other emotion in a case of ice.

He was slightly taller than Theseus but with skin the color of mocha and dark hair that was short along the sides and longer on top. Giant, feathered wings were pulled in tight to his body, the tips a few inches above the floor. They looked like they were painted with splattered ink. It was like darkness lived within their veins, and if I focused, I could see the darkness shifting and ebbing. That's when I realized, his wings weren't black at all, but a deep grey.

"And Torm, Prince of Sky, the eldest." I frowned, feeling darkness shrouding the princes even as they greeted their parents with obvious affection, and then dispersed into the crowd to dance with the many ladies pining for their attention. Something was wrong here, but I couldn't put my finger on what. I just knew I needed to stay as far from the Princes of Nature as I could.

"Wink," I said turning to her as I lost sight of the terrifying males, though not before meeting the death glare of the Prince of Forest as he swept his partner away in the opposite direction. "Why else is a ball held every time all the princes are here?"

The elf hesitated again, her pale, indigo dress swaying as she spun to lead me toward another tray of drinks. "Well," she started. "It is the hope that they will meet their mates. You know, a Princess of Disaster." I'd figured that.

"Yes, but *why?* Why is that specific type of princess needed exactly," I pushed. "Is it because of the darkness that shrouds them?" Wink shot me a surprised look.

"Wait, you can you see the....? Nevermind. Yes, but honestly it isn't my place to share. The king and queen will explain it all." I frowned, even more disturbed. What exactly was going on in the Forest Kingdom? And how was I going to escape before it all came to a head?

Chapter 10

Ember

"May I?" I spun to find cold, indifferent eyes focused on me. Up close I could see that the lavender within his iris seemed to flow like clouds through the sky. It was odd and unsettling, but not as unsettling as the feeling of the blood cells in my veins freezing one by one. I must have stared too long because Wink nudged me toward the Prince of Sky.

"She would love to Prince Torm," she exclaimed. I threw her a pleading look, but she was already backing away. "It's tradition and an honor," she mouthed to me. Yeah, sure. Throw the human into the arms of a bunch of dark princes and see if she survives.

I couldn't meet his eyes as one hand went around my waist and the other took my hand. I fought hard against the desire to recoil from his touch. I couldn't afford to insult the cold prince. Before I knew it, we were spinning across the ballroom floor, so graceful that I almost forgot I didn't know how to dance. I couldn't even focus on not stepping on toes when I felt like I was fighting the coldness trying to seep into my skin and turn me to ice. How that ice didn't freeze the wings obviously strong enough to carry him was beyond me.

"So you are the princess who's supposed to save my youngest brother." I jumped, my eyes shooting up to meet his contemplative ones.

"You say that as if you think it is bunch of horse shit," I replied before I could stop myself. I tensed waiting for his rebuke. Where the hell did that come from? This was the worst possible time to be mouthing off. And yet...the Prince of Sky's lips twitched as if amused.

"You'll need that fire to survive my brother either way," he said, tilting his head. "But I wonder, do you believe you are who they say you are?" I snorted before I could stop myself.

"I am just a human girl trying to wield the crappy hand she's been dealt." He studied me for a moment.

"Crappy hand or no, human girl you are not." He glanced down at my dress. "More like a fiery female who is attempting to hide the power simmering below the surface."

I frowned as he spun us again. "I have no power over the fire," I insisted. "I started a fire in my family's orchard and it accidentally spread. That is all." It was the only explanation I could come up with. Anything else was simply inconceivable.

But his gaze didn't falter, and he must have seen something else I didn't because he inclined his head as we came to a stop. "That is not the power I speak of Princess. And whether you are my brother's saving grace or not, I have an inkling that this won't be the last time we meet." He bowed. "Until then."

And then he was gone, and the male with long white locs was bowing to me next.

"Princess," the Prince of Sea greeted, extending his hand. Still in a daze from what his brother had said, I took it and was swept away into a new dance. I was grateful for the lack of ice radiating off this prince, and he too danced gracefully, fluid like water. But there was a raging storm in his gray, almost silver eyes. I felt like he was moments from destroying everything around him despite the casual way he held me. But it wasn't rage I felt dominating in him, but a debilitating sadness.

"See something you like?" the Sea Prince asked, his lips lifted in a dark smirk. I gulped and looked away. "No, don't lose your nerve now Princess. The world of Fae will eat you and spit you back out otherwise."

"I don't know what you're talking about Prince, "I mumbled. He chuckled.

"First, you may call me Theseus. Secondly, you have questions you wish to ask, so ask them." I glanced up at him skeptically.

"And you will answer them?" He inclined his head.

"I will answer those I can." Still doubtful, I fished for a question that wouldn't immediately get me killed.

"So...why must you all dance with me at this ball even though I'm human?"

Theseus chuckled. "Didn't Torm tell you? You're anything but human Princess. We just don't know if you're who our parents believe you are." His calloused hands, rubbing against mine as he spun me out and back to him, reminded me that I was talking to a warrior and not just a prince. I swallowed nervously.

"What does that have to do with *dancing* with me?" I pushed.

"It is tradition. It is said, by touch alone a bond can be revealed. My parents are...hopeful." I frowned.

"But they believe I've formed this "bond" with your youngest brother, and yet they have you all dance with me." My eyes widened in horror. "Wait, *do* I have to dance with *all* four of you?" Theseus chuckled again, but there was an undercurrent of madness in it. What exactly ailed these tormented princes to give them all this cloak of darkness and resigned pain?

"Yes, and yes." Oh gods. I scanned the crowd as if I could escape this ball despite so many Fae watching me.

"Can you bond with more than one?" I asked tentatively. It would be just my luck that they would think I was bonded to more than one of the dark princes, but the Prince of Sea shook his head.

"No Princess. One bond is enough for any one person to handle." We slowed until we came to a stop as the song ended.

"And if I don't want this so called bond?" I insisted. "What if I just want to go home?" Theseus gave me a sad smile, and my heart sank. He dropped a kiss onto my hand as he bowed.

"May you find that which you are looking for Princess. At least one of us shall." I frowned, even more confused by that response than I was by the Prince of Sky's. What was up with the cryptic warnings and comments from these people? Could no one say what they meant?

"Princess," a deep, rumbling voice growled, and I froze in terror. His light brown eyes were as unyielding as stone, and he was so much larger up close than he'd been across the room. Plus, unlike his older brothers, the Prince of Mountains was doing nothing to conceal his utter loathing of my presence. I wanted to scream and run from the waves of aggression hitting me like an avalanche, tumbling, building, until I thought I was going to be swept away.

"Princess," he snapped again, and I startled out of my daze. "May I?" I took his hand even though it was the very last thing I wanted. How different the brothers were. Torm's anger was cold as ice, Theseus's the calm before the storm, but Therek's was a crushing weight.

"Why do you hate me so much?" I whispered. "You don't know me." Oh gods, why did I ask that? But I had to know. What in the world was causing all the princes to feel this same dark fury that, if Wink was to be believed, was centuries old?

"You shouldn't be here," The Prince of Mountains growled. "You may have our parents convinced of your innocence, and your role in our lives, but I am not fooled."

I winced as he gripped my hand and waist so tightly I thought my bones would snap. "I am not who they say I am," I said through gritted teeth, trying to ignore the pain.

"Oh, I'm aware," Therek mocked. "And if you do anything to betray or cause harm to come to my brother, I will hunt you down and bury you alive." I gasped in horror, my eyes wide as he abruptly stopped the dance and stalked off. I was going to be sick. I rushed to the nearest door, and suddenly Wink was at my side. One glance at my face and she was guiding me down the hall.

"This way Princess," she said pulling me into a washroom. I barely made it to the toilet before I was spewing everything I'd eaten. I coughed and gagged, trying to expel the terror pressing down on me still, but three princes' worth of darkness was debilitating. And I still had one left to endure.

"I can't do this," I whimpered. Wink was at my side in an instant, a cloth, and a cup of water in her hands. She dabbed at my mouth and forehead.

"You must Ember," she said softly. "Just one more." I groaned.

"I can't handle one more," I told her, taking the water and gargling. I spat the foul tasting water into the toilet with everything else. "Thatch likely hates me more than his brothers combined because of who your king and queen think I am to him. And if that is so...I'm going to die."

Wink eyed me worriedly but helped me to my feet. "Thatch won't kill you. The king and queen won't allow it." I glared at her. Was that supposed to be comforting?

"Will the king and queen be going on this expedition?" Her silence was answer enough. "So there is no true way to know whether he'll listen, is there?" Wink shook her head, her long, white twists bobbing.

"He would never kill you. Scare yes. Prank and try to make your life difficult yes, but the Prince of Forest has always been mischievous. His antics have just become.... darker over the centuries."

I scoffed. "You say that as if that's supposed to be comforting." She only stared at me, shaking her head.

"He...he hasn't fallen that far." I frowned. Fallen? As in, he used to be nicer? I found that difficult to believe. And why did it sound like she was trying to convince herself as well?

Wink seemed to shake herself out of whatever dark thoughts she was reliving. "Let's freshen you up so you can return to the ball."

Sooner than I'd liked, I was back in the ballroom waiting for the last prince to show so I could finally escape to my rooms.

"Princess Ember." I turned to find Queen Sequoia gesturing for me to come to her. I shot Wink a confused look and she shrugged. I made my way to the throne and curtsied.

"Your Majesty?"

"Ember, I hope you have enjoyed your time at the ball." I hesitated but nodded.

"Yes, Your Majesty, it has been a unique experience." The queen lifted a brow and laughed softly.

"Already learning to speak like the Fae I see." She smiled sadly at me. "I must apologize for my sons' rudeness. They have had a...difficult few centuries and unfortunately, my youngest is using that as an excuse to leave you without a final dance this night." I blinked, not understanding.

"He...he left?" I asked, realizing I hadn't even spotted the Prince of Forest in a while. Queen Sequoia sighed.

"Yes, but do not worry. You will have plenty of time to get to know my wayward son. For now, go, rest. The day after tomorrow you will start your journey and all will become clear."

I curtsied but as I was escorted back to my rooms, I couldn't tell if the feeling in my chest was relief ...or disappointment.

Chapter 11

Thatch

"Bold move brother," Theseus said with a raised brow as we sat in my rooms. He lifted his glass of nightgaze to his lips as he studied me. The drink made of night berries and fairy dust was his and Torm's favorite, but Therek sat drinking a dark liquor as strong as the rage he carried. All wine was good wine to me, but then, I hadn't had as long to "refine my pallet" as Torm liked to tell me.

"Thatch!" said brother snapped, bringing me back to the conversation at hand. I shrugged.

"So I left the dance early. So what?" Theseus snorted, and Torm scowled. Therek was too busy trying to drown his wrath in liquor after his own reprimand from our parents. Apparently, threatening the new princess with death was looked down upon, especially when she was believed to be a prophesied one.

"You know what," Torm growled. "Mother and Father will only give you so much leeway brother."

"Yeah, well, if they wanted me to behave like a respectable prince, then they should have never caused us to be cursed," I shot back.

Theseus chuckled. "You act as if you were ever the respectable prince." I grinned broadly at him. He had always been a kindred spirit when it came to my shenanigans, even assisting me in some of my pranks. Had they become darker…more dangerous as time progressed? Maybe. But who was to blame for that?

Torm sighed. "This is different Thatch. Our parents are unyielding on this. I spoke to them, and they whole-heartedly believe she is the lost princess and that your bond has already begun to form."

I snorted in disgust. "It's just a tattoo. I have plenty of those." I gestured to the one on my left bicep that incorporated all of our kingdoms. Each of my brothers had one, each slightly different from the others.

"Yeah, but none that just magically appeared at the touch of a female," Theseus pointed out. I turned to glare at him, and he held up his hands. "Relax brother. We're not saying she's your fated mate, just that Mother and Father believe that she is."

"Meaning, you won't be able to simply get rid of her and get away with it," Torm growled at me, but his hard stare was on Therek.

Therek glared back. "It was just a warning," he snarled, but we all knew better. We would do anything to protect the other, even kill the princess our parents favored.

"So, I'll make it discreet," I said with a shrug. Torm growled deep and long, and I felt an icy rage flood my veins. I swallowed uneasily, not wanting to acknowledge the curse reflected back at me in his frozen gaze.

"I won't kill her," I assured him and the ice melted. I relaxed slightly. "But I take no responsibility for what others do to her." My eldest brother sighed and stared out the window. I frowned. He and Theseus had been acting weird since dancing with the princess. What had she said? Or was it something they'd seen? Did it really matter?

I stood to my feet, ignoring their questioning looks. "I need to pack." With that, I escaped into my room, but I couldn't shake the feeling that this trip was going to be more than I bargained for. The tattoo over my heart started to burn and I could feel it as another branch grew.

Chapter 12

Ember

I stared at the bag Wink had packed for me this morning in preparation for whatever journey the king and queen had planned for me and Thatch. Wink had said our "bond" had to be tested to snap fully into place. Something about the tribulation leading to a bond that could withstand time or some crap like that. She was very disappointed she couldn't come along for the ride. Honestly, I was too. It would have been nice to have at least one ally on this trip.

Not that anyone had been openly hostile towards me. But I'd felt the rage pouring off Thatch the other day, despite him not bothering to acknowledge me, and I still couldn't get Therek's threat to stop echoing through my head. I was terrified to be alone with another male who loathed me. Would he be as aggressive and dangerous as my father? Or was he much worse? The aura I saw around Thatch and his brothers told me it might be the latter, but there was this hidden layer underneath that made me doubt that assumption. Maybe it was the way the two eldest had treated me cordially, but I had a feeling I only had a few pieces of the puzzle.

I spun to face the door as Wink entered my rooms, a grin on her face. "Great you're dressed!" I glanced down at my comfortable black pants and dark green blouse paired with a black cape. Hunter green boots rose halfway up my legs and felt like walking on air. The entire outfit was finer than any clothes I'd ever owned, but I'd been told this was dressing down. Considering the dress they'd had me wear during the ball, I guess it was.

"Come! King Hyperion and Queen Sequoia await!"

I followed her quietly down the long stone hallway, taking in the giant open windows and lavish tapestries depicting nature. Every part of this castle depicted or incorporated some form of nature whether a forest in various seasons, towering mountain ranges, beautiful depictions of the sea, or sunrises and sunsets that could make you weep with their vividness. I'd learned in the warmer seasons, the castle windows were usually left completely open to the elements, and the birds and plants that often weaved through the halls made it feel like you were perpetually a part of nature yourself. It was beautiful and filled my heart with the desire for the peace it whispered of.

How I'd missed all of this on my first day, I knew not, but then again, I had just awoken in the world of Fae and been told to meet the king and queen. Now I'd been here for over two weeks and was still no closer to figuring out how to escape the predicament I was in. It might help if I had a clear idea of what that predicament was in the first place. And whether the peace here was a wishful thought or the very escape I'd been craving my entire life.

Once we reached the throne room, I quickly took in the giant stone pillars in the corners, more windows allowing for vines to twist in and out of the room, and the unique throne chairs. I curtsied and stood once motioned to do so.

"Princess of Fire, Ember of Earth," Queen Sequoia greeted me, but I flinched at the title. It didn't get any easier to hear. "It is time for you and our son Prince Thatch to embark on your journey." I swallowed past the lump in my throat.

"And what will this journey entail, Your Majesty?" I asked shakily, hoping to finally gain some answers. I'd already glanced around to find the prince nowhere to be seen. How was I going to get out of this? Maybe I could escape at some point during the ride?

"You will travel to the end of the Forest Kingdom with our son while he seeks to quell the rumors of unrest and hidden adversaries that are spreading throughout the kingdom," King Hyperion declared. "It is vast with many challenges and joys, but it is something he must do as his princely duties, and you will join him."

"By quell, you mean?" I swallowed uncomfortably. The king considered me quietly.

"Remove the threats as needed. Permanently." I fought the flinch at his matter-of-fact tone. So rarely had he spoken to me, but every time he did, I fought not to crash to my knees under his gaze.

"And what if this journey reveals that I'm just a normal human?" I asked softly. I stiffened as the throne room doors slammed open and the Prince of Forest strolled in. Thatch stopped to my right, once again ignoring me as he bowed to his parents. He said nothing, but I could still feel the animosity permeating the air. I gulped.

"If by the end, you are not fully mated and the curse is not broken, then we will return you to your home," The king stated plainly. I breathed a small sigh of relief. All I had to do was survive a walk across a forest, avoid whoever these adversaries the prince needed to remove were, and then I could go home. *Go home to what?* My subconscious reminded me, but I pushed that thought to the back of my mind. I'll deal with it tomorrow when I got there.

"And Thatch," he turned to the bristling prince at my side. "You will ensure she returns alive." The prince snorted in disgust.

"So not only am I to suffer her presence, but her incompetence as well." I stiffened at his malicious tone. King Hyperion tensed and narrowed his eyes at his son.

"Because you are not yourself, I will hold back from reprimanding you harshly but remember who you are and who we raised you to be. A curse does not change this." Thatch seemed to tense even further and clenched his fists. I fought a frown. What did the king mean? This was the second time a curse had been mentioned. At first, I'd assumed it was a euphemism for something. Now, I wasn't so sure.

"A curse changes a whole lot," Thatch mumbled bitterly, but I knew the royals heard him because they both suddenly had a flash of regret and sadness pass through their eyes. What was going on? As if hearing my question, Queen Sequoia turned to me.

"I know you wonder why we must test you this way child."

"It's none of her concern," Thatch gritted out. The king shot him another reprimanding glare, but it was the queen who answered.

"If she is to travel across this vast kingdom with your less than savory demeanor, she has every right to know why," she snapped. Surprisingly, the prince relented with a stiff incline of his head.

"A long time ago," she continued, turning back to me. "A seer placed a curse on this family that affected each of our four sons. While each embodies the essence of a piece of nature – the life – they were then burdened with the opposite as well. With life comes death and with nature comes natural disasters." She paused, gazing at the plant life that seeped through the windows. I listened intently, trying to figure out what this had to do with me having to trek across a forest with a hateful prince. Was this the darkness I felt tainting each of the princes at the ball?

"Once upon a time the princes were as lively as the power of life they held," she continued. "But as they grew older, the darkness began to grow, eating away at the light within them. As it does so, nature reflects what our sons now look like on the inside." She glanced at the Prince of Forest next to me who only glared at the floor.

"They were never meant to carry both life and death. It is too great a burden, but the seer gave one bit of hope. She foretold that the daughters of the King of Disasters would be their fated mates, embodying the death so the princes could be the life, and in doing so, bring balance back to nature."

Queen Sequoia gestured at me. "That is where you come in child. Each prince is marked with the princess who is meant to be his other half, but the mark only appears when in her presence. And in order to snap your bond permanently in place, you must be tested together."

I blinked as she brought the story full circle. *I'm sorry what?* I was death and represented some natural disaster just because I accidentally spread the fire from the orchard to the forest? What girl wants to be told she embodies death? How is that a good thing?

The queen smiled sadly at me. "I can see from your eyes that you do not believe me." She gestured at Thatch. "Even our own sons don't believe in their salvation."

"Regardless, you will *both* travel to the end of the Forest Kingdom and remove these threats as you do so," King Hyperion cut in with a soft growl aimed at the Prince of Forest. Thatch lifted his head and scowled at his father but said nothing else. The king narrowed his eyes, then waved an impatient hand. "Be on your way Prince of Forest, Princess of Fire.

May you find what you're looking for, and the forces of nature have mercy on you."

I frowned. His words seemed to imply something because Thatch stiffened, before nodding and turning away. With nothing to do but follow, I curtsied to the king and queen and raced to follow him to the stables. My bags had already been attached to the powerful horses saddled and waiting for us, and I tried to hold back my panic as I waved to Wink who cheerfully saw us off despite her worried eyes.

Neither Thatch nor I said a word as we rode out of the city gates to the forest beyond. He rode with such confidence on his gorgeous, dark brown stallion. Meanwhile, I gripped the saddle horn in front of me firmly, afraid that if I fell off, I'd be trampled and left for dead. We stopped atop a hill a few miles from the city and I gasped, taking in the sea of trees before us. I couldn't see where it ended in either direction. Never had I seen a forest this massive, but with a flick of the reins, I descended into the place that would either bring me life, or end in death.

The scars I wear are many,
but they cannot be seen
not unless you look past the darkness
deep within me.

Don't bother with the tears.
They no longer fall.
And though the summer sun works hard,
its warmth,
its light,
doesn't reach me at all.

Not past the darkness,
devourer of dreams.
And not to the memories
of what I used to be.

For the scars I wear are many
etched upon my tired heart.

Summer

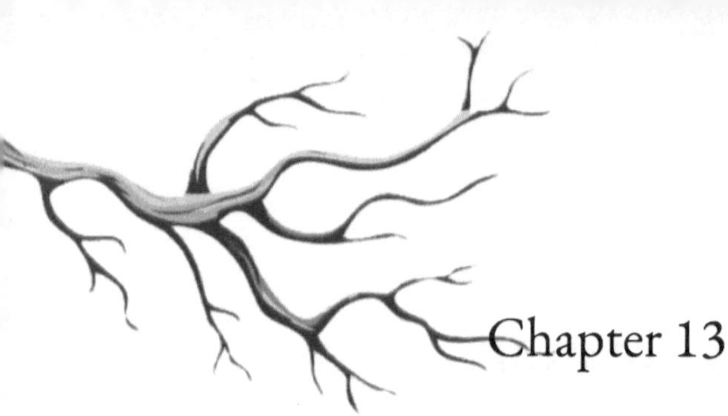

Chapter 13

Thatch

I used to love the forest. It was a part of me after all. I could feel every shrub, every tree, every vine. I could feel the birds, the deer, the insects.

I used to be life. But then I'd awoken one day in a clearing, unsure how I'd gotten there. Except it hadn't really been a clearing. It was a patch of death – all the plants dead in a black circle around and underneath me. The rest of the trees had recoiled from my presence. But I was their prince, so when I demanded the growth return, new plants had filled the clearing. That was over two centuries ago. I forgot about that incident for a while, but then it occurred more and more. Except I was no longer waking from unconsciousness with no memory of causing it... and I was no longer growing it back.

To say I'd stopped caring was not the entire truth. I cared. I did. But decade by decade, I cared just a little bit less. I began to hate my parents. For their guilt. For not telling us what they did to curse us in the first place. For encouraging such false hope. If it wasn't for our shared burden, I would likely hate my brothers as well. We met up regularly even now that we were no longer all living in Verdis. It was to check in on each other's sanity – or darkness levels – although we never said so. We knew it was only a matter of time before the darkness stopped receding and just took over for good. We never had control over the power of our respective disasters, but eventually, we wouldn't be able to command nature at all.

Honestly, I'd thought my brothers would have succumbed long before I did. We were all roughly a century and a half apart, and with Torm being just over seven centuries, I was sure as the eldest that he would have crashed first. Maybe he had more endurance. Better control.

Maybe I was just angrier. After watching my brothers' suffering, hoping it would somehow skip me or that the curse would be stopped long before it trickled down to the youngest, could you blame me? And it seemed with each son, the curse began its affliction earlier and earlier. I was only three and a half centuries and I'd already been dealing with it for most of my life.

Now here I was, riding through my withering kingdom, a mysterious female at my back who I wasn't convinced was human. My brothers definitely didn't think she was. I could sense her even when I didn't mean to. There was this light aura around her that gave off a subtle heat. I hadn't mentioned it to my parents or my brothers, and no one else had seemed to sense it.

And then there was the tattoo. It burned slightly every time a new piece grew. The tree was already taller than it had been when I'd first found her. Then, I'd found just a small sapling with the tiniest tendril of flame in the center. Since she'd burned a section of my shirt, once I'd arrived at the castle my mother had seen the tattoo and screamed, tears of relief raining down her face.

Since then, it had grown slowly larger and wider. I hadn't told anyone about that either. My brothers had seen it during our sparring but didn't know how it had changed. My parents had only seen the tattoo once...I'd made sure of that. Gods forbid they see proof of its development. They would think it meant more than it did. But then, they already did.

I peeked at the female again in my peripheral. She hung her head low, her body seeming to collapse into itself the closer we came to nightfall. She was a fragile thing. Her skin was the golden brown of the brown iris flower, and her hair was the dark auburn of fall leaves with streaks of black. She was small – but being six feet, most females were compared to me – but still curvy with ample breasts and muscle that told of hard labor.

It wasn't her body that made her fragile per se, but there was a presence about her that made me think she was seconds away from shattering into a million pieces. You would think that meant I would take pity on her. Wrong. Like I said, I cared for very few things these days. This was not one of them. *She* was not one of them. I couldn't afford to care for a *she* ever again.

Tilting my head to take in the rising moon peeking through the trees, I decided that it was too early on the journey for harm to come to her. I could probably explain away her disappearance in the more dangerous parts of the forest, but not here. Then again, my parents would never buy it. They'd had me trained too well to believe I'd let her fall to harm that easily. Eyeing the trees around me that made a clearing just large enough for the two of us and a small fire, I halted Cerberus. In the distance, I could hear water. This would do.

"We stop here tonight." I ignored how she leapt out of her skin and almost fell off the mare I was told was named Honey. I snorted. What a stupid name for a horse. I dismounted, unburdened, and patted the neck of my own massive steed, laying my forehead against his.

"Rest now, friend," I told him. He snorted, butting me, then wandered off towards the water. I turned to find that the female still hadn't moved. Lifting a brow, I began to wonder if she could. She'd obviously never ridden a horse before, and all considering, she had done well today. She was likely stiff and sore beyond measure. Poor thing. I suppose I could be nice just this once.

"Need some help?" I offered, trying to hide my amusement. She jumped, not realizing I'd come closer to her while she still glared at the ground like it was stories away instead of a few feet.

"I...um...yeah sure." Her voice was soft like a summer breeze, but it too held a lilt of warmth as if there was more under the surface. It made something shift inside me and I frowned. Stepping to her side, I glanced up into piercing, hazel eyes that did nothing to hide her fear. But then I could smell it too, along with the scent of.... vanilla. She smelled like fear and cherry blossom trees. And a hint of...was that embers? I'd thought the smell had been simply from the burning forest, but instead, it seemed to seep from the female herself. Interesting that she bore a name reflective of the very scent she carried. My frown deepening, I glared at her, then quickly gave a wicked grin.

"As you wish." Quick as lightning, I unhooked the strap of her saddle. She screamed as she suddenly slid off one side of the mare to the ground. Still grinning, I lifted the rest of the saddle off Honey and sent her after Cerberus. I glanced down at the female sprawled on the ground, pain twisting her face into a scowl.

"There. I helped." I walked away, noting the look of utter disbelief and hint of anger as I did. Hmm, maybe she had a backbone after all. The darkness reveled in her pain, but a small part of the old me.... that small part hung his head in shame.

Chapter 14

Thatch

Someone was screaming. At first, I thought it was me, but no, I'd escaped the night without *that* particular dream. Even still it took a while for me to reorient myself. Did I have another episode? They didn't happen very often anymore. Now I was very much awake when the darkness within me wanted to destroy.

I blinked as I sat up, gazing around the clearing. The horses rested not far away, exhausted from how hard I'd pushed them the last few days. I was determined to get this journey over with as soon as possible. Hopefully, the rumors of enemies creeping through the kingdom were just that.

I continued my perusal, but my eyes shot to the shivering bundle opposite the fire. She lay in the fetal position, her back to me, and every few seconds, a tortured whimper would escape her. I watched her, not knowing whether it was worth waking her. Before I could decide, she cried out and sat up with a start. Her eyes were frantic as she scanned the forest, her chest heaving with fear. Realizing she wasn't where she thought she was, she took a deep, shaky breath and pulled her knees to her chest. She stared forlornly into the fire as I studied her curiously.

Were the flames leaning towards her? What had she dreamed about? Something in my gut twisted at the sight of her fear and pain. It reminded me of...

Well, I didn't want to think about what it reminded me of, but there was a part of me that recognized her despair all the same.

In a rare moment of humility, I addressed her but kept my eyes on the flames. "I used to think dreams were a way to escape reality for a moment, like reading a fictional book." She was quiet for so long, I didn't think she would answer.

"Now?" she asked so softly that the wind had to carry the sound.

"Now, I wonder if dreams are only there to remind me of my failures, so I won't make them again. To punish me by making me relive them again and again so that being awake is the escape." She shifted, and I could feel her heavy gaze, but I continued to stare into the flames.

Damn. I shouldn't have said that. It was too revealing. More vulnerable than I'd been in centuries. Even my brothers and I didn't talk openly about the shadows that haunted our sleep. We all dealt with them in our unique way. Considering the hostile aura constantly permeating around Therek, some of us did so more aggressively than others.

"Those are nightmares," she said resolutely. "Dreams are those few moments where you're reminded that life – that you – are more than your failures. That there's a such thing as peace. Where you are allowed to imagine whatever you want." I snorted in disgust.

"That sounds like the thoughts of a child."

"No, it's the thoughts of an adult who hasn't had a dream in a very long time." I stiffened at the melancholy in her voice. She sounded much older than her current years, and I couldn't help wondering what made her sound that way. I raised my eyes to study her again, but she had already turned away from me and was now lying with her back to the fire. Curiosity had me asking despite her dismissal.

"If you no longer dream, where do you escape?" Her answer had the bottom falling out of my stomach and my heart racing, the tattoo over it burning as if in confirmation.

"The forest."

I didn't know how to respond. Didn't know what to make of this feeling that her words had sparked. So I turned away, and with a heavy sigh, returned to the land of sleep, hoping for silence. For I too had gone a long time without a dream.

Was the darkness trying to make up for my little slip a couple of nights before? Maybe. Maybe not. Had I been kind to her since then? No, I hadn't. And maybe having her ride through a mountain on a path that even the most surefooted horses struggled with was a bit much. Considering she had no riding experience, it was also probably taking it too far, but I couldn't help watching to see how she would respond. Would she snap at me, or just continue to fume in silence? Would she break down into tears and run back to the castle, or would she continue this silent treatment?

Considering how she'd appeared fragile to me from day one, I'd expected her to crack days ago. Preferably before we reached the cities and towns I had to visit. But alas, no such luck. Maybe the heat I sensed around her indicated more of a fiery heart than she was letting on. Maybe....maybe she just hadn't been pushed to the point of letting it out.

Was this what my older brothers had noticed? Despite myself, I wanted to see how much pushing I could do before her inner fire revealed itself. If she wasn't going to quit, then I could at least get some entertainment on this trip.

We were almost to Gris, but I was too impatient to take the longer, safer path, so when the trails branched off, I led us down the right. It was older and would likely be destroyed in an avalanche eventually, but currently, it was still the quickest route. After we'd made it about halfway down, I could feel the tension radiating off the female behind me grow.

"Should have gone around," she muttered grumpily, but I could hear the slight fear in her voice as the ground beneath us crumpled underneath the horses' hooves. Okay, so maybe we should have used a different route, but what was the fun in that?

The horses carefully weaved around the mountain pass, snorting occasionally when they triggered mini landslides. The pathway was narrow and the forest waiting several feet below held its breath. I could feel it. That sixth sense that I'd made a mistake. But the pathway was just about to widen up ahead. It was just a few more feet. Except those few feet were far enough for the mare behind me to slip, whinnying fearfully with her ears flattened. The female riding her, apparently not prepared for the quick way the mare corrected herself, slipped right off.... and over the edge of the cliff.

My eyes widened in shock as I watched her tumble out of sight, screaming. Blinking, I froze. "Well *fuck*. That just happened," I mumbled in disbelief.

"Help! Help Thatch, please!" I jolted. That was the first time I'd ever heard her call me by name. She'd barely spoken at all over the last week, and I'd avoided her altogether in Verdis. For some reason, the sound of my name on her lips had me reacting before I could think better of it. I jumped off my mount and leaned over the cliff to see her barely hanging on to a tree root. She was terrified, but she didn't cry as she desperately attempted to gain footing on the rock face.

"You promised!" The female...Ember...shrieked when I didn't immediately reach out to her. "You promised to get me back alive!" I scoffed. I'd actually never promised anything. My father had just demanded it like the king he was.

"I never promised you would go unscathed. The king did." She glared at me fiercely.

"I think I've been scathed," she bit out, pointedly eyeing the scrapes all over her arms and legs from trying to get back up the cliff. "Don't think *the king* would be pleased." Touché. But I still didn't reach for her.

Then suddenly the root was loosening, and she was falling again. My stomach dropped. Screams ended abruptly as I caught her, barely managing not to tumble over myself. My muscles burned and protested as I lifted her one-handed back over the cliff so that she fell against me. I tensed as I felt the curse recoil from her. *What the hell?* She immediately rolled off me, and we both lay there panting up at the sky, but for different reasons.

"I would say thank you, but you looked like you were going to leave me there," she snapped bitterly. I glanced over at her to see her sitting up. I smirked.

"But did I though?" Ember shot me a dirty look, and my grin grew. Hmm, I liked this fierier side of her better. Made things way more interesting. Maybe she wasn't some quiet wallflower after all.

As we both stood to our feet and walked the horses the rest of the way, I considered the reason she'd been quiet all this time. I suppose it was a lot to take in going from the human world to this one, just to immediately be told you're some prophesied princess and sent on a journey. Had she been processing all this time? Or had something in her life trained her to keep her true reactions close to her chest? I knew the fear was real, but for some reason, I had a feeling it didn't all have to do with me.

The curse wanted to pick at her more. The terror and the fire. It wanted to know which one it could get to flare more. If I was being honest, so did I. My brothers had told me to have some fun. Keeping her "alive" didn't mean I couldn't play with her too. I smiled wickedly to myself. The trees bowed away from me, but I was too distracted to care. For once I had another focus beyond the forest around me, and I was going to enjoy watching her break.

Chapter 15

Ember

That bastard almost let me die. I was still shaking...from shock and anger. That saying "see your life flash before your eyes" almost came to pass, but at the last moment, I'd grabbed the tree root. But Thatch would have let me fall if I hadn't reminded him of why he needed to save me. I wanted to scream at him, and the only thing that held me back was that Wink had explained how the Forest Prince had changed from the supposedly sweet and caring one to one where it was hit or miss whether he saved you or watched you die. I'd seen it myself when he'd gone from making me fall from my horse to connecting with me over dreams.

Also, when he'd grabbed me, I'd felt something. It was like the darkness in him retreated. Weird I know. Yet, he'd tensed, just for a moment, so maybe I hadn't imagined it. And I couldn't say I wasn't affected after having my body flush against the very firm male, his toned arms wrapped around me. For a split second, we'd both froze, the connection sending shivers through my body in an unfamiliar, exhilarating way. But still.... he'd almost let me die.

I wasn't sure what to think, but cowering wasn't going to make this journey any easier. I'd tried that before and look at what I'd endured. I would have to stand up for myself if I wanted to survive. I sighed. Not a new concept, just one that had to be navigated carefully. I didn't know what length this male would go if angered. I'd seen what evil men were capable of, but I refused to be a victim of another male's hatred. I didn't leave my father only to be crushed under the darkness of a Fae prince, even one who was much more powerful than me.

I'd spent too much of my life hiding my true thoughts, worried that it would result in an injury I couldn't recover from. But it was like that last interaction with my father had flipped a switch within me. There was this inner voice...this simmering foreign power that refused to back down. It was scary even as it was empowering.

As we descended the mountain path into a city Thatch had said was called Gris, I prepared to hold my ground against the angry male. Gris was.... well it was unlike any city I'd ever seen. We passed gates where the guard posts were basically treehouses – elaborate, fortress worthy treehouses, but treehouses just the same. Then, once we entered the city itself, it was as if a metropolis had been airlifted to the middle of the forest. While not as large as the ones back home, it was still impressive.

The further we traveled down the stone pathway, the homes and stores on either side of us became fancier and larger, often three or four levels with tunnels made of branches connecting some. They reminded me of an old movie I'd seen as a kid, Swiss Family Robinson, where the family built an elaborate treehouse home.

In the distance, I could make out a much larger structure that was the size of a small mansion. At least it was smaller than the castle in Verdis. The true kicker was that the entire city was within the trees. Wooden bridges – often simply the branches of the trees themselves, wide and smooth – mimicked alleyways and streets winding through the forest. It was intricate and so fluid that you would think the city naturally grew from the forest this way. The air itself was fragrant from the lovely, deep purple flowers that bloomed throughout the city.

It wasn't long before we were dismounting and handing off our horses to a young, stable boy – a small thing with sharp pointed ears – because all the livestock and horses remained on the ground. I watched as he led them away to a large stable also weaved from trees. Various pathways branched off into separate pastures for different animals – some of which I didn't even recognize – and even further down I saw hints of fields of plants that likely grew food for the people above it.

Forced to blink to wet my burning, dry eyes from staring wide-eyed, I followed after Thatch as he ascended to the treetops in a lift. It was powered by what I assumed were solar lights, as there were balls of light all along the "streets" and in the trees themselves. I tried to keep my eyes from popping out of my head as I watched the Fae go about their daily lives, chatting cheerily at a storefront here, greeting a friend from their house window there.

It was truly like a normal city even if the people were nothing like I was accustomed to. Their skin were of various shades and their bodies seemed to embody whatever creature or plant from nature they favored, same as they had at the ball. I tried not to stare at a female whose dark hair shifted like slithering snakes, or at a male who wielded a long bushy tail and ears resembling a wolf.

What I found even more interesting was how they greeted Thatch. While some bowed, curtsied, and called out his name in greeting, others avoided making eye contact and scurried out of his way as if afraid to draw his attention. I watched him closely since this was the first time I'd seen him interact with his people. But the prince before me was not the dark, angry male that had been my companion for the last week. No, this one smiled and greeted those who greeted him. He inquired about their loved ones and businesses. He winked mischievously and smirked at young females who blushed and giggled. He ruffled the hair of the children brave enough to run up to hug his calf.

My jaw dropped, and I blinked in disbelief. Was this the same male? Yes, there was still a wicked gleam in his dark eyes. Just enough that I knew that this was just a peek of the male present when the darkness wasn't completely in command. If he could switch it on and off at will, how much of the way he'd treated me was a choice?

Now I wasn't naïve. I knew the prince didn't like me, and I honestly couldn't say I was fond of him. But was he really under the control of a curse? If so, was it not necessarily that he could switch it on and off, but that once it was on, it was becoming more difficult to turn it off again? And was there really some magical bond that connected us that could counteract it...if the curse really did exist?

The idea that a trip across a forest would tell whether a bond existed between the dark prince and me was laughable. If I hadn't seen the serious expressions on the king and queen's faces myself, I'd thought this was some joke. But no. They thought I was their son's only hope of returning to who he used to be. Whoever that was. It wasn't my job to save a male who didn't want saving. I just needed to make it to the end of this stupid forest so I could go home and finally get on with my life. Not that I knew what I would do once I did make it home. I could never return to the orchard. There was always the slim chance that Dad made it out of the fire.

I shuddered, his screams bouncing around my head. But then...according to the Fae, he wasn't even my biological father. I mean if you took what they said at face value. But did it really make me feel better to think my real father was some mythical king who didn't care enough to raise me? If I thought about it – really thought about it – it was almost a relief to know I wasn't related to such evil. Except. I frowned. King of Disasters. With a title like that, how good was my supposed biological father?

I shook my head to clear it. I was going down a rabbit hole and right now I didn't have a way to find the answers I needed besides keeping up with the male in front of me. I blinked and glanced around. A male I no longer had sight of.

"Crap, crap, crap," I muttered to myself, trying not to panic. "Okay Ember. If you were an arrogant, dark prince in a treehouse city, where would you go?" I continued down the wooden streets, my head bouncing from side to side as I studied the buildings in front of me. I froze as I heard rowdy laughter and glass breaking. My eyes narrowed.

"You've got to be kidding me," I gritted out as I took in what was obviously a brothel. Because of course, those existed here too. I stormed up to the door where a sign read *The Red Room* and narrowed my eyes further. Without taking too long to consider, I strode in with a scowl. I tried not to stare at the women – or females rather – as they danced or served refreshments to the males who either watched them, played card games, or were in deep discussions.

This was *not* my scene, especially as I noticed more unrecognizable Fae. The male over there was pale as moonlight, and did that male have bat wings? I was pretty sure the bartender had green skin with vines for hair, and when he smiled at a guest, I noticed all his teeth were sharpened to deadly points. And why, oh why were so many people basically naked?

I blushed at the level of groans coming from one of the corners as a massive male took a small elven female from behind. That ever-present sliver of shame and disgust trickled down my spine, especially as a part of me looked on in averse interest.

I gulped and made my way quickly through the room, trying to catch sight of at least Thatch's green quiver. I needed to get out of here as quickly as possible before I was drowned in memories...or something worse.

"Need help with something sweetheart." I turned and came face to face with the devious grin of a tall Fae male. His hair was dark green and his skin dark brown, almost as if he could camouflage into the trees themselves. *What was up with the weird colored people around here?*

Around his waist were several daggers, along with a wicked looking broadsword down his back. A soldier most likely. A powerful one at that, if the bulging muscles were any indicator. A shot of panic flooded my veins as his eyes trailed down my body, and I fought a shiver and nausea. Something worse it was.

"You seem a little lost." His eyes focused on my chest where I knew I was generously gifted. "And a little overdressed." I swallowed around my revulsion and apprehension. *Tease. Slut.* I tried to ignore the words replaying in my head as I backed away.

"I'm good. I'm here with someone," I managed shakily, glancing around desperately for Thatch. Suddenly, he seemed like the safer option. Better the devil you know.

"Aww, come on sweetheart. Don't be like that. I'm sure they won't mind sharing." I turned around and flinched. When had he moved closer? Now I was pressed against a wall in what just so happened to be a darker part of the room. How did I always end up in bad situations like this? I flinched again as he stroked a finger down my cheek to my collarbone, and lower still until he was caressing my breast. Gods, his hands were cold even through my shirt, and I fought hard not to puke as shame and disgust flooded me. Not again. Please not again.

"Come now. Why don't you let me show you a good time." He grinned broadly, and that grin only seemed to grow when he noticed the terror holding me captive. Did he think I was faking? Some kind of role play? Considering I was in a brothel, I couldn't dismiss it. Fight or flight and I'd chosen freeze. Apparently, I'd used up the rest of my fight back home. Where was that inner power I'd been feeling now?

I tried not to gag as I smelled whatever alcohol the male had consumed, and before I could react, his lips were smashed against mine. I didn't think. I bit his tongue...hard and kneed him in the balls. Swearing, he pulled away. I should have seen it coming. I'd lived my entire life with it after all, but Fae were faster than humans, and before I could consider whether I'd made a mistake, I was on the ground with a throbbing cheek and blood in my mouth. My head was spinning so badly, I was sure I was going to pass out.

"Now, I'll also have to teach you some manners," he sneered, reaching for me. I closed my eyes and tensed, still trying to steady my spinning head. There were shouts and pained swearing, and then I was being lifted from the floor. Distantly, my brain registered that I no longer smelled the dirt and sour alcohol, but citrus and fresh cut wood, yet I still didn't open my eyes. I couldn't. I was too busy falling into the familiar respite of darkness.

Chapter 16

Thatch

Rage like I've never known was still racing through my veins. It fed the darkness to the point where I was considering going back and breaking a few more bones of the stupid male. I glanced down at the female on the bed. Her cheek was red and swollen, and she hadn't stirred since I'd lifted her. I gritted my teeth so hard, I was afraid one would crack.

He'd hit, kissed, and attempted to force himself on her. But that wasn't what had my blood boiling. Not even close. No, what made me want to go and pummel the male to release some of this pressure under my skin was her face. She hadn't fought him besides the bite and kick, but her face and body told of shame and helplessness. They told of the fact that this wasn't the first time she'd been violently accosted by a male. I had a feeling it wasn't the second, third, or fourth time. The terror I'd seen told of trauma that went back years. *Years.*

How long? How long had she been abused? Had she been.... I couldn't even finish the thought before my vision went black. I took deep breaths to control the darkness I knew was leaking into the forest around me. If I didn't get ahold of myself, I would crumple Gris to the ground overnight. I didn't need the death of my people on my conscience as well as the forest. I took several breaths before my vision finally cleared. A soft moan filled the room, and I turned to find her stirring. She opened her eyes and flinched as her hand shot to her face.

"Ow," Ember whispered, and my gut twisted at that soft exclamation. Her eyes scanned the room, her brows knitted in confusion, but she stiffened when she spotted me. Then, my blood was boiling all over again because she was looking at me as if she couldn't decide if I was friend or foe. As if I would ever strike her like that.

You did let her go over the cliff, I thought. But I was going to save her. I just wanted to scare her a little bit.

"You shouldn't have followed me," I snapped at her, needing to quiet my thoughts. She recoiled, and I instantly regretted it as her fear and anger permeated the room, burning my nose. *Gods*, I'd basically just told her getting assaulted was her fault.

"Well, if you didn't leave me in the middle of Gris and wander into a brothel, I wouldn't have had to follow you!" she snapped, sitting up. "Forgive me for being born female and entering a place where males have no qualms about objectifying them!"

It was my turn to flinch, but a part of me still reveled at the fire in her voice. I'd rather she stood up to me than cowered, but I realized now it was an oddity that she did so.

"That's not what I meant," I growled. "The females there know what they're getting into. They enjoy their work." Ember jumped from the bed and stomped over to me with a dark glare.

"Oh, and just because they enjoy it, that makes them and any female that walks in open for any old treatment?"

"No, that's not what I'm said."

"Oh, so you're saying, I should have been prepared to kiss that male back instead of biting him to stop his unwanted attention. That I shouldn't have kneed him in the balls for pushing his disgusting tongue into my mouth, because gods forbid it be unwanted since I asked for it, right?" We were both panting, rage making us face off in the middle of the room.

"No! Stop! I didn't say any of that."

"Then what are you trying to say Thatch! Because it sounds like to me that you think I deserved to be treated that way." And then the hurt and shame was flashing across her face so vividly I felt as if I'd been kicked in the gut.

"No one deserves to be treated that way. He had no right to touch you if you didn't want to be touched." I swallowed. "It's why I broke his hand and his jaw." Surprise flitted across her face before she turned away.

"Yeah, okay. Thanks, I guess," she muttered quietly after a moment. My fists clenched and unclenched as I watched her fold in on herself. Once again, I wondered how many times she'd been in that situation, and who'd put her there in the first place.

"That wasn't the first time, was it? That's why you're being so defensive?" I asked softly. She stiffened.

"That's none of your business Prince. And anyway, I don't see why you suddenly care. I'm just some female you need to escort across the kingdom, right? So don't worry about me. I'll be fine. I can look out for myself. I've made it this far alone, and I'll keep making it despite males like you and them."

I didn't like how she'd put me in the same category as the males who'd hurt her, even if I'd done my share of harm. "I'm not them," I gritted out. She sniffed, back still to me.

"Yeah, well, you could have fooled me."

Gritting my teeth against the retort I desperately wanted to make, I stalked from the room and into the sitting room, slamming the door behind me.

"Well, that went well." I turned to glare at the male in maroon and black hunter gear reclining on my couch like he owned the place. He held up his hands in surrender at my expression. "I'm just saying that blaming her for being attacked maybe wasn't the best idea." I snarled and I saw him tense even though the teasing smirk on his face didn't waver.

"Careful Lurk. I'm not in the mood for your BS," I growled. He shrugged, but nothing about the power radiating off him implied calm.

"It's not me you're still angry at," my best friend reminded me. His already dark eyes darkened until they were almost black. "If I had my way, Terc would have more than just a broken hand."

"I did break his jaw," I reminded him. Lurk growled low.

"Not nearly enough."

"Agreed, but Terc is still captain of the guard in Gris. Despite his obvious lapse in judgment, he is still damn good at his job." Lurk grumbled something under his breath, clearly not appeased. My eyes narrowed. "Plus, I made it very clear what would happen next time he decided to forget which kingdom he represented." His eyes lit up in understanding.

"That explains the pile of goop that looked mysteriously like metal," he said with a wicked gleam. I shrugged nonchalantly. I may have used the darkness to melt his favorite blade. At least the curse served a purpose this time.

"It could have easily been bone." Lurk chuckled.

"My how dark and ruthless you've become." His smile grew. "I approve." I raised a brow and Lurk waved his hand dismissively. "Yeah, yeah. Minus the little death you're causing the forest."

"It's not a little damage," I said quietly, sitting across from him and crossing my arms.

"Isn't that what the female is supposed to be for?" He said it mockingly, knowing the likelihood of a female from the human world being my savior to be slim to none.

"Forget Ember," I growled, not wanting to talk about my impending doom any longer. "What of the rumors you were telling me about before I had to rescue her?" Lurk gave me a knowing look.

"So Ember is her name." I scowled at him and he grinned and relaxed against the couch again. He knew very well what her name was.

"You're not going to like it," Lurk told me, his tone turning serious. I raised a brow again. "There have been tales of unknown figures traveling throughout the kingdom causing havoc. Homes have been destroyed, livestock slaughtered, and entire sections of the forest lost. And get this..." I gave him a questioning look.

"The destruction is made to either appear as if your power has done it...or fire." I blinked. Someone was mimicking my curse? How? Why? And fire?

"Why fire?" I wondered aloud. Lurk leaned his elbows on his knees, a frown on his face making the scar cutting down the left side from his eyebrow to his jaw jump. The warrior was one of my best, but that scar always reminded me to never take our experience for granted. The day you consider yourself infallible and become complacent is the day you are bested.

"That's one of the parts you aren't going to like. There are rumors that it is you and your mate causing the damage." My vision went black for a moment, and my senses dulled until all I could hear was this whooshing sound. When they returned I found Lurk frozen, watching me as if I was moments away from destroying the world like the rumors claimed.

"Who's spreading these rumors?" I snarled, my fists clenched tightly as I fought to stop the trembling I could feel spidering throughout the city. If I didn't stop, I would kill every plant here...and then the people.

"Right now, the foreigners, but no one seems ready to truly believe them as of yet. But that's not what worries me Thatch," Lurk said sullenly. "They've been spreading rumors of your supposed mate before she even came to this world. Even if we don't know who she is for sure..."

"How do they? And how did they know she was coming?" I finished. He nodded grimly. I frowned as I considered what he implied. "There's something bigger going on here," I said contemplatively.

"What do you want me to do?"

"Observe and collect intel. I have to travel through all four arcs before I return to the capital. By then, I expect to be bringing our king and queen news of an adversary defeated, not a kingdom destroyed." *At least not by anyone else but me*, I thought bitterly.

"And the princess?" I snorted in annoyance. If I hadn't already been around Ember, I'd think she had a hand in this, but no, if anything, she was just as much a victim here as the people being attacked.

"I'll handle her. Regardless of whether she's really the princess, she's been assigned to accompany me. Even if she's a part of this, she can't do anything with me watching her." Lurk nodded.

"So we wait."

"We wait."

We were back to not talking. I couldn't tell how much of that was because of what had happened in Gris or what I'd said, but as we left the city, I found myself glancing at her more often. I kept arguing with myself over whether I should explain why I was in the brothel to begin with. It wasn't for the females...although they were a bonus. It was a great place for gossip and a few of my men who patrolled this section of the forest loved to meet there.

Honestly, I hadn't thought about how it would look for her to walk into the brothel. I hadn't even noticed she was no longer behind me. I'd been too focused on Lurk telling me about the area around the summer court rotting rapidly. It made sense. The summer court was closest to the capital where I mainly resided. Any effects from the curse spidering out would reach them first.

While the effect of the curse wasn't as bad in the other seasons, it was only a matter of time before it spread further. Especially with me making my routine journey through them. It would likely spread more if I had to fight this threat being whispered throughout the kingdom. A threat that for once, wasn't caused by me...at least not directly. I didn't know if this unseen adversary was here because I was losing control of my power, but the fact they were causing damage and framing me was concerning.

There was a time when our enemies wouldn't have dared to enter our kingdom, but despite the curse growing in power each day, King Hyperion and Queen Sequoia were leaving more and more of my birthright for me to govern in preparation for when they deemed me ready to claim Alyvia's throne. Unfortunately, it appeared my pending rule was seen as more of an opportunity than a hindrance.

When I'd brought this concern to the king shortly before leaving, my father had simply reminded me of the lessons he'd given me and my brothers when we were each younger.

"A king is not simply a king because he is given a throne, or even because he conquers it. It is what he does with the power and responsibility that determines what kind of king he will become.

"You have my title and reputation behind you, but for your own rule to be successful and prosperous, you must create your own. You, like your brothers, believe that this curse prevents your mother and I from anointing you ruler over your respective kingdoms, when in fact it is your surrender to its inevitability that prevents your defeat of the curse and the claim of your crowns."

He'd placed a hand on my shoulder as I'd glared out the window of his chamber, his words as heavy as the crown he wore. His eyes had softened as I'd met his gaze. "I look forward to the day when you finally see what your mother and I have always known."

"What?" I'd asked tentatively.

"That you are only limited by the restraints you place on yourself. You and your brothers will do great things, and it is because I believe this that I'm already proud of the male you will become."

I'd been filled with shame because I knew I hadn't been living up to his expectations for a long time. He was right. I spent too much time blaming him and my mother for our predicament instead of fighting to overcome it. But it felt too late to change the bad habits I'd fallen into. To become the male my father was... who I wished I could be.

I glanced up at the canopy where redwoods, oaks, maples, and others swayed in the breeze. They still seemed to recoil from me, and the calls of the animals were silent. Once upon a time, the forest came alive in my presence. Now it only represented death, and nature seemed to sense that. The forest that used to be my escape now feared *me.* How did one reconcile that?

"Why was it so much warmer in Gris?" I startled, shooting a glance at the female who'd ridden up beside me. Ember was getting better at riding despite my lack of assistance. She looked almost regal as if she truly was a princess riding through her kingdom.

I frowned. What was I thinking? She was still just a normal female. A female with an aura that gave off more heat than the first time we'd met. A female that had triggered the tattoo to grow another branch while we were in Gris. I hadn't told Lurk about the tattoo's growth, although he'd already heard about my parents' reaction to seeing it.

"What?" I replied, forgetting what she'd asked. Damn, my brain was so scattered today. Dangerous for trekking through a forest with unknown adversaries.

"In Gris. It was warmer than it had been at the castle. Why?" I blinked. She'd noticed that, huh? Well, it wouldn't hurt to answer her this. I owed her some level of decency after what I'd said in the city.

And why do you care? I thought bitterly. I shook my head before considering her.

"Alyvia is broken up into seasons. The thin strip of forest around the capital, Verdis, and at the border of the kingdom itself surrounds all four. The rest of the forest breaks off in an expanding arc between them. The first is summer." She turned to watch me, and I gestured to the trees around us.

"The trees, animals, and Fae that reside there tend to change within each season. The next arc is autumn, then winter, and finally spring. Only once we have passed through all four will we have journeyed the breadth of the Forest Kingdom." She frowned thoughtfully as she glanced around us, taking in the plants.

"How often do you travel through...the arcs?"

"At least once a year since it's part of my princely duties," I replied. I shrugged. "Although, I'm usually gone for months when I do."

"Months?" I heard her whisper in horror. Ember shuddered slightly but eyed me curiously. I tried not to flinch under her stare. She seemed to see more than I wanted her to. It was confirmed with her next question.

"Does it take months to trek, or do you just prefer not being home?" I sucked in a startled breath but managed to keep my face indifferent.

"It does not take months to trek, no. Not if I travel straight through, hitting only the main cities," I answered simply. I waited for her to dig further – the truth was nowadays I lingered in the arcs to avoid the sad and disappointed gazes of my parents – but she only nodded.

"Which is your favorite season?" I turned to her surprised, but she wasn't looking at me. "Mine was always spring. There's something magical in watching nature come back to life after a season of death. Each new sprout of green against the brown and grey is like a fresh breath of air."

All I could do was stare at her in shock....and a little bit of awe. I couldn't have described it better myself. Honestly, I loved each season for a different reason...or at least I used to.

"Used to be late spring into early summer," I found myself answering. It was the time of breeding where young were everywhere. "I used to slip through the forest as a child, trying to spot the new offspring of all the animals that lived here. I'd earned their respect – their trust – and most, if not all, would let me get close, even hold their young." I swallowed and looked away from the female who kept reminding me of a better time. When was the last time the animals of the forest trusted me near their young? When was the last time I cared about them at all?

"You said used to be. What is it now?" She asked, still curious, still prodding the ache building in my chest.

"Dead of winter," I replied as the ache grew. She tilted her head, a frown twisting her brow.

"Why?" I didn't meet her eyes as I raised a fist to press hard against the pain in my chest.

"Because it's the only time I can't destroy." Not wanting to answer any more questions, I clucked, pushing Cerberus into a canter. I heard her yelp as her mare sped up to follow me, but all I could see were the memories of who I used to be....and who I would never be again.

Chapter 17

Ember

As we traveled through the summer arc – which was apparently, the largest arc – I couldn't help but think there was more to the dark prince than I'd originally thought. As much as I tried to ignore him, I couldn't help but feel the aura around him. It was an ability I'd always held, but Thatch's was more evident to me than any other I'd ever seen. Yes, it held darkness, but I also sensed...sadness, guilt, and resignation.

It was almost as if Thatch had given up on ever breaking the hold the darkness had on him. Because it did have a hold on him. During the brief moments where I saw him interact with his people, first in Gris, and now in this small village we'd just visited– and even during the rare times he was kind to me – I could see the aura around him was grass green but edged with jagged black. At times the black and green switched places, and maybe this was the result of this so-called curse.

Could I deny there was something off about how Thatch's behavior flip-flopped when I could see his aura for myself? I mean I'd never even explained to my friends at school, or my mom and brother, how I could always tell a little about the character of a person by their aura. My mother's had been gentle pink...my father, a violent crimson. If I could do some paranormal things, could I really deny the claims that a curse was causing Thatch to act out of character?

I shot a look across the fire at the fierce male who currently twisted some type of rodent-looking thing, that reminded me of a groundhog, over the flames. I still didn't believe I was the cure for what ailed him. What if it wasn't about a bond at all, but about convincing the resigned male to fight the darkness? I mean, I knew a little bit about believing things weren't going to get any better. You become so used to the darkness that you start to forget there's light. I know I had.

Despite the uncertainty that came from being in the Fae world, it had still been a better experience, even in the short time I'd been here, than the life I'd lived the last few years. I sighed. What did that say about me? I'd rather travel gods knew where with a dark prince I didn't know, and face his equally dark brothers, than be home with an abusive father and his touchy feely friends?

I was so lost in my thoughts, it took me a moment to realize the forest had gone quiet. Well, it had been quiet before, as it was in the prince's presence, but this was different. This was "calm before the storm" quiet.

I glanced up, startled, only to meet his tense gaze across the fire. Thatch slowly lifted a finger to his lips as he reached his other hand towards his bow laying at his side. I nodded stiffly, fear and something else flooding my veins. He stood slowly, pulling his bow around and notching it. I glanced to the side to see the horses had disappeared. I frowned and shot a glance back to Thatch. He shook his head once.

Don't move, his eyes seemed to say and I tried to obey, but I could feel a heat rushing over me as a presence burned into my back. I took deep, shaky breaths as I slowly glanced over my shoulder. The moon was bright, but I could still barely see anything. Well, nothing but glowing eyes between the trees.

I blinked. Eyes? I looked again and now the eyes were over a grinning ring of sharp teeth. My own widened in horror as I slowly scanned the trees to find more and more eyes watching us. When my gaze finally met the dark green ones of the prince, his horror matched my own.

"Get down," he mouthed, right as the first wolves jumped out of the trees. I bit back a scream as I dropped to the ground beside the log. I stared in terror as wolves as big as bulls and twice as deadly came at him from all sides. He was effectively shooting them down one by one and somehow avoiding getting sliced or ripped to shreds in the process.

I was so focused on him, I didn't notice the looming gray wolf above me until viscous drool dripped onto my cheek. Rubbing it off, I turned to meet its snarling grin. I did scream this time, and Thatch spun to face me just as the wolf went to bite my face off. But one minute it was lunging and the next it was a dead weight on top of me. Breathing hard, I managed to push it off and stared wide-eyed at the arrow through its head.

"Ember! To me! Come to me!" Jolted out of my rising panic by my name, I turned to see Thatch still franticly fighting off the wolfpack. He had his long dagger now that he was using to swipe out as he fought to reach me. He was battling hard, but he was outnumbered. A bigger wolf than all the others appeared on the sidelines, its eyes pinned on the prince. It prowled closer, the other wolves parting to give it room. Thatch was still fighting and didn't see it. He *did* see the ones coming for me though.

"Ember!" I spun as three wolves leapt towards me at the same time that the alpha landed on Thatch's back. I screamed...and the night turned to day. There were whimpers and cries, and then the forest was silent. I lay on my side panting, unwilling to open my eyes. I startled and screamed again when something cool touched my cheek, trying to roll into a ball.

"Hey. Hey. Easy. It's just me. Open your eyes Princess." Princess? Confused, I slowly opened them and blinked up at the dark prince kneeling before me.

"Are they gone?" I whispered. Thatch grimaced as if in pain but nodded.

"They're gone." I sat up slowly and glanced around us, shock making my eyes widen. Several bodies lay around us.... burnt to a crisp. My eyes shot back to his.

"What happened?" He glanced around at the carnage and small patches of flames still burning.

"Well, as much as I hate to admit it, I think my parents are right." He made a face and shook his head in disbelief, but I wasn't following.

"Right about what exactly?" I insisted. He looked at me then.... like *really* looked at me as if this was the first time he was seeing me. A part of me felt unnerved, but another part felt a flicker of heat at his perusal.

"You can summon flames. You are indeed the Princess of Fire." I blinked, then I was shaking my head in denial.

"No. No, that can't be. I can't summon fire. I'm not some mythical princess. I'm human." I scooted back away from him. "No. Even if I could summon fire, how is that proof I'm the Princess of Fire? I'm sure there are several Fae that can do that." But Thatch was already shaking his head.

"Manipulate flames that already exist, yes. But the ability to create fire from nothing, there is only one being who is said to hold such power." I shook my head. This couldn't be real. I was stuck in another nightmare. In another dimension. Something. Because I was one hundred percent human and I could not summon fire.

"You're wrong. It's impossible. It's.... Thatch? Are you okay?" The prince gave me a funny look, even as he swayed.

"I'm fine," he snapped. Then, his eyes rolled to the back of his head, and he collapsed beside me. It was only then that I remembered what I'd forgotten. He'd been attacked by the giant wolf and now blood was gushing from beneath him so violently I was surprised he'd lasted this long without fainting. Hell, I was about to join him because *gods* that was *a lot* of blood. It pooled around him, unable to seep into the soil fast enough. I bit back my panic and shook my head.

"No," I reprimanded myself. "He needs you. You need to get it together. This isn't the first wound you've had to treat."

Although none had been this intense, with that peptalk I swiftly moved to his packs and dug around until I found what appeared to be a first aid kit. I didn't recognize some of the contents, but bandages were universal, so I grabbed a roll of it, and what looked like salve and hurried back to him. Realizing I needed to clean the wound first, I quickly ran back to his pack, grabbed the largest bowl I could find, filled it with water, and then tore off cloth from one of his extra shirts to use as a towel.

I quickly used his dagger to cut off the strips of his shirt in the front, before carefully shifting him onto his belly and out of the bloodbath. He groaned in deep agony but did not wake, and I pulled the remaining pieces of his shirt away to assess the damage. Sucking in a sharp breath, I fought the nausea that threatened as I took in the five deep slash marks that now marred his back. They cut right through a hawk, wings outstretched, tattooed across his entire back. Gods, that had to hurt.

Not stopping to think about how much blood he was still losing, I quickly washed the wounds as best I could. He growled incoherently and tensed at the pain, but despite the fluttering under his eyelids, he didn't open them. I gingerly rubbed the salve in as his body jerked with every sweep. Finally, I managed, with much huffing and puffing, to get the bandage wrapped around his back. By the time I was finished, the agony on his face seemed to have lessened, and he was breathing steadily again, so I took that as a good sign.

Only after I had cleaned up the supplies, covered him with a blanket, and buried the blood pool with dirt did I consider the clearing around us. The fire had burned so hot that all that was left of the giant wolves were piles of ash. Chills ran through me. I had done *that*? Me? I quickly grabbed a stick with branches of leaves and scattered the ashes until the dirt around us concealed them. Relieved to not have to stare at them anymore, I grabbed some dried meat from Thatch's bag, grimacing at our destroyed dinner, and sat cross-legged next to his head. His body had relaxed some more, so maybe the salve was helping.

Absentmindedly, as I nibbled on the dried meat, I ran a hand through his unruly, midnight black hair. It was surprisingly soft, and Thatch seemed to sigh, and then relax at the contact, so I continued to comb it. I'd never purposely been this close to him, and I couldn't help taking in the firmness of his body. Here was a male who had muscles not from a gym but from legit life and you could tell he'd fought hard to get it if the scars crisscrossing him were any indication.

His tattoos matched him as well. A tattoo depicting a mountain rising out of the sea and piercing a cloud covered his left bicep. A representation of his brothers maybe? There was a vine of roses that encircled his right arm. The details so vivid that it almost looked like you would actually get pricked by the thorns there. The vine continued over his shoulder and down his entire right side, spanning into half his chest, before disappearing into his pants. I was almost curious enough to see how far down it traveled. Almost. Instead, I took in his long eyelashes, his sharp cheekbones, full lips, and dark mahogany colored skin. It was a color fitting a prince of the forest. Staring down at him in all his ruggedness, I had to admit he was handsome. In a brutal, dark way.

I found myself remembering how he'd protected me without hesitation this time. It made me wonder if my previous assessment had been correct. Was Thatch so resigned to his fate that he didn't realize how much control he actually had? Or was there something that had caused him to give up in the first place?

I wouldn't know unless he told me, and despite myself, I truly wanted to. I wanted to understand the dark prince who was sometimes not so dark. Who'd broken another male's hand and jaw because he'd touched me without my permission. No one had ever done that for me. Given me pitying looks and empty apologies, but never redemption.

Who'd let me fall off my horse but saved me from falling off a cliff. Who'd taken a wolf to the back. His behavior was so contradictory. His darkness and sheer power terrified me, but at the same time, I felt safer with him than I'd ever felt around a male. How was that even possible?

Thatch grunted and groaned. My eyes shot to his as they fluttered open. He stared at me for several, long seconds before he finally shifted. Holding my breath, I watched as he gingerly moved until he was sitting against the log next to me. He sighed once he was settled and took in the clearing around us.

"You buried them." It wasn't a question or an accusation, and I wasn't sure what response he was looking for, but I nodded. "And bandaged my back." Still not a question, but I nodded again. He didn't say anything for a while, then. "I probably should thank you, huh?" I blinked and considered him, my brow raised.

Thatch glanced at me and winced. "What I meant to say was, thank you for not leaving me to bleed out." I frowned. I hadn't even considered that I could have used this time to escape. Where would I go? It was the middle of the night and only one being was obligated to protect me at all.

"It's I who should be thanking you," I said softly. "You took a demon wolf to the back while I cowered beside a log." I scowled in disgust at myself. He snorted in amusement.

"They're called dyrewolves and if you remember, I told you to get down. You were doing exactly what you were supposed to do."

"But you were outnumbered," I pointed out. "And then you were attacked...."

"And then you saved me and yourself," he cut in. I froze. Thatch studied me and smirked. "I thought you were some weak, defenseless human, and you took out half a pack of dyrewolves to the point where only ash remained. It's not often I admit I'm wrong but in this case." He shrugged, then, winced.

"Are you alright?" I asked, glancing at his back.

"Oh, this?" He gestured at his back. "The salve will heal it in a couple of days. My mother has a way with healing, and with sons who tend to get into everything, she's perfected it over the years."

"It still probably hurts though," I insisted. He glanced at me and relented.

"A little, yes. But it could have been worse." Yeah, he could have been eaten by wolves or left to die.

"True. It can always be worse." I smiled tentatively, and he shook his head with a small smile. We were quiet for a while, just listening to the wind weave through the trees as the flames danced.

"What now?" I whispered. He didn't have to ask what I meant.

"Now, we sleep," he replied quietly. "And then we continue our journey through the kingdom." He glanced at me. "We'll need to add some lessons in along the way. Can't have you roasting me randomly." I snorted in reluctant amusement.

"Maybe with the threat of fire, you'll be nicer," I retorted softly. Thatch's smile dropped, and he stared at me intently, a serious expression on his face.

"I can't promise you that Ember," he said quietly. "Don't mistake me for a friend just because I fought for you. I am still the same cursed prince you've known over the last few weeks. Nothing will change that."

"What if that could change?" I asked softly, but he shook his head.

"I'm not that prince anymore. I can't promise to be nice to you. I don't have it in me to give that part of myself again." I frowned, not fully understanding what he meant.

"So, what? Despite what we've gone through, you're going to pretend to not care about whether I live or die? To not care about your people or this forest?" Thatch shook his head again.

"I don't care Ember. I protect you because my father demands I bring you back as unscathed as possible. It is a duty, that is all."

"And your people?" I insisted, not ready to believe the peeks of good I'd seen were only him fulfilling a duty.

"My people recognize that there will come a day when I will leave rather than destroy their homes completely." I stared at him in shock and horror. A kingdom without the Prince of Forest to rule it?

"You're giving up? Why? Do you not want to beat this curse?" He smiled sadly.

"Even if you truly are the Princess of Fire, that doesn't make us mates, and there is no beating this curse. I accepted that a long time ago."

"But why? Why do you so readily accept death?" I said exasperated, unable to believe the warrior in him could quit so easily.

"I learned what happens if I try to combat the curse. I learned what happens when I dream Ember, so I stopped dreaming. There was only regret and sorrow, so I won't do that...not again." He whispered the last two words, and I fought for words of my own, but I had none. How could I convince him to walk out of the darkness when I myself could barely recognize the light?

He scooted down and laid on his side, his back to me. "Sleep, Princess. We still have a long way to go before you can go home." You, not we. Thatch didn't believe he had a home to return to, no more than I did, and as I turned to lie down as well, I shed a tear for both of us. For the children inside who'd forgotten what it felt like to dream...to truly live. As I closed my eyes, distantly, I found myself wondering why he would have a tree with a heart of fire tattooed over his heart.

Chapter 18

Thatch

Gods my back hurt like I'd been stung by several hornets. It had to be residual pain because the wounds had completely healed a few days ago, just as I said they would. I would need to get Lurk to fill in my hawk next I saw him.

Or maybe it was more centered in the chest area because something kept shooting pain there that spidered out from the tattoo over my heart. I didn't dare speculate too closely on what that could mean. Not when Ember had insisted on cleaning my wounds and reapplying my salve twice a day. Not when her fingers almost as callused as my own, but still soft, trailed along my skin. The pain from my wounds was nothing like the pain from the enjoyment of having someone care for me.

Not someone. Her. The normal female who I was now convinced was anything but. I could tell she was wary of males, but when she touched me...suddenly I didn't feel like the monster I'd been towards her and everyone in my life for centuries. In fact, despite my denial, the darkness settled around her. I could even feel the flicker of life in my core that used to thrive. It was a euphoric sensation that almost made me desperate for an excuse to touch her again.

I shook my head to clear it. Shifting uncomfortably on Cerberus, I fought the desire to glance at the female who now rode at my side. Whether this was because she felt safer there or to keep a closer eye on my back as I rode, I wasn't sure. And honestly, it shouldn't matter. She was still a means to an end. No matter the fact she could summon fire – which I really needed to train her on before she burned down my forest – or that the darkness responded to her touch, it was not to be between us. I couldn't allow it.

I would train her. I would protect her. Try my darnedest not to harm her too permanently, but at the end of this journey she would be going home and I... well I wasn't sure where I would be. Not here for sure. I could care long enough to leave. I owed my kingdom at least that.

And the female at my side. I stole a glance at Ember despite my better judgment. Gods, she was a complication I wasn't fully sure how to handle. I fought the urge to rub at my chest as more pain shot from around my heart. Rage, dark, unrelenting rage, arrowed through me in answer obliterating my word to bring her as little harm as possible. The darkness knew what she did and for some reason I wasn't ready to face, it knew the meaning of the tattoo too. It was in its best interest to get rid of her as soon as possible...just as it had done before.

Gritting my teeth, I fought the wave of power ricocheting out of me, but it was too late. The forest groaned, the animals cried out, and every living thing besides our little group shriveled and died within a one mile radius.

There was a sharp gasp from beside me, but I was still hunched over my horse, eyes squeezed shut as I fought the power still radiating out of me, and the shock of so much death. I could feel the curse yanking as it laughed at my torment. Did I say I cared? Silly me. Caring is how the life around me died. No, caring was dangerous. If I shut it off, then it wouldn't hurt so much to feel and see the forest I loved so much destroyed by my own hands. Yes, that's it. I just needed to shut it off for a while.

I jerked as a small hand touched my arm. My eyes shot open to meet concerned hazel eyes. Were those flecks of green in her irises? Green like fresh spring leaves? I shook my head, but her gaze stayed fixed on me.

"Thatch, are you okay? Is it your back? Did that wave of darkness hurt you too?" I snorted. If only the nonexistent pain in my back was my only problem. No, turn it off. Don't let her touch get to you. Turn it off. *Turn it off.*

I sat up straighter, my face clearing as the waves of power stopped. I could feel the death around me, but I no longer cared. "Fine," I told her simply. Then, I rode ahead, stepping over the decay now scattered all around us, the darkness once again a blanket around my pain.

Ember watched me closely as I went through business in Laark. Meeting with the leaders there, this time with her standing against the treehouse wall behind me, was something I could very much do without. They continued to share reports of the damage to the forest, to their crops, and I stared at them with a bored expression as I reclined in my chair with one arm thrown over the back. I could feel her growing disapproval as I continued to blatantly dismiss the city leaders' concerns. I could even feel the heat in the room start to rise as I only blinked at their report of the water supply drying up.

"The river used to be raging, Your Highness," an older female Fae pointed out for the millionth time. "Now, it is a creek that ambles by. We've managed to source water from elsewhere, but it's not sustainable long term."

I waved a hand. "So, you've handled the problem." I went to stand, bored with this conversation. She shook her head insistently, her cobalt eyes stricken.

"You misheard me Your Highness. I said it's unsustainable. Without the river returning, we won't have enough water to maintain the city within the next year." The other leaders nodded their agreement. I scowled.

"And what do you expect me to do about it?" I growled, growing impatient. They blanched and some straight out recoiled. I knew they could feel the darkness rising, threatening to rot their city until it crumbled to the ground below. "You have the situation handled from what I hear. Keep handling it." With that, I walked out.

I didn't acknowledge the furious steps that followed me, not until we reached the townhouse that I usually stayed in. I stalked to the nauseatingly exquisite bedroom, surprised when she followed me inside.

"If you have something you want to say, then say it," I growled over my shoulder. "Unless you're too much of a wallflower to speak your mind. But see, I don't think that's the case. I think you hold back because you're afraid of what will happen if you do speak." I shrugged nonchalantly. "I don't care what you have to say. It doesn't affect me one way or another, so speak."

There was silence before the princess moved so that she stood in front of me. Her eyes were blazing, her fists balled and she bristled with such heat that she just might burn this city down before I decimated it myself.

"Why do you do that?" Ember snapped. I blinked lazily.

"Do what?"

"Switch your personality like that?" I lifted a brow.

"I don't know what you mean." Her eyes flashed and my power – the one buried deep – flickered in response to the heat raging in them.

"I think you do. I saw you in Gris." I frowned, but she continued. "I saw you in the small villages after that. Who I saw out there today." she pointed furiously at the door. "He is not the same prince. The prince I saw before would have never dismissed the struggles of his people. The prince I saw before cared and felt guilt over the destruction of the forest."

I plucked nonexistent lint off my tunic. "Maybe you don't know the Prince of Forest as well as you think you do," I suggested. I glanced at her and held my arms out wide. "This is me Princess. You may be new to Alyvia but make no misconceptions, the prince who cures the woes of this forest has been gone for over two centuries. You've never met him, and honestly, you never will."

I went to step around her, but she moved in front of me again. I lifted a brow. Bold, considering I saw a flash of uncertainty in her gaze and the tension in her body. Apparently, it didn't overshadow her grievances with my behavior because she still held her head high as she spoke.

"Bullshit." I blinked.

"Say again."

"I call bullshit. You want the world to believe that the prince you used to be is gone, but I don't believe that. If that was so, the guilt and regret I've seen wouldn't exist. The attentiveness to his people wouldn't exist. And he definitely wouldn't have taken on a dyrewolf attack for a human he didn't know."

I tensed, the darkness racing through my veins as I narrowed my eyes. I stalked towards her, causing her to back up until her back met the wall. She gasped, but her determined eyes didn't leave mine and if anything, the heat in them rose, even as her heart rate started racing and a tinge of fear entered her expressive eyes. I placed a hand on either side of her head and leaned in close.

"You. Don't. Know. Me. Princess," I growled quietly. "I bring death everywhere I go. The lively Prince of Forest is *dead*. This is all who's left. I only waste my time catering to the people, when I have the patience for it, so they will leave me alone. I only saved you because my father, the king, ordered it done, and so that I can be rid of you when we return. I am not a good male. Haven't been for a very long time. Stop trying to make me into someone I'm not."

She was breathing hard, her heart rate still racing, unease still seeping from her pores, but she still whispered, "I don't believe that." I gritted my teeth, ready to snap at her, but then she did something so unexpected I fought back a wince. She placed a shaky hand right over my heart. "And right here, deep inside, I don't think you believe that either." She was grasping for straws and her hand on my body made the darkness rage. It flared around us and she jerked her hand away in terror.

"You're afraid of me," I growled. She shook her head in denial, but I'd seen it. "You are, and you should be. This is your final warning. Don't expect me to be this nice Prince Charming from your human fairytales. That's not me. I. *Will*. Hurt. You. Don't ever doubt that." I pushed away from her, suddenly wanting to see something else besides the fear leaking from her. I needed to burn off this energy before I did something worse than destroy a mile of forest.

But as I reached for the door to stroll out, I heard her whisper so softly, I almost thought I'd imagined it. "I learned a long time ago, that fairy tales don't exist. No one ever came to save me." My darkness blanketed heart clenched, and I slammed the door behind me so hard it shook, but no matter how much her words affected me, I couldn't save her. I couldn't even save myself.

Chapter 19

Thatch

"Thatch." I raised my head from the almost empty glass of liquor in my hand. Lurk slipped into the seat across from me. He shot the drink in my hand a questioning look. "Rough night?"

"Rough century." He snorted, but the dark-eyed male knew it for the truth it was. Lurk gestured for the barmaid to bring him a drink and refill mine. She grinned broadly at me, her long red hair barely concealing her bodice as she leaned over the table to do so. I kept my eyes on Lurk, but they narrowed as his knowing grin grew broader and broader.

"Thank you darling," he drawled with a wink, and the faerie giggled and blushed, her translucent wings fluttering. I rolled my eyes and bit back a growl. "So touchy tonight My Prince," Lurk teased, taking a sip.

"Oh shut up," I growled.

"My, my. What a bad mood we're in. Have you ever considered just fucking her?" I choked on the sip I was taking. He watched in amusement as I coughed to clear my lungs.

"Bastard," I snarled when I could breathe again, but he only grinned.

"Come now Thatch. I've never seen you this irritated over a female." I scoffed.

"This has nothing to do with Ember." Lurk lifted a brow, a teasing smirk still on his face.

"You sure?" I growled a warning and he shrugged.

"Fine, should we talk about how you left Laark with a life threatening water issue instead?" I glared at him. "You know, the one Hyperion sent you to fix?"

"Father sent me to hunt down these foreigners spreading deceit and unrest in the kingdom, not...."

"Fix the damage you've caused," Lurk finished, cutting me off. Deep shame speared through me, but I kept my face indifferent. His eyes softened slightly. "Thatch..."

"Don't," I replied quietly. "This isn't why I called you here." He studied me for several moments. I knew he wanted to argue his point, but he sighed.

"What is it you need?" Regret clenched my chest, but I took a drink to wash it down.

"Did you bring your tattoo kit?" Lurk frowned.

"Yeah, why? What did you do now?" I stared at him incredulously.

"What makes you think *I* did something?" He lifted a brow and I snorted. "Fair enough, but it wasn't my doing. We were attacked by dyrewolves a week ago and they caught me down my back." He nodded in understanding.

"Shall we?" Grabbing our drinks and gesturing to the barmaid to bring us more refills, we retreated to one of the back rooms. Wordlessly, as Lurk pulled out his kit, I grabbed a chair and spun it backwards before pulling my tunic over my head and sitting. I shot back the rest of my glass and set it aside.

"Shit Thatch." I glanced over my shoulder to see him staring wide-eyed at the five claw marks scarring my back. He raised his surprised gaze to mine. "How the hell didn't you bleed out?"

I thought back to the feeling of fingers combing through my hair as the coolness of the salve fought against the agony ripping my back apart. For a moment there was no curse coursing through my veins, just the sweet smell of cherry blossoms and embers. I shook my head to clear it.

"Let's just say a certain princess does have fire abilities after all."

"Shit," Lurk swore. "So it's true? She's the King of Disaster's daughter?" It still blew my mind, but I nodded. "So, she's..."

"No, she's not!" I snapped, but his gaze shot down to the tattoo over my heart. It was larger still. The kernel of flames now reaching halfway up the tree trunk. There were several small branches, and even the root system spread down my chest. It was well on its way to covering my entire left pec.

"Okay, I know you don't want to consider it, but the prophecy mentioned that the Princess of Disaster would lift the curse," Lurk pointed out carefully. "Ember is the Princess of Fire, the very element that would complement a prince over the forest. So, is there a chance that she may have the ability to at least help save the forest?"

What a diplomatic way of phrasing that question. We both knew the true way to save the forest was to either save or remove me. The former was impossible, the latter...well if she was here to destroy me, for the sake of my kingdom, I just might let her.

"That's not what I meant Thatch," Lurk said quietly, but he lifted the inking needle. I spun to face the chair again, unflinching as he filled in the hawk on my back. It had always reminded me of freedom. The freedom to view my beloved forest from above, to appreciate its vastness and beauty, and to also call it home. I loved Alyvia. I hadn't shown it so in decades, but it didn't make the fact less true. In the end, would my parents and Lurk be right? Was she my and my kingdom's salvation? Or our demise?

Chapter 20

Ember

Someone was here. I could feel them shifting through the townhouse on silent feet. What were they looking for? *Who* were they looking for? For a moment I thought Thatch had returned. He had been gone for almost two days. Maybe I'd pushed too hard. I thought he was going to strike me down, but in the end, he'd stormed out. At first, I'd waited, but when he hadn't returned, I'd gone out searching for him, only to get lost for hours. By the time I found the house again, I was too relieved to leave its walls.

Now someone besides Thatch stalked the halls, and I had no way to protect myself and no one to turn to. Not that the latter was anything new, but I felt even more helpless in this world where everyone seemed to have more abilities than humans could ever dream of.

"I'm not here to harm you Princess," came a deep whisper. I spun to find a tall male with dark eyes and short black hair watching me. He wore a dark brown tunic and pants with a bow at his back and a jagged scar cutting down the left side of his face.

"Who are you?" I whispered, wishing my voice sounded stronger. Wishing I *could* control the heat simmering in my veins.

"I am Lurk Sempris, Your Highness. I'm a close friend of Thatch." I snorted.

"Is that supposed to make me feel better?" He chuckled and shifted so the moonlight from the window illuminated him better. I could now see that his eyes weren't black like I'd thought, but a deep maroon. They were odd, but all I saw in them was a rare kindness.

"No, I suppose not, but I truly mean you no harm." I studied him, taking in the winding tattoos down both his bare arms that depicted thorned vines. They reminded me of another set of vine tattoos.

"You did Thatch's tattoos?" He glanced down at his arm and chuckled again.

"Good eye. Yes, I do all our tattoos, including those worn by the other Princes of Nature."

"You're all friends?" I asked skeptically, and he nodded. "How?" His eyes filled with sadness and he glanced down briefly before meeting my gaze again.

"They weren't always the dark males you've met," he said softly.

"The curse." It wasn't a question, but I was interested in hearing this male's take on it.

"I grew up with them," he explained. "So I had a front row seat to how their normal tendencies were twisted and morphed into a darker, angrier, more unforgiving version." Sadness flashed across his face again.

"You don't understand. You never knew them when they were the princes of life, so you don't know what the kingdoms lost as the curse ate away at them. It was worse as they gave up hope...as we gave up hope. The waves of darkness grew more frequent, and they stopped working to reverse them."

I gasped. So it *had* been Thatch who'd killed the forest all those days ago. I'd hoped that the wave of darkness was a separate thing, not his own power twisted into death.

Lurk studied me then, with a gaze that was both hopeful and wary. "And then came you," he whispered.

"Me? What can I do?" He smiled.

"You give us hope for the first time in centuries. And if you save my best friend...you will have my loyalty and depthless gratitude for eternity."

"But why? I'm just a normal girl." His smile grew as he shook his head.

"No Ember. You are the flicker of light in the darkness. Once you both believe that, there is nothing you can't do." I blinked, unable to come up with a reply, but it didn't matter. Between one blink and another, he was gone, leaving me to wonder if he'd been there at all. Then I noticed the parchment sitting on the windowsill.

Grabbing it, I took in the drawing of the most beautiful tattoo I'd ever seen. Something about it spoke to a deeper part of me that I couldn't explain. There was a rightness to it I didn't understand. And then I read the words underneath.

"I'll gladly tattoo this for you when the time is right. I drew this many years ago, waiting for the perfect person to wear it. It was always meant to be yours."

I didn't know what to make of the words or the drawing, but I secured it away anyway until the day I understood what the pull in my core was trying to tell me. And why I wanted to answer it.

Chapter 21

Ember

"Today we start your training."

My hand paused on its way to my mouth as I looked over the tavern table at Thatch. His face was neutral as he considered me with those dark green eyes that were too close to black for comfort. I'd begun to notice that they became darker whenever he succumbed to "the curse.

I could no longer deny it after speaking to Lurk or watching Thatch travel from city to city with various levels of indifference or outright hostility. I had hoped Laark was a fluke, but no, he had continued to dismiss his people's concerns or simply ignore them.

Every now and again, I'd see a flash of...life, of emotion, and he'd shut it down almost immediately. It was like he couldn't bear to care. For the sake of Alyvia, and my survival, he needed to. If the destruction we'd seen in the cities, from the demolished homes to the dwindling resources, were any indicator, someone or something was tearing this kingdom apart piece by piece.

Burdened by the darkness I could feel feasting on him now that I'd accepted the curse's presence, Thatch was too lost to see that the threat his parents sent him to solve was evident in every city and village we entered. To make matters worse, he didn't even bother to remedy it. Just shrugged off the people's concerns one by one. What will happen to his kingdom once we've reached the end of the arcs if he hasn't stopped this unknown enemy? Or healed the damage the curse was inflicting? What will happen to me?

Just yesterday, we'd entered Sorlic to have a trio of beautiful elven sisters drop to their knees at Thatch's feet. They'd implored him to heal the rot destroying their family's home. Thatch had only stared at them in disgust as if their pleas were offensive to his ears. His lips had pulled back in a silent snarl that made the sisters cringe in fear even as they remained at his feet.

Unable to stand watching him dismiss them so carelessly, and afraid of what he may do now that I recognized the waves of darkness he often expelled, I'd discreetly bumped into his shoulder. Thatch's eyes had shot to mine, the darkness in them lightening to a lighter green for a brief second. He'd frowned as if confused and then turned back to the elves.

"Give me until tomorrow so that I may consider your request," he'd finally answered. Despite the maybe which I knew meant no unless I could change his mind by tomorrow, the sisters had thanked him profusely before racing gracefully away.

Now I stared at him as he waited for my acknowledgement of his statement. I chewed slowly, trying to determine how I could use this to my advantage without having him turn on me next. I didn't need that dark power of his used against me. I knew it would be worse than anything my father could do to me. I gulped, trying to swallow past the sudden lump in my throat. I had to help them though. Whether Thatch showed it or not, he would regret his treatment of his people if someone didn't try to temper him. I had to at least try. No matter how much the thought terrified me.

I met his eyes which were narrowed in annoyance. "Well? Are you going to say something?" I swallowed again and then sat up straight, drawing strength from the fire simmering in my veins.

"I can't start training until something else is handled first," I said quietly but firmly. Thatch's eyes narrowed further.

"And what exactly needs to be *handled first?*" he almost growled.

"There's the matter of the elven family who asked for your assistance yesterday. Once their home is healed, I can focus on working on my fire training." He lifted a brow, wicked mirth on his face, and I fought the shiver of apprehension slithering down my spine.

"And you think you can negotiate on their behalf?" At my serious – and likely still uneasy expression – he burst out laughing. There was nothing friendly in it. I could feel the eyes of others around us as they pretended not to listen. I wanted to hide. If he wasn't hesitant to treat his own people like garbage right now, how would he treat me? I couldn't even control the fire we both reluctantly accepted I possessed. But I couldn't afford to stand down.

"Yes," I told him. "Someone has to." He lifted a brow.

"What do I get in return?" I frowned.

"I thought you wanted me to start training." The smile on his face gave me chills. What exactly was I about to agree to?

"That's more for you than me. What I want is a favor, to be collected whenever I deem to request it." My frown deepened. Something told me that I should decline. That it was too broad an agreement.

"And if I say no?" I dared ask. His smile grew.

"Then you can explain to those elven sisters that their home will belong to the forest soon." Cruel wasn't a strong enough word to describe Thatch in curse form. I couldn't allow another family to suffer, so even though everything in me was telling me not to, I nodded.

"Fine. Deal."

"Say it."

"Say what?" I asked confused.

"Say the specific words." Now I knew it was a trap.

"I agree to start training with my fire and to owe you a favor to be collected whenever you deem to do so in exchange for you repairing any damage to the forest that we come across and resolving any issues your people face to the best of your ability."

Thatch froze, shock plain on his face. It was a brave addition, but I knew I was giving up something significant by owing him a favor. I had to make sure it was worth it. He growled low and menacingly so loudly that the entire tavern went silent. A few Fae slipped quietly out the door or up the stairs. I fought the fear flooding my veins as I waited for him to either attack me or agree.

"If you want that, it will cost you three favors." I swallowed, and I could see on his face that he didn't expect me to accept.

"Fine," I spat and repeated the statement with the new stipulation. He snarled but repeated his own agreement, and like that, I'd made a deal with the devil. Only time would tell if it was worth it.

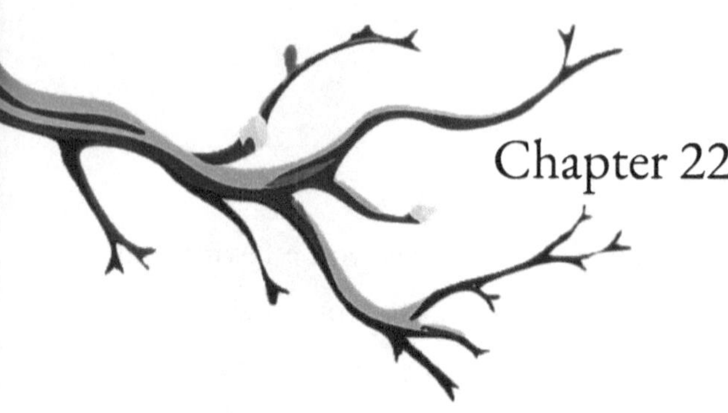

Chapter 22

Thatch

She'd fought back. Unlike everyone else who'd been shaking in my presence and avoiding my gaze, she'd maintained eye contact, even as she noticeably fought the shivers racking her body. The darkness enjoyed her fear, but I found myself hoping she maintained her bravery. The agreement she'd made with me was unwise. You should never let a Fae have such open-ended favors, and she'd given me three. Although, she was making me work for them. Did she not know that I could make her life a living hell? What did she think she would gain? Except.... she hadn't asked for anything for herself, only for my people.

Sighing, I eyed the female at my side as we strolled to the edges of Sorlic. Begrudgingly I had to respect her spirit. Why did she care what happened to my kingdom when she desired to go home at the end of this trip? It made no sense, and yet I couldn't help but wonder what would come from this agreement between us.

I saw nothing of the city as we walked, and when we finally reached the treehouse that I was to restore, it took a vast amount of effort to focus in on it. When I finally did, I felt like heavy stones had dropped into the pit of my stomach. The treehouse at one point must have been a proud four stories – a floor for each member of the family – but now the massive oak holding it up folded in on itself, making the upper stories unlevel and uninhabitable.

The branches were noticeably brittle and the floors had to have cracks spidering throughout the foundation. There were barely any leaves remaining on the rotting tree, and the ground around it was barren despite once being a vibrant flower garden. Their home was seconds from succumbing to the death permeating each vascular bundle – the veins barely able to provide the necessary nutrients pass the black sludge traveling through them instead.

I swallowed past the lump in my throat, that inner part of me shaking in absolute horror. Here was a visual representation of the destruction occurring all over Alyvia. Destruction that the curse allowed me to forget until I was directly faced with it thanks to a certain fiery hearted princess. I swallowed again, trying to calm the pounding in my heart that screamed for me to fix it, heal it... or run.

"My Prince?" It took a significant amount of effort to draw my eyes from the treehouse to the family at my feet. I met the gaze of the stricken father as he kneeled slightly in front of his family. "Forgive us My Prince. I apologize for the badgering my daughters have bestowed upon you. Please understand that it was only done out of desperation for our lives."

The male was withering away like the tree barely holding his home, but then that was the way of the wood Fae. Their lives were tied to the tree of which they built their house. To allow the tree to die would be to murder the entire family. I wondered how many of the wood Fae bordering Sorlic were experiencing the same thing... and how many had already succumbed to the call of nature.

"If you see fit to save us, My Prince," the male continued in an exhausted voice. "We will be forever in your debt." I scanned the rest of the family, his mate barely able to maintain her bow with her body withering away, and the three elven sisters tried their best to contain the shivers tormenting their bodies.

I was quiet for several seconds before I asked, "How many?" Despite the darkness telling me I cared not, I had to know. The male knew what I meant.

"All My Prince. It has worsened over the last few months and a few...a few could not withstand it." A soft sob came from behind him and left no doubt that they'd personally known some of those who'd succumbed. I turned away from them to look at Ember at my side and felt a sharp pain shoot through me at the sight of the tears streaking down her cheeks, her long hair a curtain around her sorrow stricken face.

Why was it that the sight of her sorrow for those she did not know hit me harder than the sight of the death before me? It was enough to crack the ice-cold wall I'd constructed, and despite the curse raging in my blood, I stepped around the family and walked until I stood next to the trunk of the oak.

I felt their eyes on me, especially hers, but I ignored them. Instead, I lifted a hand and placed it onto the trunk of the tree and closed my eyes. I felt it shudder, the life in the tree recoiling from the death within me, but if I was to save it, for once I needed to fight the curse. So, for the first time in a long time, I purposely reached past the darkness to the low light flickering behind it. I felt the curse revolt, but I fought it, fought to feel beyond the dark emotions I wore like armor.

It seemed a lifetime before I was finally able to draw the light to the forefront. And when I firmly held it in my grasp, I spoke, feeling the power radiate outwards from my hand.

"Ancient oak tree, I beseech thee. Though your pain I have caused, I have come to beg your forgiveness, and to heal thee. By the forces of nature, let it be."

And then I sang in the ancient words of healing, praying that the flickering light within me was still strong enough for this. Willing it to be. I heard the wood elves behind me join me in song, their voices weak, but it grew in strength as I felt the death retreat from the tree. Slowly, oh so slowly, I could feel the sluggish flow of darkness being washed away until the water and nutrients flowed freely again.

I felt the tree grow beneath my hand and although I could hear the creaking and swaying as the house itself straightened again, I did not open my eyes, nor did I stop singing. Only when the tree swayed to my song and the wood elves' voices became the soft, lyrical ones that spoke of new life again, did I open my eyes and step away.

Before me stood an oak, strong and tall that would stand against many more disasters to come. The green of its leaves was as vibrant as the grass now blanketing the ground around it. The array of flowers grew big and lush again and filled the area with the sweet aroma of life.

I turned to find the family still bowing, but they too were stronger, their pleas now words of praise. They tried to thank me, but I stepped around them, making my way further along the border. The wall keeping my emotions at bay was only cracked, but I could still feel the pain of the forest seeping through. I did not deserve their gratitude. I did not deserve their praise. I had almost killed them...*me. And I hadn't cared.* It mattered not that I had now saved them.

Distantly, I became aware of Ember almost jogging to keep up with me. The reason I felt anything at all. The only reason I'd saved them. That didn't sit well even as a part of me was grateful that she'd convinced me to help. I slowed my pace so she could walk at my side.

"Where...where are you going?" she panted, pushing those stunning auburn waves from her face to openly gaze at me. "Why didn't you stay?" Stay and take their thanks...the thanks that weren't mine to accept. I had to do more...*fix* more...before this darkness filled in the cracks again.

"There are others," I told her simply. As if understanding how close I was to losing it, she gave me an understanding nod. And she remained there at my side as I waved away the plea of every wood Fae around Sorlic and healed their homes. She remained when I could not bear their tears of joy and fled to heal the next one until the entire perimeter had been restored.

And when despite my exhaustion, I collected our belongings and had us make camp miles away outside of Sorlic, she remained, a silent flame keeping that inner flickering light still burning through the night. Until I could no longer hold it back, and the darkness seeped through the cracks and I felt nothing once again.

Chapter 23

Ember

The last few weeks had been torture to say the least. I feared my assessment of Thatch giving up was becoming more evident with each day. He lashed out regularly and continued to do spiteful things just to mess with me. He treated his people with disdain even as he assisted their cities and hunted for their enemies.

What was even weirder was that his people didn't even hate him for it. Feared his moods and darkness, yes. Gave him pitying and melancholy glances, definitely. But none of them seemed to hold it against the prince. It was as if they knew this wasn't him. That he was under the control of a higher power. It reinforced my theory that Thatch was good at heart, and the crushing fear I used to feel in his presence was diminishing the longer we were together. I had yet to truly feel threatened by him despite the curse. This helped to reinforce my theory even the more.

The more he fixed though, the more I could sense that he wasn't able to fully block out his emotions as he had before. The prince was determined to quit, but my deal prevented him from doing so – even if it had added additional time to our journey – holding him at the edge of despair and hope. But there was only so far I could push him before his curse retaliated too harshly and he fell off one end or the other. Hell, I could barely handle these training sessions he'd insisted on daily.

Every morning, before we headed out, no matter whether we were in town or on the trail, Thatch would lead me to a clearing and try to get me to summon my fire. The operative word being tried. I hadn't summoned the flames again since that night with the dyrewolves, and I desperately wished I could if only to get him off my back and to have some type of protection for myself. Instead, every day for what felt like hours, but was probably only like two, Thatch would have me meditate with these special breathing exercises and attempt to summon something. He never outright showed his annoyance, but I could feel it in how his aura would darken.

Today was no different, and I found myself desperately feeling for this mythical power on my own as we traveled to the edge of the summer arc. I already felt the difference in the air, but suddenly, it grew cooler, with a chilly breeze that ruffled my hair, and colorful hues that adorned the trees. The ground was crunchy with layered dead leaves, and I felt the spirit of winding down that usually followed the beginning of fall. I pulled out my cloak from the saddlebags and draped it around my shoulders as we continued on, taking in a soothing breath of the forest.

That evening I watched Thatch sweep away leaves to make a large circle, while also ensuring the ring of rocks he always magically had was unbroken and at least two layers thick. Obviously, he was more concerned about the fire spreading than his dark power... or it was simply a habit. Either way, soon a fire was steadily burning, and he stood to his feet. For the first time all day, Thatch studied me as he tilted his head contemplatively.

"We're going to try something different tonight. Come here." I blinked, swallowed hard, but didn't move. His eyes narrowed. "Come here, Ember." I shivered at my name but tried to hide it as I rose to my feet and slowly stepped up to the fire so that we stared at each other over it.

His eyes flashed when I didn't move around the fire to join him. "Trying my patience today aren't you?" I shrugged and said before I could stop myself.

"You could have said please." I stiffened, my eyes wide as I instinctively waited for the backhand I was used to receiving. Except it never came. In fact, not once had the Prince of Forest ever raised a hand against me. Pranked me yes, but never physical abuse. Instead, I saw a flicker of amusement in his eyes as he rounded the fire and stepped to my side. I looked up at him as his lips lifted in a wicked smirk.

"Let's see if that fiery heart of yours can manifest its flames outwardly, Princess." Thatch tilted his head towards the fire in front of us. "Reach out to the flames. *Please*." His lips twitched at the word, and my eyes widened in surprise, but then I frowned.

"What exactly do you want me to do?" I asked confused. He gestured at the fire.

"Maybe I started too advanced. I know you can summon fire, but you don't have the basic knowledge of how to manipulate it in the first place, so we're going back to step one. I want you to reach for the flames. Try to feel it. And when you do, when you recognize that it's just an extension of yourself, I want you to will it to move." I hesitated, considering what he said.

"Is that what you do? Connect and *will* the plants to move?" He shrugged.

"At first, yes. Now, I can feel every cell, every drop of water, of life in every plant and animal around me. If I will them – *ask them* – to do my bidding, they will. You have to understand them – *be one with them* – completely. Then, it becomes as simple as breathing."

"But that's different. Fire isn't alive," I insisted. He lifted a brow and gestured at the flames again.

"You sure about that?" Deciding to humor him, I stared into the flames, watching how it devoured the logs. How it licked the moisture beading on some that wasn't completely dry. How it danced in the air, shifting from red to yellow, to blue, to some combination of all three. It crackled and popped the air pockets in the wood, shooting sparks into the air as if delighted. I was wrong. It was very much alive. Maybe not in the traditional sense, but fire had the power to destroy life. Didn't that mean that it lived?

"Do you see it? Do you feel it?" Thatch whispered, his breath tickling my ear. I hadn't even realized that he'd moved closer to me. He stood behind me, looking over my shoulder. Normally I would flinch away or feel the normal fear a male's presence summoned, but I was mesmerized by the flames in front of me and warmed by the strength behind me. I nodded. His fingers trailed down my arm, making goosebumps jump all along my skin until his hand covered mine. He lifted it so that it reached out for the flames.

"Feel it, Ember," he whispered against me. "Then will it." I shivered, but I couldn't tell if it was from the male almost pressed completely to my back or the power I felt rising under my skin. Deciding to go for it, I embraced the feeling, even sinking deeper into the strong male behind me. My eyes went half lidded as I continued to watch the flames dancing beyond our interlocked hands.

I felt his other hand land on my stomach, pulling me even closer so our bodies molded together like a puzzle falling into place, and the heat in my blood rose. Then, he started to move our hands from side to side, and I willed the flames to follow like a cat stalking its toy. It did so, swaying from side to side, rising until it roared louder but didn't reach out for us. We stayed like that for a while, Thatch's hand still on mine as I weaved the fire into pattern after pattern.

Finally, his lips brushed my ear as he said, "Now, let it go Princess." I shivered, still feeling drunk.... off the power, off life, off him. But I did as he asked and released the flames. They flickered, then returned to their normal state. As it did, it was like I came out of a trance. Suddenly, I was very much aware of the hard male pressing up against me, and the warmth of his hand holding me to him. I tensed and jerked away, almost stumbling over my own feet into the fire as I did. He watched me with wicked amusement in his slightly dilated eyes. There were plenty of things I should have said, but what came out was none of them.

"You shouldn't be touching me," I snapped, but it came out breathy. He smirked and tilted his head.

"Trust me Princess, I don't touch females who don't welcome it." I glared at him, trying to get my composure back, but his words resonated. Polar opposite to what I'd come to expect from males. And even with his dark behavior....I believed him, but I wasn't going to tell him that. Things could change at any moment.

"I did not welcome it. Why would I want you touching me? *You*, who made it plain that you only keep me alive so that you don't have to deal with your father's wrath when you get home?" Thatch's smirk only grew.

"You were the one who pressed against me." He ignored the rest of my comments and my eyes flashed.

"You gripped my arm and wrapped around my waist," I accused. He shrugged and I fumed.

"You were overthinking. I was just guiding you along. It's not my fault that you wanted to get closer to me when I did." I bristled in disbelief, but I couldn't really blame him wholly. I *had* pressed up against him first, and if I dared to admit it, for those brief moments I hadn't wanted to be anywhere else but in his arms. What did that say about me?

"What you should be saying is thank you Thatch." I narrowed my eyes.

"*Thank you Thatch*, but now that I know what my power feels like, I don't need you to *guide me along*." A full grin spread across his face and my heart broke into a gallop.

"Tsk. Tsk. Such an ungrateful, fiery princess." He turned away and headed towards the forest. "Someday, you'll thank me properly." I glared after him as he disappeared to hunt.

"Whatever helps you sleep at night," I grumbled, but I couldn't help wondering how it would feel to have all of him in his masculine glory wrapped around me as I slept. Instead of a wave of disgust, the thought sent a delicious dark shiver down my spine.

"Tell me again why we have to travel on foot." I followed the male who was steadily walking in front of me as the ground gradually sloped upwards. Despite all the work I did growing up, I was horribly ill equipped to handle the amount of riding and hiking we'd done these weeks. Although, I had started building muscle.

"Because the mountain part we need to pass can't be done by horses," Thatch shot over his shoulder.

"Then maybe we shouldn't be passing it either," I mumbled to myself trying hard not to stare at his muscles as they shifted as he climbed. I swallowed hard. These thoughts had to stop, but ever since I'd experienced being in his embrace, I couldn't stop my brain from going there at inappropriate times. So, basically all the time. Meanwhile, he acted like nothing had happened a couple of nights ago. Frustrating male.

I didn't have time to worry about his body as we started basically climbing a freaking mountain. What the hell was up with this prince and impassable mountainous areas? Also, why did this forest have so many gods damn mountains in the first place?

Too many times, I found myself slipping slightly as I followed after him, sometimes having to go on all fours to keep myself from falling. Finally, I could see a ledge where the trail must even out again, but I didn't dare look below me. We were too high for comfort now, and with all the rocks around us, I was afraid what would happen if we had a repeat of me falling off a cliff.

I watched with annoyance as he easily climbed onto the ledge and stared down at me. "Hurry up Princess. I want to reach town by nightfall."

"Sure he does," I grumbled to myself. "Sure, I'll speed up. It's not like I'm rock climbing without gear or anything."

I'd almost reached the ledge when exactly what I'd feared happened. I reached for the edge, but the rocks under both my feet gave out. My eyes widened in horror, and then I was falling backwards into empty air.

Chapter 24

Thatch

She was in my arms again, every soft part of her, pressed up against every hard part of me. All blood rushed south, and I bit back a groan. Forget the fact that she'd almost fallen off another mountain. Forget that I was supposed to hate her. I'd been secretly wanting a reason to touch her again since the other night if only to see how she'd react. It wasn't because I enjoyed the feel of her against me. No, definitely not. But as she gripped onto my shirt and panted in my arms, I couldn't help pulling her closer. Ember stared up at me, the fear of almost falling still present in her gaze. But was she still afraid of me?

"If I didn't know better, I would say you're looking for excuses to be in my arms. I only did so to break you in, but seems like to me, you really did enjoy the touch."

She immediately stiffened and shoved away from me so hard that I released her. I fought to keep my teasing smirk on my face, but internally I was reeling from her aggressive reaction. She wasn't looking at me now as she marched down the path towards town, but right before she'd shoved away I'd seen a flicker of recognition and horror. What had I said that triggered her? Why was she triggered in the first place? Concerned, I followed after her.

She refused to acknowledge me as I caught up to her, but I wasn't letting this one go. I had to know. "Hey, slow down, Princess. What's gotten into you?"

"Nothing," she snapped as she continued marching on, but her body was tense like she was preparing for an attack, and she kept shooting glances around us like she was expecting something to jump out at her.

"Sure doesn't look like it Princess," I pushed. She spun to face me suddenly.

"I'm not a princess!" she screamed. "And why do you care anyway? I thought you didn't care about anything and anyone anymore."

I flinched. I didn't mean to, but her words hit like an electric shock. I should know. I'd been hit with one over a decade ago during battle. Knocked me flat on my back. Not a good time.

But she was right. Why *did* I care? I couldn't explain it. The curse prevented me from getting too close to people...and yet I found myself needing to know what was wrong. Touching her must have made the curse rescind some. And the usage of my power to heal the land was preventing me from withdrawing fully back into the darkness. Leaving me to feel way more than I wanted to...care more than I wanted to.

"Okay, *Princess*," I stated just to mess with her. "No need to get hostile. I just wanted to know if there's a threat I need to be watching out for." There. That didn't sound like I was concerned right? Just my responsibility as guard like dear old Dad wanted. I groaned internally. Yeah, she was definitely getting to me.

Ember glared at me, but I saw the terror and shame in them, even as the heat around her rose. I hadn't seen that look in a while now. Not even with how often I snapped or messed with her. What had I said to bring it back?

"No, there's no threat besides the dark prince in front of me." I fought another wince. She wasn't wrong. She turned and started walking again. "Just let it go Thatch. We both know you wouldn't do anything about it even if there was something."

Wrong. If another male was threatening her, I would do the same thing I did in Gris, curse or no curse, but we were reaching Hoark so I held my tongue.

As we entered the small city, I knew immediately that something was up. Not long after we'd ascended to the treehouses, after checking on the horses who'd found their own way here, another of my closest friends, Wolf, was storming towards me. I frowned. He was supposed to be at the castle right now. What had made him race to meet us here?

The residents greeted me in much the same way as they had the last couple of weeks, but I only had eyes for the scowling Fae male in front of me. Barely stopping to address me, he gestured at the large three storied treehouse reserved for my visits.

"We need to talk," he said firmly. He glanced at the still tense female at my side and his scowl deepened. "Now." I nodded and we followed him. Thankfully she stayed silent.

We entered behind Wolf, and I waited as he locked the door before turning to me. I barely took in the four bedroom treehouse decorated with rich crimson and black before folding my arms across my chest and considering him.

"What's this about? Why aren't you at the capital?" I demanded. He shook his head in annoyance, his blond hair in its usual braids shifting violently at the movement.

"You're not going to like it." I snorted. What was with my men starting with that phrase lately?

"Do I ever?"

"There's a price on her head." I stiffened, my power rolling under my skin. There was only one female near me that would warrant a warning from the capital. But an assassin attempt? Damn.

"How much?"

"Does it matter?" No, it didn't, but it would tell me how serious a threat it was.

"How much Wolf?" Hard, cobalt blue eyes shot to her before turning back to me.

"Ten thousand gold coins." My eyes widened in shock.

"You've got to be kidding me," I breathed in disbelief. He shrugged but he was anything but relaxed.

"She's technically royalty, and you know who the king and queen believe she is. Somehow word got around." He glanced at Ember again, before his voice hardened. "Someone really doesn't want you to break the curse."

"She's not going to break the gods damned curse," I growled in exasperation. Wolf held up his hands in surrender.

"Regardless, some people believe she can and want her dead. They're using the rumors of her bringing destruction to the forest to lift morale." I growled in annoyance. This was getting out of hand, and so far I'd yet to run across the foreigners actually causing the destruction or spreading the rumors. It did explain some of the odd looks she'd received at the last couple of cities.

"I'm sorry, but it sounded like you just said that there's an assassin running around trying to kill me because they think I'm some mythical princess with fire abilities who can somehow prevent the Prince of Forest from destroying the forest." We both turned to stare at her, and she glanced between us in disbelief.

"That's correct," Wolf finally said. He glanced at me. "They came through a couple of days ago, interrogating the citizens about your whereabouts, but of course, you hadn't made it here yet. And with your love of taking unmarked trails..." My love of unmarked trails was likely the only reason we hadn't been attacked by assassins sooner...or our impersonators.

"That's bullshit." Wolf turned back to her, his brows rising to his hair. "If they wanted me gone all they had to do was ask. I don't want to be around the dark prince of doom for longer than necessary anyway." She scanned me up and down. "No offense." I fought a smirk despite myself.

"None taken." Wolf snorted a laugh and pointed a thumb at her, relaxing for the first time since we'd arrived.

"I like her." I scowled at him as he smiled at her like she was his new favorite toy. He was like a brother to me, but I was about to send him flying out of this house if he didn't take his eyes off her.

"Warning received Wolf. You can go." He shot me an amused look, but it dropped when he took in my expression. He knew me enough to know when to back down. He nodded.

"Stay safe Thatch. I don't want to hear they're sending one after you next." I smiled smugly.

"You know they wouldn't dare try me." He laughed darkly, remembering very well what happened to the last one who'd tried. I was sure a section of my carpet was still stained with blood back at the castle.

"Thrive well brother." I inclined my head.

"Thrive well." As quickly as he appeared, he was gone again. It was silent for several minutes, and I walked towards the kitchen area to pour a glass of nightgaze. I swirled the contents around, staring down at the black liquid with white sparkles that looked like the night sky. I'd just taken a sip when Ember finally decided to speak.

"So, an assassin huh?" She sounded indifferent, but I could hear an undercurrent of.... something. I turned to study her. She still stood in the middle of the sitting area watching me. Her arms were crossed over her hunter green tunic. The tunic and matching pants hugged her frame nicely. In fact, she'd been wearing a combination of my colors this entire trip, likely on orders of my mother. I shook my head unsure whether I enjoyed seeing her in them or if it annoyed me.

"Thatch?"

"Hmm?" I jerked my eyes back to hers to see a brow lifted. Crap. I'd been caught staring.

"That assassin. What do you plan on doing about him?"

"Nothing." Ember blinked, her hands falling to her sides.

"Nothing?" I took another sip of my drink.

"Nothing." She stared at me in disbelief, her jaw hanging open.

"Do you truly hate me that much?" she snapped, but I could hear the hurt in her tone. My heart clenched at the sound, but I shrugged.

"Why hunt him down when he's going to come to us anyway?" Her eyes widened in understanding.

"You're going to use me as bait?"

"Why not?"

"You cold hearted bastard!" she spat. "What is wrong with you? I know you don't want this curse broken, but do you have to treat me this way? It's not like I believe I'm the cure." She scowled at me. "I meant what I said. It'll be too soon for me to never have to see you again." She marched away to one of the bedrooms and slammed the door shut.

"Hmm, such a dramatic fiery princess," I muttered into my drink.

"I told you to go home." Wolf gave me a knowing smile as I slipped into the chair across from him at the tavern.

"I figured you'd want to take a break from her at some point, and I wanted to talk to you." I took a long sip of my drink.

"Am I going to want to talk about whatever you came to say?" I asked grouchily. He chuckled.

"No." I sighed. Why was I constantly getting bad news lately? I waved a hand.

"Get on with it then."

"I didn't see you before you left on patrol of the arcs." I lifted a brow when he didn't say anything else. "You didn't invite me." Ah. It was true he normally accompanied me on my yearly princely duty...along with Lurk – when he wasn't with Therek – and a couple of others. This time, my parents had insisted I take only the princess.

"I was ordered to go alone. Likely my mother's attempt to force me to interact with our Fire Princess and see if she could break the curse." Wolf snorted.

"What? The queen thought we'd distract you and prevent the bond from snapping into place?"

"Exactly," I replied, chugging my drink. Wolf shook his head in disbelief.

"Isn't she only a human though? Your brothers told me after you'd left that there was no definitive proof that she could summon fire."

"There wasn't...until we were attacked by a dyrewolf pack and she fried every last one of them." His eyes widened in shock as his jaw dropped.

"She can actually summon flames?" he shouted, and I gave him a pointed look. Glancing around to ensure no one was listening he leaned over the table towards me. "What are you saying? Is she truly the Princess of Fire?"

I tapped my glass as I considered how best to answer him. I went with the truth. "Yes, she must be. The way she summoned it from nothing and the fact that I've seen her manipulate present flames, leaves no doubt that she is the famed princess." He stared at me in disbelief.

"So then..."

"No," I interjected. "I said she was the princess, not that she was my mate. Not that she was some magical cure for the curse. Gods, you're as bad as Lurk and my parents." He scratched at his beard which he honestly should have trimmed by now, but still held on to. Likely, to symbolize his ability to shapeshift to a dyrewolf, but I'd always been more of a short to non-existent beard person myself.

"But if she's the Princess of Fire, the prophecy says that she's the Prince of Forest's fated mate, and hence the cure for the curse. How can she be one, but not the others?"

"There is no cure for this curse," I growled, feeling the power rising under my skin. "My brothers and I know this. You know this." Wolf still stared at me as if seeing me for the first time. As if.... there was hope. It was the same look Lurk had given me, and I loathed it. There was no room for hope in my life anymore.

"But...but what if there *is*? What if it's *her*? I mean, yeah in the past we doubted it, but with this new evidence," Wolf insisted, his fists clenched on the table as he leaned toward me.

"Let it go Wolf," I snapped. He flinched as a dark power wave rolled over him and he leaned back again. Immediately, I regretted it. "She can't be it," I said more quietly. Instantly his eyes softened in understanding.

"That was an accident," Wolf insisted. "If she's truly your mate, that won't happen. She would be able to counteract it." A pause. "And fated mates wouldn't betray each other." Pain and regret flashed through me.

"Do we know that for certain? Can you tell me without a lick of doubt that she's my fated mate?" He said nothing. "I won't risk her life to test it no matter how I feel about her. No one deserves that. Not Ember. And definitely not my kingdom."

Our time in Hoark turned out to be uneventful. I would think Wolf was mistaken about the threat over our heads if it wasn't for the unease of the residents and the forest around us. The trees could feel the threat in the air and although we were now riding away from Hoark, I knew that didn't mean the threat would disappear. No. Now it meant we would face whoever it was out on the road. Fine by me. It didn't matter one way or another. The assassins would meet the same fate as the last one if they stood against me. I supposed that went for the princess as well, even if I didn't tell her that.

No, Ember had continued to stew the last few days, even refusing to acknowledge me despite my knowledge that she watched my every move. Whether it was curiosity or only apprehension, several times I'd caught her considering me with a furrow in her brow. Whenever she did, I found myself wondering what she saw when she gazed at me. Somehow

I doubted it was only the male I now portrayed. It was like she could see deep into my core where the old me slumbered. I wasn't sure if that scared or pleased me.

I knew the darkness didn't like it. It continued to lash out at things around me as if to remind the kind-hearted female that I would never be her knight in shining armor. Despite this, I couldn't help looking forward to interacting with her the longer we were together. She seemed to be gaining more confidence and the fact she called me out instead of just buckling under my episodes, was refreshing.

"You would think knowing that someone wants you gone enough to sabotage you would be enough to change your behavior," I heard her mumble across the fire. I lifted my eyes to her angry ones. She was bundled up in a thick blanket and sat closer to the fire than normal due to the unexpected swim we'd taken earlier. By we, I mean her when Cerberus had spooked her mare while crossing the river. I may have caused him to shift suddenly which led to said spook. Oops.

"You would think traveling with me all these weeks would have taught you otherwise." She scowled at me and I smirked. "Don't worry oh fiery one, you can continue to reprimand me to your heart's desire," I assured her. Ember scoffed.

"If I'm so fiery, maybe you should heed me more. Or at least that of your precious forest." She gestured at the trees around us. "Do you truly wish to see it die? To burst into flames?" My smile faded. "For once, be honest with me Thatch, and not just say what the darkness wants you to say."

My gut twisted. Gods, she had a way of stabbing a male where it hurt. I exhaled heavily but didn't look away from her. "No, I do not wish to see it destroyed." She sat up straighter in surprise.

"Then, why...?"

"Because there's nothing I can do," I told her cutting her off. "I'll only make it worse. Those I care about will only be destroyed." It didn't escape me how bitter my voice sounded.

"What makes you think that?"

"Because it's happened in the past." I swallowed, finally looking away. I didn't want to talk about this. "I burn everything I touch." I waved a hand. "Not literally of course. That's your thing." She didn't laugh or scowl, just tilted her head like she was trying to figure me out. Somehow that felt worse.

"Fire is cleansing. Sometimes you have to burn away the old to make room for the new." My eyes shot to hers as the tattoo at my heart burned. Something in her words nagged at me, but I couldn't quite grasp it. Instead, I turned it around on her.

"Is that why you were running from the fires you set when I found you?" Her eyes lowered to the flames between us, and I saw her fold into herself.

"Kind of," she whispered. "But sometimes fire isn't enough." Suddenly, I wanted to pull her into my arms and take on the weight that was now dragging her shoulders down. I didn't move though. Just stared at her for several moments.

"I've made some mistakes," I told her finally. "Serious mistakes. Things I can't return from." She glanced at me, a small smile on her lips.

"Even with fire?" That jolt again as if her words were trying to tell me something.

"I haven't tried fire," I admitted, not knowing what else to say.

"And I haven't tried growing anything."

"We can't both be death," I pointed out. She snorted.

"I've been death my entire life. You'll have to be the life." She yawned and laid out by the fire. "Goodnight Prince of Forest."

"Goodnight Princess of Fire," I answered. She snorted again but said nothing else, and I was left reeling.

"I've been death my entire life. You'll have to be the life."

Her words, like the others, triggered something in me that made me wonder. Wonder if I was wrong about who she was. About the curse being unbreakable. About my soul being lost.

I see them.
The tendrils of what could be.
One full of buds.
One full of shadows.
Possibilities.
Death.

Before I had accepted the inevitable.
That night was eternal.
But now, the stars remind me
That fire lights even the darkest shadows.
That it burns brighter until night becomes day.

And now I see them.
The tendrils of who I could be.
So maybe....
Just maybe...
I'll try one more time,
to follow the light.

Autumn

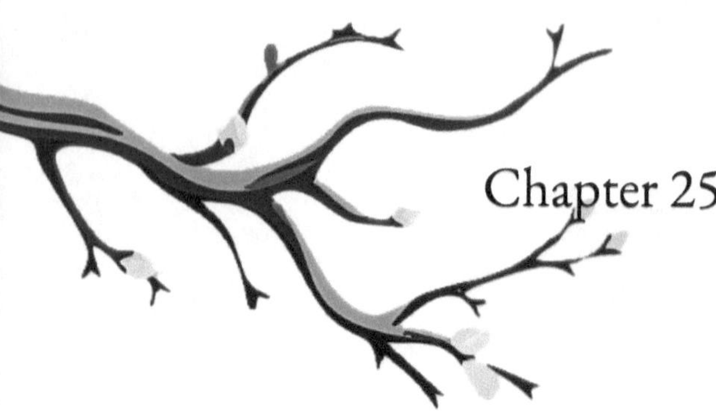

Chapter 25

Thatch

The forest screamed at me that something was seriously wrong. We were only a mile or so into the autumn arc, but the forest was begging for my attention. Something it rarely did these days, afraid of what came from encouraging the curse's interest. No matter the darkness seeping through my veins, I could not ignore its cry. I turned Cerberus towards its call. Concerned, Ember stopped Honey and turned to watch me.

"What's wrong?" she asked, scanning the forest as if she too could feel its unease.

"I'm not sure." I said nothing else as I let the forest lead us down the summer-autumn line, pushing Cerberus into a trot, and then a gallop as the forest's desperation grew.

"Hurry Prince. Hurry," It implored me. I could feel the dread growing the closer I came, the curse giddy within me as it fed off the despair I could feel seeping through the ground. It turned to outright devious joy as I felt a piece of my soul wither away.

"Too late Prince. Too late," the forest sullenly told me. I heard Ember's sharp gasp of horror and despair beside me, but I couldn't take my eyes away from the town in front of me. Everyone and everything had been

burned away, and the town lay in a withered circle of death. I barely registered dismounting. I wandered the town, desperately hoping to find the life I knew was no longer present. The ground was warm. Too warm.

I dropped to my knees in the middle of the town and reached out tendrils of hope at least a mile around us, searching.... searching. But they were gone. Those who'd lived here, and those who'd snuffed out their lives like it was nothing. Minutes. I'd missed them by minutes. Would it have been enough to save my people? Or just enough to capture those who'd murdered them? It didn't matter, because in the end, I'd failed. I hadn't even sensed the danger. Hadn't even seen the fire.

I raised my head from the ash covered ground and spotted the remains of a kid's forgotten toy. The grief and guilt ripped through me then. I could feel it rising like a tidal wave until I couldn't contain the anguish. Power blasted from me as I bellowed my torment to the sky. Too late I realized my mistake. The darkness curled around the power, twisting it so instead of an outburst of life, it morphed to death, and I wiped out the very sections of the forest that had begged for my help.

Chapter 26

Ember

Nothing could explain the level of dismay rushing through me as I gazed at the lost town. Here was the damage Wolf had warned the foreigners caused as the assassins searched for Thatch and me. An entire town burned to the ground to prove a point. To cause a war. To break the prince whose heart I could see shattering before me.

I could barely see past the tears raining down my cheeks as I watched Thatch dismount. I followed him, not sure why but not wanting him to bear witness to this alone. I watched as he walked the entire town looking for life we both knew was long gone. I knew the heat and ashes layering the dirt beneath us was what remained of it. I could feel the fire still crackling in the ground, but something told me that it was only used to cover up what had actually killed these people. How I knew this, I wasn't sure, but I knew Thatch saw the parallels of the withered ground around us to his own destruction.

When he fell to his knees in the middle of town, defeat bending his shoulders and head forward, I didn't know what to do or say. I felt the wave of power he sent out, no doubt hoping for something that was long gone. We'd galloped here full speed. He'd tried. I'd watched the desperation of which he rode, the desire for life that kept slipping through his grasp. I'd felt the darkness in him celebrating, but he'd *tried*. I knew there was little consolation in that when he'd still been too late. And not by much if the heat of the earth was any indicator. That alone had to be eating Thatch alive.

It was confirmed when a tsunami of power rose and exploded from him as he bellowed into the forest. I recoiled and gasped as I felt the power change as it rippled from him. Alarmed, I watched as the wave of what should have been light, turned to darkness and the forest around us died. I gaped at the sheer diameter of destruction. I could just make out the trees miles from us. *Oh gods.* If the Prince of Forest could harm so extensively, what was he capable of when he wasn't cursed?

My eyes shot to his anguished ones when his agonized bellows grew as he realized what he'd done. More twisted power rippled from him, but he was too lost to stop it. I had to do something before he did the very thing he feared. *Destroyed the entire kingdom.* But what? My eyes widened. Maybe....

I didn't think further than that before I was launching myself at Thatch and wrapping my entire body around his front, straddling him to the point that I even crossed my ankles behind his back. His bellows abruptly ceased, and he fought to loosen my grip on him, but I held him tighter. I could feel the darkness in him writhing and screaming, but it slowly, reluctantly, recoiled from my presence as it had done in the past.

Thatch was shaking as it did so, and it took me several minutes through my own tears to realize he was sobbing. His arms finally gripped me to him instead of working to push me away, and his face was pressed into my hair as his body shuddered around me. I held him impossibly closer, offering him what little comfort I could.

It was nightfall before the defeated warrior decided to move. Our tears had stopped long ago, and my muscles were seconds from spasming from holding the same position for so long. Gently, he unwound my limbs from around him. He didn't say anything as he lifted us to our feet and led the way back to the horses. The blankness in his dark green eyes bothered me more than anything. He was escaping deep inside himself. What would happen if he fully withdrew?

When he went to mount his horse, I frowned. I glanced back at the town and back to the cursed prince. "Can't you do something for them?" I whispered, my voice thick with grief. Thatch froze, his eyes lifting to the devastation all around us. I saw the regret in them before he closed his eyes and started mumbling something to himself. At first, nothing happened, and I saw his brows knit together and his hands tighten on his reins as he focused harder.

A gentle breeze picked up and the ground shuddered. Then there were plants shooting out of the dirt: trees, flowers, and bushes. Large vines twisted from the ground to overtake the buildings still standing. When the land stilled again, everything around us was green, and the town was buried under a blanket of life.

"They belong to the forest now." I turned to watch the Prince of Forest ride away, the trees bowing in reverence and shared grief as he passed.

Chapter 27

Ember

The feel of the cool breeze of autumn on my skin was heavenly after the suffocating heat of summer. I suppose if I was the legendary Princess of Fire then I should be immune to it, but the humid heat of summer and the warm comforting heat of a fire was two different things.

But no amount of cool air could erase the loss Thatch was likely feeling. He hadn't spoken in days, just indicated with a gesture of his head or hands when we needed to change direction or stop for the day. I wish I had words to comfort him. Seeing the powerful warrior succumb to tears had taken my heart and shattered it into pieces.

This was a male who loved his people despite the curse bleeding through his veins. I was worried about his reaction to what he'd likely viewed as a failure on his part. It was a prince's job to protect his people. He was beating himself up enough about his own destruction of his kingdom. This group fighting to undermine him was unfortunately succeeding. And who killed children just to prove a point? Monsters obviously.

I found myself wishing I had control over the flames so that I could help Thatch seek the vengeance he likely desired. I wanted desperately to help him save his forest, if only because no one had ever saved me. I understood how it felt to be hopeless and alone. Even if I wasn't some mythical princess, surely I could find a way to help Thatch anyway. First I needed to help him recover from the loss of the town. I had no idea how I was going to do that. Maybe I should start by convincing him to talk. It couldn't be healthy to walk around with that level of regret and grief inside.

I was so distracted by my musings, I didn't notice the split in the pathway until it grew steadily narrower and darker. There was a feel to this part of the forest that had my instincts screaming for me to leave. I stopped Honey and glanced around me warily.

"Thatch?" I called, wondering how I far I'd traveled without noticing. "Thatch?" I called again, scanning the pathway in front and behind me, but I couldn't make out anything through the trees. Should I turn around? I glanced forward again, and my instincts screamed. Okay, turn around it was.

Honey whinnied softly as we made our way back. She sidestepped every now and again as if she too could sense that something was wrong. I bit my lip, trying not to panic, but I didn't know these woods. I didn't know all the beings who inhabited it. And then I remembered the assassins who were supposedly after me. I gulped and urged Honey faster. It was with relief that I found the correct path to take at the split, but it felt like the ominous feeling was following me.

My mare whinnied again, breaking into a trot as she tossed her head anxiously. Her eyes were wide, and I scanned the trees trying to find what terrified her.

"Thatch!" I called again. How far had he made it down the path before I noticed my mistake? Would he even come back if he realized I was gone?

I tensed and my heart skipped a beat. What if he left me out here? "Oh gods," I whispered, fighting the panic squeezing my chest.

Then, something large snapped to my right, and Honey whinnied in fear. Her ears were pinned to her skull now. Another snap, this time from behind us. And then to our left. Biting back a scream, I held tight as Honey went from trot to full out gallop in seconds. Trees crashed around us, dropped by an unknown force, and Honey leapt over their protruding branches. I heard them then, the heavy footsteps of something after us. They were coming from all around us, and herding us no doubt, because suddenly we charged between the trees as Honey jumped off the path.

I hung on desperately, but when I saw what was following us, my muscles almost locked. They were easily twenty feet tall with rough, gnarly skin, and ginormous feet. They each held a club larger than my entire body and their evil eyes were pinned on me. Ogres. Giant ugly ogres.

"Help me. Somebody help me please," I begged, but I couldn't manage to get my voice above a squeak.

It happened too quickly for me to see it coming. One minute I was riding Honey, the next she was crying out in pain and we were flying in separate directions. My momentum took me rolling and slamming into a giant trunk that knocked the air from my lungs and almost caused me to black out. I didn't move for several seconds. Everything hurt. I swear even the movement of my eyes to search for the ogres and my mare was excruciating. The pain of seeing my horse on the ground lifeless with a crater sized dent in her side from a club hurt worse.

I lifted my eyes to meet the gaze of the five beasts thirsty for my death. Blood dripped from the club of the middle one, and he smiled to reveal black, rotting teeth. I swore I saw maggots crawling in between them. Using whatever energy I had left, I sucked in one last breath... and screamed.

The ogres growled and the bloody club was drawn back. I watched through vision framed in black as it descended toward me in slow motion. *This is it*, I thought sullenly. *This is how I die.* I closed my eyes, only opening them again when I heard the frustrated, and then agony filled cries of the beasts before me. My addled brain couldn't make sense of the vines wrapped around the club preventing it from hitting me.

Suddenly, more thorned vines thick as tree trunks were rising from the ground and embedding the ogres. Their cries of terror could probably be heard for miles, but I just watched in horrified fascination as the vines completely covered them until they were pulled down and buried beneath the ground.

"Ember!" I blinked. When had my eyes closed? "Ember, can you hear me?" I frowned, trying to focus on the fuzzy male in front of me. He looked familiar and he smelled like sandalwood and spice, like safety. His eyes were the most beautiful green I'd ever seen. They almost glowed with life.

"Thatch?" I whispered. I felt calloused fingers caress my cheek.

"Come on Princess," he said softly, his face twisted with concern. "Stay awake for me." I frowned again, my eyes already closing.

"Can't. Sleepy," I told him. Then fear gripped me and my eyes shot open. "Please don't leave me alone," I begged him. "Bad things always happen when I'm alone." His fingers grew still, but he didn't move.

"I'm not going anywhere. I swear it by the forces of nature."

"Okay," I sighed, eyes already closing again. The darkness enveloped me then, and I let it. Only barely making out his next whisper.

"Dream Wildfire. Dream for both of us."

Chapter 28

Thatch

She'd almost died, and it would have been my fault. I had been so busy wallowing in self-pity that I'd completely missed the fact that she was no longer behind me. It wasn't until I'd felt the tattoo over my heart burn and a yank in the opposite direction that I noticed. Then, something I couldn't explain had me hurriedly galloping back down the pathway.

"Hurry Prince. Hurry!" The forest had told me, and it was like the town all over again as I raced towards the danger, begging the God above all to let me get there in time.

"Please," I'd implored. "I can't be too late again." And then I'd heard her scream, and something inside of me responded. Seconds. I'd caught the club seconds before the ogre smashed her to death as they had her horse. The beautiful mare lay in a pool of blood, her lifeless eyes still wide with terror. Time seemed to slow down as I was consumed with rage, my eyes taking in the crumpled female at the ogres' feet.

I'd gritted my teeth as pure wrath flooded my veins, but it was not darkness that shot out with my release of power, but more and more *green* vines.

"Absorb them. Destroy them," I'd ordered the forest, and it had complied until the ogres were buried underneath the ground. I'd reached Ember just as she was losing consciousness.

I stared down at her now, her face twisted in pain despite being unconscious. Afraid of injuring her, I summoned thinner, thornless vines to wrap around every inch of her. Forehead scrunched in concentration, I carefully, slowly, shifted her until she lay flat against the ground. She whimpered in her sleep but didn't wake.

I swallowed hard, still fighting the rage racing through my body. I needed to calm down if I was going to examine her with minimal pain. I needed to make sure she didn't have anything broken. I swallowed again, and then I was carefully pressing into her skin from head to toe. Pained whimpers revealed bruised ribs and back, a large knot on the back of her head, and cuts and scrapes across her arms and legs – which I cleaned and bandaged – but thankfully no broken bones. I'd still rather not move her just yet. Hopefully, with her Fae heritage, she would start healing soon enough.

Standing, I glanced around the area. My heart clenched as my gaze fell upon Honey and I went to her side. Kneeling beside her, and laying my hand on her flank, I thanked her for her sacrifice and then wrapped her in green until she was once again a part of the forest.

It was late evening when the Princess of Fire finally stirred.

"Thatch?" came the tentative whisper that had my tattoo burning and my heart rate picking up.

"I'm here," I told her, and she opened her beautiful eyes to meet mine. We stared at each other for several minutes. There was something like relief in hers. Had she expected me to be gone when she woke? The thought didn't sit well with me.

"You didn't leave." Rage flooded me again as she confirmed my thoughts. "They always leave," she whispered to herself frowning and my gut twisted.

"Who?" I asked, wanting to hit something. She startled as if she hadn't realized I'd heard her. "Who left?" I asked again, already knowing I wasn't going to like the answer. Her eyes lowered and she looked away.

"My mother. And my brother." My chest was tight.

"When?" I managed to get out.

"When I was nine and then about six years ago when I turned fifteen." Her voice was small, defeated, and all I wanted to do was go berate the people who'd left her alone to deal with whoever had abused her. Would she tell me who it was if I asked? I could feel her shutting down, sinking into herself. No, today was not the day, but someday soon I would avenge the scarred female before me.

"I stayed," I told her simply. Her eyes rose to mine again, and I could see the battle happening behind them, even if I couldn't tell what it was about.

"You stayed," she agreed, a small smile lifting her lips. And then she closed her eyes again and left me wondering why a part of me wanted to ensure I always did.

"They shouldn't have even been here," I muttered to myself with a frown as we continued onwards the next day. Ember sat in front of me on Cerberus, holding her body as apart from me as she could despite the soreness still likely afflicting her body. I would get her another horse at the next town, but I couldn't help wanting to wrap an arm around her waist and pull her snug against me.

Only to mess with her of course. The curse loved to make her uncomfortable...no that was all me. The curse didn't like having her so close, but the mischievous side of me loved to push her to see what it took to bring out that fiery attitude of hers she concealed so well.

It had been suppressed in her past life, I could tell, because the longer she was around me, the more I could feel the heat rising off her. A strength that was likely the reason she'd survived this long in a life that had no qualms about hurting her. It still blew my mind the few times she'd stood up to me despite the wariness still permeating her being. A lifetime's worth made worse by the darkness I couldn't help inflicting on those around me.

Ember shifted on the saddle bringing me out of my revelry. "What?" she asked, confusion marring her too sensual face. It took me a second to remember what I'd said.

"I said they shouldn't have been there," I repeated. "The ogres."

"Why? Because they don't live in this part of the forest?" she asked curiously. I bristled as I considered the magnitude of the situation.

"No, because they don't live in the forest at all. They are of the mountain kingdom, my brother Therek's domain. They shouldn't be this deep in the forest unless..."

The truth had me tensing and the power under my skin roiling in anticipation. I scanned the forest with new eyes, suddenly way more concerned about the threats I'd been unable to sense.

Ember turned slightly in the saddle to glance up at me with wide eyes. "Are you saying what I think you're saying?" I nodded solemnly. "So someone not only has been masquerading as us and destroying parts of the forest, but now they are dropping ogres in an entirely different kingdom to kill me?" I nodded again, watching as her breathing accelerated.

"Stop the horse," Ember whispered, her heart pounding erratically.

"What?" I asked confused. She was hyperventilating now, her eyes wider still.

"Stop. The. Horse," she all but screamed, and I jerked Cerberus to a halt. He snorted in irritation, but I was too focused on the female who threw herself off the horse and fell to her knees just in time to expel her breakfast into the bushes. Swearing, I swung off after her and reached to pull her hair out of the way. She flinched at my touch but was too busy hacking her guts out to push me away.

When she finally stopped, she was dripping with sweat and shaking like a leaf. Had she been triggered again? Or was it the simple idea that someone was going to such trouble to hunt me down and assassinate her? Either way, I found myself wanting to wrap her in my arms and promise her that I wouldn't let them, but I held myself back. She was not mine to protect, and I could not and *would not* give her the idea that I was some hero.

So I let her compose herself and then mounted Cerberus again. Glancing down at her on her knees, I flashed back to when she had dared hug me in my grief. My heart and gut clenched, my tattoo burning again as if to reprimand me for not returning the favor. I gritted my teeth against the sensation and pull of the female before me.

"Come Princess. We must reach Dirk before nightfall. I need to contact my brother." She raised bloodshot eyes to mine as she managed to rise to her feet. She glared at me with a mixture of disdain and disappointment as she made her way back to the stallion. I fought the wave of shame as I pulled her up in front of me.

"Why?"

"Because this is not just about the Forest Kingdom anymore. Someone is manipulating the forces of nature, and it's past time we stopped them."

Chapter 29

Ember

What had I expected? That he would pull me into his arms and comfort me? Thatch had made it abundantly clear that he did just enough to prevent permanent harm from coming to me per his father's orders. Anything extra was an unexpected treat that should never be assumed to occur again.

But he'd *saved* me. Came racing through the forest just in time to stop the ogres from killing me. Because they were going to kill me. Simply because I was prophesied to save this dark prince from his curse. I was being harmed for merely existing once again.

Then he'd held my hair back as I vomited at the revelation that I'd jumped from one bad situation to another. How could I escape the abusive home of my childhood just to enter a land with even worse beings determined to snuff out my life? Gods, what were the odds?

I bit back a groan, my brain aching with these conflicting views. The prince leading Cerberus by the reins at my side had both vowed to save me, but also to care little for my wellbeing. Maybe I was the one cursed and not him. I sighed, trying to focus on just putting one foot in front of the other as Thatch handed off the stallion to a stableboy and led me into another massive treehouse meant for visiting royalty.

Dirk was a beautiful city. Being in the autumn arc, its trees were adorned with leaves in vivid reds, oranges, and yellows. There were vines of twinkling lights wrapped around all the branches over the "streets" and the smell of cider and pumpkin filled the air. The patch of pumpkins decorating the space between several of the trees helped. Overall, the city as a whole had such a cozy feeling to it that reminded me of happier days reading by the fire with my mother.

You would think the homey atmosphere would have improved the mood of the forest prince before me, but no. The curse must be bothering him again because the lighter green I'd seen in his eyes was darker today and the aura he gave off was dark with green edges.

I said nothing as Thatch stalked into his room, mumbling incoherently to himself. I just simply went to another on the opposite end of the treehouse to drop off my bags. I noticed a red spot of blood still on one of the straps, and grief shot through me at the thought of Honey being killed because of me. Not wanting to linger in my room with those thoughts, I quickly returned to the living room to see Thatch speaking to another male through a flickering portal on the wooden wall.

"I need you here brother, if you are able." The massive male in the portal inclined his head, the handles of his twin axes peeking over his shoulders.

"I will be there within the hour. I happen to not be far from Dirk at the moment." I noticed Thatch jerk in surprise as he considered his brother.

"What? Why?"

"That is something best discussed in person. See you soon." Thatch inclined his head and the portal closed, returning to undisturbed wood as if it had never existed. Weird. I should be freaking out more about their mode of communication, but my freak-out-the-meter was full. Or maybe the oddities of this world no longer surprised me. Thatch ignored me as he reclined on the couch to wait for his older brother to arrive. Biting my lip to hold in a scalding remark at his behavior, I retreated to my room again.

As promised, within an hour a pounding knock came at the front door. Curious, I returned to the living room as Thatch opened the door to reveal Prince Therek scowling on the other side. I couldn't help taking an involuntary step back at the level of wrath I could feel rumbling under his skin. I couldn't get over how he was built like a damn mountain himself, and his twin axes looked sharp enough to cut down trees as easy as wheat. His light brown eyes were hard and unforgiving, but his spikey brown hair gave him an almost playful look. It was confusing because after meeting the Prince of Mountains at the ball, he gave all new meaning to the word terrifying.

Why were the other two brothers less imposing than this one? Were the younger ones just angrier? Or had the eldest learned to conceal their rage more effectively with age? Thinking back to the undercurrent darkness wrapped around them all, I knew it was the latter. But something was different about the younger princes. The curse seemed to weigh heavier on them. Therek's aura was a brown so dark it was almost black. Only the edges held a lighter tan color that hinted at what the male used to be before the curse took hold.

"Still alive is she?" his gravelly voice had me jumping out of my skin. The mountain prince scanned me up and down, obvious disdain in his eyes despite the smirk on his lips. I hadn't forgotten the threat he'd tossed my way the last we spoke. "Why didn't you just feed her to the ogres?" All the air fled my lungs.

Chapter 30

Thatch

Rage overtook me so fast, I had blasted Therek with a wave of dark power before I could think. There was a small scream behind me and it was only then I realized Therek's ax lay at my throat and my long dagger at his. *What the hell?* Why? Because he'd suggested harming Ember? The snarl on his face was likely a mirror of my own as I sensed the darkness in him rising to challenge mine.

"You will kill me, for what? A female who is likely working with our enemies to set you up?" he growled. I frowned, but I withdrew my dagger.

"Why do you say that?" I asked as he sheathed his weapon.

"It is why I am in this forest instead of up in the mountains. Someone is out for our blood. They have been sneaking into each of our kingdoms, capturing our people, and placing them elsewhere to cause chaos in each other's land. It is how the ogres came to be here. And why I just had to kill a pack of rabid dyrewolves in my kingdom."

Therek stalked to the bar and poured himself a glass of dark liquor. He shot back the entire thing before pouring another.

"What does this have to do with her?" I asked following him and taking the glass he poured me next. I could see Ember in my peripheral, posed to run at any perceived threat from the mountain prince. A piece of me reveled at the lack of fear directed towards me despite my brisk manner the last few days. Seems the fire princess had learned to roll with the punches.

Therek turned to her, a murderous glare on his face. I tensed, my hand moving to hover over my dagger again before I could think better of it. "The attacks on your kingdom grew worse right after *she* came to be in this world. The attacks that were made to look like fire also began once *she* arrived."

Ember was already shaking her head across the room. "That wasn't me," we both heard her whisper. My brother snarled at her, his power causing the ground beneath the city to rumble slightly.

"No, but you were sent to distract him so that the people who are doing this can catch and destroy him. Once the Prince of Forest is out of the way, it would allow for them to take over. If they were to take all four kingdoms, the forces of nature would crumble and die."

Therek pointed an accusing finger at Ember. "Your presence had the king and queen insisting my little brother travel through the arcs *alone* instead of with his normal warriors, making him vulnerable while he determined whether you are who you're rumored to be."

My gut clenched in trepidation as I glanced from the shaking female to my raging brother. Could it be true? Was I being played so my kingdom would fall to another entity instead of by my own hand? Was the fear and care for my people only an act by the female in front of me? The tattoo burned again, reminding me of the new branches and roots I'd noticed this morning. Some of the roots were extending down towards my abdomen now. The flames in the hearth reminded me of something else as well.

"Her intentions may be false, but her identity is not." Therek turned back to me in shock.

"What? You can't mean..."

I nodded, finishing my drink before pouring another.

"She can control and call forth the flames. She is indeed a daughter of the King of Disasters. She is the Princess of Fire." Therek stared at me aghast. The rumbling ceased and I felt the relief in the trees around us.

"You know this for sure?"

"I do." I quickly explained about the dyrewolves and training her with the flames, leaving out how intimate it had become in my desire to mess with her at the same time.

"This should be impossible," he said breathlessly, sinking into a chair, one hand rubbing through his short hair, wrath forgotten for the moment. "If she exists, then...."

I watched as the realization flashed across his face, and he met my gaze. If one princess truly existed, it meant the other three did as well. The Princess of Storms, the Princess of Hurricanes... and the Princess of Earthquakes, the match to the mountain prince himself.

"And the tattoo?" My gaze shot to Ember, who frowned in confusion as her eyes fell to the spot right over my heart. When had she seen the tattoo? Did she know what it represented?

As much as I didn't want to admit it, if the princesses were real, the appearance of one of them likely symbolized what my brothers would be facing next. I nodded. Therek swore fiercely, jumping to his feet and pacing across the living room.

"Have you told Theseus and Torm yet?" I shook my head.

"I didn't think it necessary until your ogres showed up in the middle of the forest." I glanced at Ember. "And I'd planned to tell them about the princess's ability when we met up in a few weeks." He nodded, deep in thought.

"I'll tell them. I was headed to their kingdoms next to warn them anyway."

"I'll come along," I offered, but Therek was already shaking his head.

"No, more is going on than we know. You are needed in the Forest Kingdom." He glanced narrowed eyes at the princess still watching us. "You need to finish your rounds. See if you can draw out whoever is hunting you down with the pretense of hunting *her*, and then destroy them."

He moved closer to me so only I heard his next words. "Keep her close. But brother, if she betrays you in any way... kill her." The tattoo screamed with dismay.

Chapter 31

Ember

If she betrays you in any way, kill her.

I couldn't get those words out of my head, especially knowing I wasn't meant to hear them in the first place. Even long after the Prince of Mountains left and I lay in bed staring at the ceiling, I couldn't sleep, afraid that Thatch would decide I wasn't worth the risk and prematurely kill me.

They believed me to be the daughter of this mythical Zeus, but didn't believe the rest of the prophecy? What kind of messed up crap was that? I was good enough to be the Princess of Fire, but not good enough to also be Thatch's salvation? I rolled over in annoyance, putting my back to the door I'd shoved a couch against. Pointless really. If he so desired, the powerful male could simply shove it aside or use his vines to pull it out of the way.

Why did it bother me so much that he believed I would betray him? Was he so determined to keep his curse that a few words from his brother were enough for him to overlook everything I'd done these few weeks to indicate otherwise? I've found myself falling in love with Alyvia and its people without trying. There was just something about this place that felt like home, despite the concern that another male would do to me what my father and his friend did. Despite the fear, now almost nonexistent, that the male who traveled with me would be the one to break me for good.

Now Thatch thought I was assisting in some complicated plot to destroy him so some other ruler could take over the kingdom. How exactly could I be doing that when I'd been human not so long ago? When would I have had time to plan such things while fighting to survive?

I sighed again. But he didn't know that. I'd told him little to nothing about where I came from. Of course, there hadn't been much opportunity to tell him the depth of my scars. He knew I worked on an orchard and that I'd been abandoned...even by the workers at the end. But I'd never outright told him what happened to me to make me feel incapable of running away. What would he say if he knew? Would his eyes fill with disgust and disdain? Would he feed me to more ogres or leave me for the assassins? What would a prince want with damaged goods anyway?

I felt it in my soul. That desperate need to be wanted by someone. Needed by someone. I was afraid of the depth of the feelings growing in me, and gods I was tired of being scared. And I was so sick and tired of being sick and tired. I turned over again and eyed the door. But what if...

I sighed and closed my weary eyes. No, what ifs were for those who had the luxury of dreaming of something better. The best I could hope for was coming out of this experience alive.

"Hi beautiful." I started, turning to see the sheriff standing in the doorway of the kitchen. I tried to glance behind him, but my father was not there.

"Is there anything I can get you?" I asked, trying to keep my voice steady. "More dessert? A beer?" Please be the only thing you want.

He smiled darkly at me, shifting a step closer. "Now Ember, surely you can offer me something better than that. You have, after all, bloomed into a lovely young woman." Revulsion coated my skin like oil, and I backed away from him towards the back door. His smile grew.

"Your father had to step out for a few minutes. Why don't you keep me occupied in the meantime?"

My eyes darted towards the doorway, and when his hand shot out, I was already running. I screamed as he slammed me into the door, his hand wrapping around my mouth.

"Now, now. Don't be like that. Eventually, a wild thing like you has to be broken in. I'm doing you a favor."

I tried not to vomit as his other hand trailed over my breast, squeezing it roughly so that I flinched in pain, and then down lower until it was tracing between my thighs. I fought to break his hold, but his entire body was pressing me against the hard wood, and he had at least a hundred pounds on me. Bile rose in my throat the more he stroked, and I felt something hard pressing against my back.

"Oh gods. Someone help me. Please, help me," I cried silently, tears rolling down my face.

"That's it beautiful," he breathed into my ear as he started to unbutton my pants. His hot, whiskey breath made me gag. "I'll make it good for both of us, just you wait." Out of breath, I stopped struggling. He must have taken that to mean my surrender because the hand over my mouth lowered to help loosen my pants further so he could reach into them.

His breathing picked up and he grinded against me. I was really going to vomit now, but I took advantage of his distraction. I shoved my elbow back into his stomach as hard as I could. Surprised, he stepped back just enough for me to spin and knee him directly in the balls.

Cries of pain echoed around the kitchen, but I was already running. I could still hear him cussing me out and calling for me as I ran and ran until the forest enveloped me, hiding me from my purser. Then, I collapsed against a tree and vomited my shame onto its roots.

I jerked awake, my heart beating a hundred miles per hour and humiliation and disgust flooding my system. I couldn't breathe and I realized that not only was there an arm gripped around my chest, but a hand covered my mouth all over again. I struggled franticly still trying to throw off the lingering sluggishness of sleep as nausea rose, but faster than I would have thought possible, I was being dragged out the window onto a tree branch. I fought hard, trying to kick my attacker in the knees, the groin, anywhere, but they hit me in the side of the head and everything went black.

"Wake up Princess," someone sneered, and I fought the grogginess pulling me down to pry my eyes open. I was being carried through the forest over the shoulder of one of my assailants. I could just make out the second one walking slightly behind the first, snarling down at me. I blinked to clear the glaze from my eyes. Both males wore all black, but a silver emblem depicting crossed hammers inside a circle sat on the shoulder of the one staring at me. Both were obviously trained if the wicked daggers at their sides were any indicator.

I shifted slightly, trying to ignore the slamming of my stomach on the shoulder of my kidnapper as I observed our surroundings. How far away from Dirk were we? And where was Thatch? My heart jumped at the thought of the forest prince. Would he think I ran off to betray him and kill me?

I was surprised when we stopped shortly after and the males tied me to a tree with iron chains. The feel of them inflicted such a slimy feeling along my skin and nausea in my gut that I leaned over and vomited all over the grass.

"Not a pleasant feeling is it, iron?" I lifted teary eyes to the smirking male in front of me. What was wrong with me? "You're Fae sweetheart. Iron and Fae don't mix." Well, that explained that, but who were these guys?

As if reading my mind, his eyes trailed down my body in a way that had more bile rising to my throat, before saying, "You're probably wondering who we are." He stepped closer, and I gagged at the wrongness of his scent. It wasn't bad per se, just not the one I instinctively recognized now. The pure evilness permeating his pores didn't help.

"We serve a different king than that weak prince of yours. One who's not infected with a curse or prone to being fallen by such a thing as iron." He snorted dismissively. "No, our king is all powerful and can crush nature under his pinkie finger, and what our king wants, he gets. And what he wants right now, is you."

Terror gripped me as I felt the iron sucking what energy I had left. "Who?" I managed to ask. If I survived this, maybe giving the information to Thatch would be enough to keep him from killing me.

The male grinned again, tracing another finger down my neck until his hand wrapped around my throat and squeezed. My eyes widened as I fought to breathe past the flashbacks of another night, another male pinning me to the bed as pain shot through my body.

"The King of Iron and Steel, ruler of the Metal Kingdom of course," the male before me said, but I could barely hear him past the memory of another male grunting as he squeezed my neck and clumsily thrusted into me. The memory overtook reality as my kidnapper trailed his hand down my body feeling me up as he went. I could feel the pain shooting through my gut, the blood trickling down my legs as if it was happening all over again. I was prepared for it to go farther with me helpless to stop it, but just as he reached the junction of my thighs, I saw him distantly jerk his head to the side as if hearing something. His eyes shot back to mine right as a pinprick of pain hit my thigh.

"Alas, the prince has caught up. I guess we'll have to continue another time." And then he was gone, leaving me lost in my memories with the other male sneering at me. He stalked toward me, but just as he reached to touch me, vines shot up from the ground, wrapping around his throat. The assassin gagged, hands tugging franticly at the thorned plant, but he could do nothing as they squeezed and squeezed until he wheezed and fell to the ground lifeless.

The sight of his body before me was enough to jar me back to reality just as the avenging prince stepped out of the forest. *Gods*, he was magnificent in all his dark and living glory. The power radiating off him swept the memory away until all I could focus on was the shifting of his powerful body as he stalked towards me. I held my breath as Thatch stepped right over the dead assassin to reach me and with a quick twist of his hands had the iron chains loosening and falling to the ground.

Suddenly light headed, I staggered and would have fallen to the ground if it wasn't for him catching me. Looking up into eyes that were more of a forest green than black, I almost didn't register the burning I felt flowing through my veins. I just said the first thing that came to mind.

"I didn't betray you," I muttered. His eyes flashed with something I couldn't read.

"I know," he said to my surprise. I opened my mouth to say something else, but then the burning turned into a roaring inferno that had me screaming silently before the world blissfully went black.

Chapter 32

Ember

When I woke again, the burning had stopped, and I was lying on a pile of soft furs on the forest floor. I looked up at the canopy to the dawn just rising. A gentle breeze flowed through the forest, bringing with it a scent that I breathed deep into my lungs. At least until I remembered the assassins. I shot up into a sitting position, too many memories from two different time periods warred in my head as I tried to reorient myself.

Finally, I met the green eyes of the Prince of Forest, and something within me settled. We stared at each other over the fire for several minutes, as my heart rate slowed.

"What happened?" I managed as I swallowed past my dry throat.

"You were kidnapped and poisoned. Luckily, I recognized the scent and had the antidote on hand." I swallowed again and needing to move, I slowly stood to my feet. I could feel his eyes on me as I shifted over to the packs and grabbed some water. Only after I'd drank deeply, washed my face and teeth, and came back from relieving myself did I finally find the energy to face what he'd said.

"How...how did you find me?" Something flashed across his eyes before they went carefully blank again, but I saw his hand rub against the spot over his heart almost absentmindedly.

"I have my ways," was all he said, but I felt this weird warmth in my chest that had me wondering what he wasn't telling me.

"You killed them?" I asked tentatively, taking the proffered bowl of whatever hot cereal he'd cooked over the fire. It looked like oatmeal and tasted like cream of wheat. Sweet, smooth, and warm sliding down my abused throat. Suddenly, I remembered I'd been choked, likely to blame for my soreness. I didn't meet the considering eyes of the male watching me as I ate.

"One of them. The other had left by the time I arrived." Words said bluntly and with little emotion. I swallowed down my mouthful of breakfast and raised my eyes to his. I couldn't read them.

"Did you see or hear who they worked for?" I asked tentatively. Still unsure where I stood with the detached male.

"He wore an emblem that seems faintly familiar and the chains were iron, indicating someone outside of the nature kingdoms."

"So there are others?" I asked. He inclined his head slightly even as his eyes narrowed.

"Yes, the Metal and Disaster Kingdoms. Though we do not enter them and they do not enter ours. It would mean war." I gulped. "So, by your questions, can I assume you know who they worked for?"

"Not because I'm working with them," I insisted. "But the one who left, he said he worked for the King of Iron and Steel." The first real emotion flashed through Thatch's eyes then. He blinked at me in shock before he covered it and stood to his feet. "That bad?" I whispered.

"Shouldn't you know? He came for you after all. You're his little seductress. I can smell the other male all over you." I shot to my feet, red hot anger blowing through me followed by ice cold shame.

"I was kidnapped, poisoned, and assaulted, and you think I am working with them!" I snapped at him. "You act like I wanted to be trapped in this world. Trapped traveling this kingdom with you. Hunted by other beings determined to get to you through me. I can assure you that it's the last thing I would want!" I stopped abruptly as he stalked towards me slowly, and I backed up until I hit a tree with a gasp.

Thatch leaned in closer, pinning me to the tree with his dominance, one hand pressed against the bark next to my head. I could have easily slipped away, but I couldn't move. It wasn't the same feeling as the assassin holding me to the tree. Instead of fear and nausea, desire flowed unmistakably through me.

"What *do* you want Princess?" Thatch whispered seductively. I stiffened, ignoring the cartwheels my stomach was doing. What a stupid reaction to the wicked prince in front of me.

"I'm not a princess," I snapped, but it came out breathy and he smirked. Thatch leaned even closer until his body was pressed against mine and we shared the same air.

"I don't know, my parents seem convinced." He stroked the back of his fingers down my cheek, to my neck, to my collarbone, and I sucked in a sharp breath. "That assassin sure thought you were." I stiffened again. His green eyes didn't leave mine as it continued its journey down my side next. Gods, why didn't I want to push him away? I was literally in this same position hours ago, but no negative memories bombarded me. Only the need for him to press himself closer.

"Well the assassin was mistaken and clearly after you," I bit out. He chuckled though it lacked any humor.

"You're probably right, but…" He smiled wickedly. "You want all the other privileges of being a princess, don't you?"

I scoffed. "Like what? Having to sit in boring council meetings and learn how to hold myself like a lady while catering to males' every whim? Have assassins hunt me and an arrogant prince blame me for it?" I rolled my eyes, but I was finding it difficult to concentrate with his warmth enveloping me. Thatch chuckled again.

"Sure, sure. But everyone knows princesses kiss princes and that's exactly what you want to do. I bet you've been thinking about it for weeks, haven't you?" My eyes widened in surprise and horror. *Wait what?*

"What…what gave you that idea?" I sputtered, trying to put some distance between us. He only pressed closer.

"Your heart is going a mile a minute Princess," he teased. I opened my mouth but no words came out. He was right, it was. "Is it because you're lying to me about the assassins…or you really *do* want me to kiss you?" He paused as if reading the answer on my face, and then smiled wickedly. "Don't worry. I'm feeling charitable today so I'm willing to make your dream come true."

I scoffed ready to tell him off, but then his lips were over mine, and I lost all semblance of time. They were soft but firm and as his hand slid up to cup my chin, I found myself melting into him. He smiled against my lips, then licked along the seam of my bottom lip.

"Come on Wildfire," he whispered against me. "Let me in." He pressed his lips to mine again and this time I couldn't fight the gasp that escaped, allowing him to sweep his tongue inside. He kissed me thoroughly, slowly, but firmly, exploring all of me. And gods help me, I kissed him back. I went as far as to grip him closer to me by his tunic, not realizing I had done so until he broke the kiss. I quickly dropped my hands embarrassed, too dazed to do anything but stare at him.

"There. Now you've kissed a prince." He turned away with a smirk and said over his shoulder. "You're welcome." I stared after him, stuck between my disgust at my response and his audacity, but also the need to pull him back. And as I stood there fighting with myself, I couldn't help but think he'd forced himself to walk away, because while it had started as a tease and potentially a test, I'd felt just how much he'd enjoyed it. Heard how breathless he was as he left. That in itself raised more questions than answers.

And whether he'd meant to or not, with one kiss, he'd washed away the nightmares of my memories like they'd never existed.

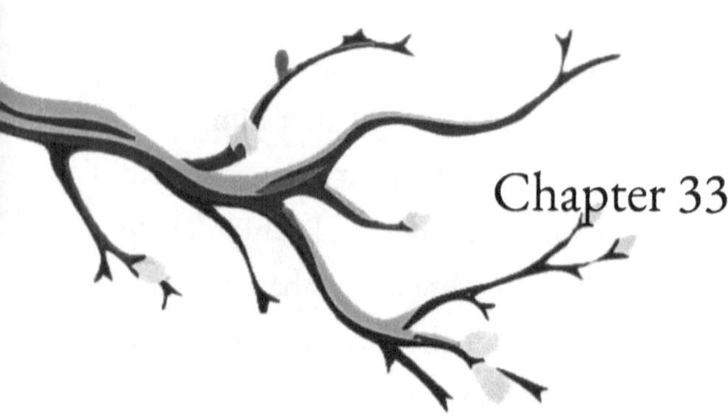

Chapter 33

Thatch

What had I been thinking? Catching her off guard, yes. Distracting her from the trauma of the assassination attempt for sure, because I had no doubt that she had nothing to do with this one. I'd tasted her terror in the air as I followed the burning pull of the tattoo over my heart to find her chained to a tree. Seen the hand marks around her throat that made me want to destroy everything around us. Yet it was the haunted look in her eyes that spoke of living nightmares that I'd wanted to erase. I had no doubt that the manhandling from the assassins had triggered bad memories.

But if all I'd wanted was to distract her, I should have stopped after the first peck. I shouldn't have pushed her against the tree until our bodies were perfectly aligned. I definitely shouldn't be this uncomfortable in my pants right now, desperate to go back and see what other sounds I could coax from those beautiful lips.

She'd never been kissed. I could tell by the way she froze and then responded clumsily at first, but the way she'd melted against me was sheer perfection. Every inch of her molded to me like we were meant to complete the other. And that kiss…I'd never enjoyed something so trivial as a kiss more in my entire existence.

I shook my head. No, not perfection. It was nothing. It had to be because to admit that I actually wanted this female was out of the question. Especially one I wasn't sure I could trust.

I froze, a hand going to the spot right over my heart. It'd burned again when I'd kissed her as if confirming something. I scowled. Yes, I was attracted to her, but no, this marking meant nothing because I could never give her what she deserved. I was too far gone and she'd had enough darkness in her life. I'd seen the arousal in her eyes as I'd leaned close. I'd also seen the fear. Fear that reminded me that she'd been in threatening positions with a male before. Enough that my closeness could be construed as either violent or welcome.

I gritted my teeth, thorns wrapping around nearby trees. The fact she didn't know whether our kiss was a threat or pleasure infuriated me like nothing else. The fact that she'd likely been in that same position right before I arrived infuriated me more.

And I shouldn't care. I growled. Gods, I wanted to fuck her so badly. Maybe that's what I needed to get this hold she had on me under control. My brothers had told me to have fun, and then Therek had told me not to trust her. Maybe if I took her to my bed, I could coax the truth out of her. Get her to tell me where her loyalties lie once and for all.

A wicked smirk grew and I licked my lips, capturing her lingering taste of fresh cherries. Yes, that's what I'll do. I'll scratch this itch and ensure the female was so satisfied with pleasure that she'd either spill her secrets or become loyal to me. Liking the idea immensely, I turned to return to camp. Suddenly the arrival at the next city couldn't come fast enough.

"We need a break," I declared a couple of nights later as she finished her bowl of jackalope stew. Riveting, hazel eyes shot to mine. Those *were* flecks of summer green leaves in them. How had I ever thought she was anything but extraordinary? Ember frowned.

"And do what exactly? I thought you were going to scope out the city tonight." I nodded in confirmation.

"Oh, I am, but you're going with me. I know a great place to gather gossip." Her nose scrunched up in disgust.

"We're not going to a brothel again are we?" I chuckled.

"No, Princess. Just a normal tavern." She stared at me skeptically but nodded after a long moment.

"Fine, let's do it. I'd like to do something besides race from city to city anyway." I grinned wickedly.

"Good, because I have just the dress."

Gods. "I think I set myself up for a long night," I muttered bitterly. I could barely take my eyes off the female in front of me. When I'd saw the dress a couple of cities back, I hadn't known why the impulse to buy it was so strong, but now, seeing it on her. Gods. I knew.

It only fell to above her knees in the front but pillowed out past her feet in the back. It was the vibrant orange and red of a sunset, making it look like she was a walking flame. She'd pulled her hair in a half up-do, leaving two strands to kiss either cheek. On anyone else, the black midcalf boots she'd chosen to wear would have been out of place, but on her....

She was stunning. Royalty in every sense of the word. I wondered if she knew that yet. That her inner power had nothing to do with the flames flickering in her veins, but her tenacity and fiery heart. Every other male in this tavern surely did, and if I didn't make it clear who she belonged to, I would be destroying more than trees tonight.

A faerie made his way towards her, his wings flickering eagerly, no doubt in anticipation of taking her to bed. A growl escaped my chest before I could stop it, and I hurried to intercept. Ember stood near the wall sipping on her mocktail and watching the crowd with barely concealed longing, but she glanced up at my presence.

"Dance with me," I told her, and she blinked in surprise.

"What?"

"Dance with me." She snorted.

"You don't want to dance with me," she said rolling her eyes. "And I can't dance." She glanced at the dance floor again and I smiled seductively at her, watching the moment she noticed how my gaze wandered the full length of her body. I did nothing to hide my desire and her pupils dilated as her heart rate picked up.

"There's not a male in here who wouldn't like to dance with you Ember. Let me have that honor." I flashed her a wicked grin. "When was the last time you let loose Wildfire?"

She swallowed, her eyes on mine before they glanced at my out-stretched hand. I willed her to take it. Daring her with my gaze. Ember narrowed her eyes at the challenge but took it anyway.

"This is a bad idea," she insisted as I swept her away. Here was the dance I should have given her at the ball, but I'd been too caught up in rebelling against my parents. Now I pulled her close to me and reveled in the feel of her in my arms.

"I don't know," I said, smiling down at her. "I think it's the best idea I've had all night." She graced me with a shy smile under long lashes. My heart damn near stopped, and I felt the pull deep within my core telling me to pull her closer. That she was *mine*. A feeling that was quickly growing out of control. This time I didn't fight it as I held her against me song after song.

I could have danced with her forever, but I was committed to the plan tonight, even if the pull was growing stronger the longer she was curled in my embrace. Needing to step away before I truly forgot the purpose of the night, I pulled us to a stop.

"Let's get a drink," I told her. She was panting, her lips slightly ajar and my gaze fell to them. Desire shot through me like a shock of lightning imploring me to steal another taste. Not yet. Not when I could use this. My lips lifted up in a smirk when I lifted my gaze to find hers riveted to my mouth.

"Ember?" Startled eyes met mine. "A drink?" She nodded slowly, clearly flustered, and I fought another smirk as I guided her with a hand on her lower back not to the bar, but to a private room.

"Why are we in here?" She questioned, still breathless from the danc-ing...and whatever was going on between us.

I moved towards the minibar and poured us both a glass of wine. I kept my back to her as I withdrew a vial and dropped three drops into hers. I spun to face her holding the glasses.

"I want you to do something for me." She froze and I hid my smirk behind my glass. She studied me, hesitant curiosity in her eyes.

"What is it you want?" she asked tentatively, eyeing the drinks in my hands with barely concealed displeasure. Hmm, interesting. She'd avoided every drink up until this point, but maybe she'd drink this one. My smile grew as I indicated the glass with a tilt of my head. The dark wine with streaks of purple running through it shimmered invitingly. If my instinct was correct, she wouldn't be able to fight the effects of the sweet wine for long, not with the dose of truth serum. It was time to interrogate my lovely, little fire princess once and for all.

"Drink with me." She lifted a brow in disbelief before eyeing the drink with hesitation.

"Really? That's it? You just want me to have a drink with you?" I shrugged.

"You may find yourself inclined to do more afterward, but yes, that's all I'm asking." Still skeptical and hesitant, Ember moved to my side, but we had a deal. She couldn't refuse without consequences and she knew it.

"Okay, your prerogative," she said, and then she took a healthy sip of the wine. I watched as she licked her lips and eyed the drink again, seemingly surprised she enjoyed it. I couldn't help the wicked grin I gave her.

"Like it?"

"Mhmm," she hummed before finishing the glass. She grabbed mine, and I quickly snatched it back before she finished it too. I wanted to test her...loosen her up some... not get her too intoxicated to participate.

"Woah, easy there Princess. This is potent stuff. Don't want to drink too much of it too soon. Here, have some nightgaze instead." Disappointment flashed through her eyes but she took the drink I poured.

"Why are we actually here Thatch?" she studied me suspiciously, even as her body heat rose from the wine. I took a sip of my own to stall. I closed my eyes in pleasure as it slid down my throat, seductive warmth flowing through me. I opened them again to find her studying my lips again. I smiled.

"I just wanted to take a breather and get to know each other better. We've spent so much time just traveling from city to city focused on the threats to the kingdom. When do we stop to just.... talk?" *And I need to know if you're my enemy,* I thought sullenly.

She scoffed. "You want to play twenty questions? Now?" I inclined my head and she sighed. "Fine, but I get to ask a question for each one answered." I hesitated, but those were fair terms.

"Deal. I'll start." I studied her, deciding to start with something easy. "Tell me about where you grew up." Ember frowned.

"I told you this already." I shrugged.

"Bits and pieces, yes, but humor me." She still eyed me with skepticism but nodded.

"I grew up in the human world on a two hundred acre apple orchard. We used to be famous back in the day. The Lanxter apples. Best apples in the state." She snorted in disgust, and I eyed her curiously.

"You didn't like growing up on an orchard?"

"No, it wasn't that. It's just...." She sighed. "When I was young I loved every aspect of having an orchard. There was something magical about working with the trees until they flourished and grew delicious fruit. Everyone loved them, and I used to brag at school about it all the time. I would bring them for lunch to share with all my friends.

"It wasn't until I grew older that I noticed the looks of pity. The undercurrent of others knowing something I didn't." Ember sucked in a shaky breath. "I wish I never found out," she whispered, her eyes far away. I swallowed uneasily. I'd asked about her past forgetting that was where her scars lie. The ones that stymied her fire, but I couldn't stop. I was dedicated now.

"What happened?" I coaxed her, hoping for her sake that she refused to tell me so I couldn't use it against her, but hoping she confided in me anyway because I desperately wanted to know more about her. I took a sip of my wine to conceal my eagerness.

"I came home one day to my dad beating the living daylights out of my mother," she said abruptly, and I almost choked on my drink. I coughed.

"What?" I managed.

"He was drunk," she muttered. "I don't know how I'd missed just how often he was. I don't even know what my mother did. I just remember jumping on his back to stop him and being thrown against the wall with a hand to my throat. I was eight."

And a year later her mother abandoned her and her brother to her father's abuse. I gripped the glass so hard in my hand, I feared it may shatter, but then she shook herself and finally glanced at me. I could see the glaze falling over her eyes. The wine was starting to work, not that she noticed how she was suddenly shifting from side to side.

"What about you?" My gaze shot up from her lips.

"What about me?" Ember raised a brow.

"You asked me three questions Thatch. It's your turn to tell me something about yourself."

"First, tell me one more thing." I needed to hurry this along. I still needed to interrogate her, and the wine was starting to take effect.

She sighed. "What?"

"Are you working for my enemies to betray me and my kingdom?" There. I'd asked, and I could tell by the hurt flashing in her eyes that Therek had been wrong. Despite everything I'd done, what I was prepared to do, she hadn't tried to harm me.

"I would never betray you Thatch," she said softly. And I believed her. She was nothing like the last female I'd trusted not to do so. And maybe that's what had me revealing the next piece of truth of my own.

"Sometimes memories that I wish were gone, come back to haunt me. To remind me of what I've become. What I've lost. Every time I think that I'm past them. That I've overcome them, they return....and then there's you."

"Me?" She twirled the drink in her hand, a lovely blush filling her cheeks.

"The thought of you getting close to me terrifies me and yet...." The darkness growled in me. And yet I desired her more than air itself. By the way she was watching me, the feeling was mutual. I swallowed the last of my drink.

I could tell the effect of the wine was getting to her, lowering her inhibitions just enough that she wouldn't fight her desire for what I was about to do. Dragon wine, aka lust wine, was great for doing that, but it only encouraged those who drank it to act on the level of their craving. I doubted that was going to be a problem.

I sat the glass down on the dresser and moved towards her. Ember saw me coming and moved away from the couch.

"What are you doing?" she asked me as I herded her towards the bed. The uncertainty mixed with arousal in her voice would have stopped a better male, but I was no longer one of those. I herded her until she hit the edge of the bed, and then faster than she could track, I pushed her gently until she fell backward onto it, grabbing her glass and setting it aside.

"Watch," I told her, my arousal raging through me, amplified by the warmth of the wine. Slowly, I undressed, reveling in the way she devoured my body with wide eyes. I growled in pure male elation and yanked her towards me so I could thrust against the apex of her thighs. My hands slipped underneath the edges of the dress, pushing it up as I leaned down and swallowed her gasp with a harsh kiss. I was determined to devour her and make her lose control like she was doing to me.

"Thatch...." she started but moaned as I pressed a finger against her bundle of nerves.

"Do you want me to stop?" I asked smoothly, rubbing more vigorously as I trailed my mouth across hers.

"I.... I..." Not wanting to give her the chance to finish her sentence I trailed my lips down her neck to her collarbone, nipping as I went. She gasped, leaning her head to the side to give me more room, and before she knew what I was doing I had lifted her gown up and over her head. I moaned at the sight of her mostly naked body below me, and I quickly slid the last bit of cloth down her legs baring her fully. Gods, she was exquisite. Every scar spoke of a female who'd been through hell and survived, and I wanted to lick and kiss each one. So I did, pulling her boots off as I worked my way down her legs.

By the time I was done, she was moaning and twisting with pleasure. Her eyes didn't leave mine as I kissed my way up her inner thigh until I hovered over her most intimate parts. I wrapped my lips around her bundle of nerves and worked her with my fingers until she fell apart under me.

Grinning wickedly, I lifted her leg and pressed my body against hers as she stopped shaking. Wide, hazel eyes shot back to me. I could see the conflicting emotions there again like she was being pulled into another memory not as pleasant as what was before her.

"Stay with me Princess," I whispered, stroking her again as I leaned down to kiss her deeply. "Feel that? You want me just as much as I want you, even if you won't admit it." With those words, I shifted until I was slowly sinking into her. Her breathing escalated, but she gripped me to her, her legs wrapping around my waist and pulling me closer. Both of us groaned when I bottomed out.

"Thatch," she moaned, her body arching underneath me.

"That's it baby," I told her, letting her feel every inch of me before I grinned again. "Now hang on." And then I took her, hard, fast, deep. It was too rough, too soon. She'd obviously never been with a male as endowed as me, but I couldn't stop. The darkness and power within me alike reveled at her cries, at the tears pouring down her eyes and I wrenched every piece of pleasure I could from her body. I nipped at her breasts, her neck, and still pounded into her relentlessly. Yet, she pulled me closer, until I felt her shatter below me. Nothing could prepare me for the feeling of her squeezing around me. I could feel something in my core attached to the tattoo over my heart flaring, confirming, and then I was roaring my release.

When I could catch my breath again, one look into those hazel eyes, one squeeze of her around me, and I was thrusting into her all over again. I had to wipe that look from her eyes. A look that was both shock and desire. A realization of what I'd stolen from her. So I pounded into her relentlessly, and when she cried out a third time, and I had released myself deep within her, I pulled away immediately. I couldn't meet her gaze, not after what I'd done. I'd wanted her out of my system. To discover the truth. I'd wanted to scare her. Instead, I'd done to her what others had done. Taken her without her consent. It didn't matter that she'd enjoyed it. And the truth I'd discovered....

I stormed into the night, swearing right then and there, curse or no curse, I would never touch her like that again, not unless she explicitly asked me to. I was a monster yes, but I couldn't be *that* kind of monster. Not now, not ever. But as I disappeared into the night, I couldn't help but wonder if I was every inch the monster she feared, especially when it took everything within me not to turn back around and take her again and again until she only had memories of me.

Chapter 34

Ember

I wasn't sure what had happened. Was it the drink or Thatch himself? I couldn't decide. And I couldn't stop the desire to feel him deep within me again. Hell, I would take being wrapped in his arms.

No. I shook my head to clear it. It was that stupid drink he'd given me. It had made me feel and want things I shouldn't. It had stopped me from fighting when he pressed into me, filling me with the need for him to make me his. *Gods*, what was in that drink? And the memories.... they'd tried to peek through but didn't get a chance. It was like the core of Thatch – the light – washed away the darkness, leaving only him, me, and rough, delicious sex. In that moment, I'd forgotten to be afraid. I didn't know the act could be enjoyable...or that a little pain could lead to that same enjoyment.

I felt the heat rise in my cheeks, but then I frowned. I'd fallen asleep almost immediately after the final time, my body too worn out to remain awake. But I'd awoken alone and embarrassed, still at the tavern he'd left me at. I'd found my beautiful dress discarded on the floor along with my boots. Too horrified to stop to shower away our combined desires, I'd quickly dressed and escaped back to the townhouse. I'd spent a long time under the cascading water before emerging to thankfully still find myself alone. I'd spent the rest of the day dreading Thatch's return.

I kept switching between anger at his abandonment and worry over the reason for his absence. Where was he? It was almost night and he still hadn't returned. I had a sinking feeling that he hadn't slept beside me last night. Was it not good for him? Did he remember how broken I was and decided I was only good for the moment? Or...or was he haunted by demons of his own? The uncertainty was worse than knowing he didn't want me. I needed to find and talk to him. Make sure we were okay, but what could I do if he didn't want to be found?

Thatch didn't return that day. Or the next. Or the one after that. I found myself in Corr alone, wandering the streets and taking in the sights. I walked in and out of shops, admiring jewelry and clothing I wasn't familiar with but thought beautiful all the same. It amazed me how friendly the people of this kingdom were. They welcomed me, an outsider, patiently explaining things to me when I asked. Those who eyed me skeptically, I avoided just in case.

Luckily Thatch had left me money, and breakfast and dinner were brought directly to the treehouse daily from some unknown service. But when four days had gone by and I still hadn't seen the Prince of Forest, my anger and worry turned to panic. Had he left me here, or was he just refusing to make himself known? Was it something I'd done?

By the evening I had gone through that night a million times, analyzing it from every angle. Suddenly, I wondered if it was because of my expression after the first time. I blushed thinking of how much I'd enjoyed the rough way he'd taken me. So much so, I had been horrified at myself.... because I'd wanted him to do it again. Had he thought it was horror and fear of him?

Gods, I was giving myself a migraine, and I was no closer to figuring out what to do when I heard the front door open and close. My heart beating out of my chest, I raced to the living room to find the dark prince himself standing there. He was disheveled, his hair wild, and he smelled like the brothel. Of course. The one place I hadn't thought to look.

"Where have you been?" I asked more harshly than I meant to. "Do you know what you put me through leaving me in that tavern to wake up like... *that* alone?" I snapped when he didn't respond, my ire rising at the memory. Thatch ignored me and moved to the bar to pour himself a drink. He drank the contents in one go before pouring another.

"Thatch," I growled again, moving to his side. "Where. Have. You. Been?" He eyed me up and down, his eyes unfocused.

"Here and there. And nowhere," he said hoarsely, then threw his drink back. My eyes widened and I stepped back, my blood running cold, anger forgotten. He was drunk. Completely and horribly drunk. I stepped back another step. I couldn't deal with this. Not again. If he was volatile sober, how would the curse make him act drunk?

"Running away now?" Thatch sneered, watching my retreat.

"You mean like you did?" Gods why didn't I keep my mouth shut? Had I forgotten how to act around drunk men in the months I'd been here? I'd allowed myself to become complacent and now I would suffer for it.

"Did you expect me to stay?" he spat harshly, and I flinched. Maybe he was the one who was disgusted by his desire to be with me. "I saw your face, afterward. Saw the conflict in your eyes. You wanted me but hated that you did. Was repulsed by what we had done." He growled in obvious agitation, and I took several steps back as he continued towards me. "Don't worry, it was mutual."

What? That he was repulsed by me? Or that he hated that he wanted me? Did I? I wasn't sure, and right now I was too afraid of what he might do to figure it out. Thatch stopped and glared at me.

"And why in the gods name do you keep running from me? Do you think I'll hurt you?"

"Yes." The word was out before I could even consider holding it back. He froze, the hostility falling from his face and replaced by a carefully blank mask.

"Why? I haven't done so yet. Why would I now?"

"Because you're drunk," I managed. "That's what they do." Thatch cocked his head and considered me.

"Who's they?" he asked quietly.

"Men," I whispered, barely able to talk past the lump forming in my throat. I should stop. I'll only make him angry and then he'll follow through with his desire to be rid of me.

He stepped towards me again until my back hit the wall, but he remained a few feet away, not touching me.

"What happened Ember?" he asked quietly. Not able to bear looking him in the eye, I stared at his feet as I shook against the wall. He moved slightly closer and tilted my head up to meet his gaze. The drunken haze was gone from his eyes now as he studied me. "Tell me Princess. Tell me who hurt you."

A tear rolled down my face then, and then another as I spoke my shame. I told him of the full extent of my father's abuse. Of how it ran everyone out of the house until it was only me. How I learned to hide the marks, but that no one ever looked too closely anyway, not even the orchard workers. I told him about the drinking, the financial struggles, and the cage I was trapped in.

And then.... I told him about that night. The night that still woke me up in a pool of sweat, terror, and helplessness. I'd thought myself safe for a while after the sheriff had made that comment about breaking me in, but I'd been wrong. So very, very wrong. I'd woken up one night to my legs tied down and my father holding my arms pinned to the bed as...as the sheriff climbed on top of me. I could still smell the sweat and whiskey on their breath. Still hear my father telling me that this was all I was good for and that I should be thankful.

"Did he..." Thatch's voice was rough as he gritted out the words. He swallowed. "Did he rape you Ember?" More tears escaped my eyes and I tried to turn away, but he wouldn't let me. His gaze implored me to answer, so I gave a single nod as a sob wretched my chest. He swore harshly under his breathe, and then pulled me into his arms.

I should be scared, should hate the idea of him touching me, especially after he'd basically stalked me across the room in his drunken state. But I suddenly felt safe and relieved. Finally, someone knew who didn't just ignore what I'd gone through or blame me for it in the first place. No, he hugged me tight and whispered words I couldn't make out into my hair as I cried. He lifted me into his arms and dropped onto the sofa with me in his lap. I wrapped my arms around his neck and sobbed into his neck. Eventually, the tears slowed and stopped, and still, he held me.

"I'm sorry," he whispered and I shifted my head to look at him in confusion. "I would have never taken you so roughly if I'd known. *Gods.* I basically coerced you into my bed." He pulled away, placing me on the sofa before pacing away. And I desperately wanted him to come back, to hold me tight until I no longer felt the sweaty hands of my memories. He paced across the room and stopped with his back to me.

"Ember, I am so sorry. I have become just as bad as the males who hurt you, and I can't even blame the curse, because I allowed it to push me this far. I even gave you aphrodisiac wine knowing what would happen. And...and I put truth serum into your drink to find out who held your loyalty."

Shame coated his words, even as hurt and rage roared through me. He'd drugged me? Had I not shown my loyalty to his kingdom all these months? To him? But even as I considered this betrayal, a part of me understood. His brother had warned him away and at the end of the day, he was responsible for an entire kingdom of people. What was the hurt of one female compared to the hurt of hundreds? But the remorse and shame in his voice. He actually regretted hurting me.

I felt my rage diminish until it only simmered. I couldn't forget what he'd done easily, but I understood why he'd done it. Now I needed to stop his downward spiral into self-loathing. I had to find what bravery that remained within me despite the rawness of my soul to tell him the truth or this would be something else he let rot him from the inside out.

"I was wrong," I said softly but firmly. His pointed ears twitched, letting me know he heard me. "You are nothing like those men. Nothing. Yes, drugging me was beyond a betrayal – and you have some serious groveling to do by the way." He tensed but didn't turn around.

"Yes, you encouraged me into your bed, but I wanted to be there. The drinks, you taking control, it just provided me the freedom to allow myself to have what I already wanted." He was still rigid, and I could tell he didn't believe me, so I moved to stand right in front of him so I could meet his eyes.

"You are nothing like them Thatch. You are everything they're not. With you, the memories tried to resurface, but you wouldn't let them.

And...and it scared me how much I wanted you, how much I liked how rough you were, so I reacted badly."

"The first time should have been gentle because they were not. You should have been with someone who could have shown you how good it could be. Who would worship you. Instead...you got me," he spat with derision. I placed a hand over his heart and felt an answering hum around my own.

"The fact that you wish you were gentle with me proves my point. You are still a good male deep down no matter how much the curse tries to change that. What will it take to get you to believe that again?"

He stared down at me, his pain and grief reflecting my own. "A force of nature," he muttered softly.

"Fire is destructive," I said softly. "But it is also light. Maybe you just need something to be the sun so life can flourish." His eyes widened, and I felt something building between us, something strong and unstoppable.

His thumb rubbed away a streak from my tears and gazed at me with a look I couldn't decipher. "Or maybe I just need your fiery heart."

A fire that simmers, still burns.

Winter

Chapter 35

Thatch

Dying screams had me jerking awake and scanning the room thoroughly, one hand gripping the sheets while the other held my favorite dagger. My chest heaved as I glanced at each corner, each offending shadow. But there was no one there waiting to hunt me. No sweet voice distracting me from nefarious intentions. I took a deep breath, trying to erase her piercing cries. Cries I'd caused. Cries I still regretted, even if she'd made me believe she loved me...and then betrayed me.

"If she betrays you, kill her." Therek's growled warning was warranted. My brothers had had to deal with the darkness that rose from the aftermath of the last female I'd let get too close. But why was this coming up now? Yes, occasionally the dreams would come back, making me relive that faithful day, but I hadn't experienced them in months. Not since....

My eyes widened, my heart beating faster and the tattoo across my heart burning. Pulling myself from the bed, I hurried to the bathroom mirror. I choked on a combination of disbelief, dismay, and that spark of hope I'd felt last night. The tree was larger still, its branches now reaching halfway across my chest and beginning to meld with the rose vines. Its roots were spreading out across my stomach. And the core of it...the flames there were also larger, seeming to feed the growth of the tree, sparks shooting up the trunk and down branches like the flames themselves were alive. There was a sheen to the tattoo now as well. I could see slivers of red, orange, and blue reflecting in the light.

What was happening to me? And how could I stop it? Did I want to stop it? Yes, yes I needed to because the wildfire next door was drawing out feelings I hadn't felt in centuries. She was burning away the darkness with simply a touch, and despite my words to never touch her again, I had this hunger to do so anyway. It would end in disaster. She had been hurt, and I couldn't be trusted to respond properly. I wanted to kiss her again and destroy her, all usually on the same day. Often at the same time.

I snorted in reluctant mirth. "She is a Daughter of Disaster," I muttered, shaking my head. But this. This visual representation of what her presence in my life was doing. Was she destroying me? Or healing me?

"The curse can't be broken," I told my reflection, but there was this growing part of me that was starting to wonder if I was wrong. If I could use her to save my kingdom, even if she couldn't save me. I narrowed my eyes. Well, I could use her to draw out this foreign group so intent on causing chaos in my forest, but I would not allow harm to come to her. Not again. The males in her life had done enough. *I* had done enough.

I turned away from the tattoo and connection I could feel growing with each passing day. I quickly washed up, changed, and went in search of breakfast. The Princess of Fire was already sitting at the kitchen table, a bowl of fruit and oatmeal in front of her. Ember looked lost in thought as she absentmindedly stirred her meal. That beautiful autumn colored hair of hers was loose, draping over her face to conceal her from the world.

It was too late. I could already see every aspect she tried to conceal. I wanted to wrap my hand around those gorgeous curls so I could see her face as I took her roughly and thoroughly. I wanted to hear her breathe out my name with desperate moans and sighs. And then I wanted to hear her scream it so the entire kingdom heard and knew who'd claimed her.

Gritting my teeth, I shook my head to clear it of the sensual image. Had I not just berated myself for touching her? Despite the curse, I couldn't shake the distaste of how she'd been treated by those human males. I wanted to hunt them down and bury my thorny vines into their skin until their tainted blood fed the ground beneath them. But I also wanted to destroy her in my own way. Not against her will. No, even with the darkness rampant in my core, I would not harm her that way. But like before...making her fall to her concealed desires, using her body to bring us both pleasure even as I milked her secrets from her cries.

I growled, the images in my head so conflicting. I couldn't even say all were due to the curse. I'd never been a gentle lover. But I'd never been cruel, and what I wanted to do to her was wicked. I wouldn't...couldn't touch her again, especially not when I planned on using her. I clenched my fists and strolled to the stove for food, ignoring the scent of cherry blossoms and embers. At least I would not touch her unless she initiated it. I smiled darkly to myself. I couldn't be faulted for what happened to her then.

Ember lifted her head to gaze at me as I finally sat down in front of her. She didn't say anything for a while, but then she sat her spoon down in frustration.

"Well?"

I glanced up casually as I spooned another helping into my mouth. I made sure to lick the spoon clean as I withdrew it and grinned wolfishly at the hard swallow she gave as her eyes watched my mouth. "Well what?" I asked finally, and the princess jerked her eyes back to mine. She scowled, likely picking up on my game.

"You said something last night about using my "fiery heart", and then you just went to bed without any explanation whatsoever." She made dramatic quotation marks with her hands.

I smiled sweetly. "And what did you think I meant Ember?" She startled slightly, as she commonly did when I used her name. I enjoyed the sight a little too much.

"I don't know, but if you are expecting to sacrifice me like some virgin sacrifice then I would like to know ahead of time."

"Then, you have nothing to worry about." She frowned.

"Why?"

"Because you're not a virgin." It was cruel. Beyond cruel. And it took several seconds for it to register down to the past me why. When it did, my blood went cold, but it was too late, she was already shooting to her feet and throwing the bowl of oatmeal in my face.

"Screw you Thatch. Screw you and that curse of yours."

"You already did, babe." Gods why couldn't I stop? The light in me was screaming for me to do so, but the darkness was front and center as usual. I saw the pain and wrath flash across her face, and the flames in the living room flickered and flared.

She shot me a hateful glare and stormed from the room and out of the townhouse. I took a moment to wipe her meal from my clothes and finish my own before going after her. It took me much longer than I anticipated to find her. It finally took me reluctantly tuning in to what was between us for me to locate her deep in the forest at the bank of a bubbling creek. Ember sat with her arms wrapped around her knees as she stared into its depths. The forest was quiet, likely waiting to see how I would respond today.

"If you came to berate me more, you can leave," she snapped, but I could taste her tears in the air. My gut twisted.

"You wouldn't make it out of this kingdom alive," I told her. She might, especially if she gained confidence in that fire of hers. She snorted in disgust.

"You'd like that wouldn't you?" I opened my mouth and closed it again. Deciding to take a different approach, I gazed towards the forest before sighing.

"I owe you another apology," I said quietly, sinking to sit at her side. She didn't acknowledge me but continued to glare into the water. I could still smell the tears she'd hurried to wipe from her eyes, and my gut twisted. "Ember?"

"What?!" She snapped, turning to face me. "What can you possibly want from me? One minute you're treating me like you enjoy having me around, and the next you're spewing derogatory comments like I haven't shared my scars with you.

"You convince me to partake in wine *knowing* I don't like to drink. You put truth serum in said wine because you *still* don't believe me when I say I have no idea who these people are trying to destroy your kingdom. And while I understand the need to protect your people, I would think after spending *months* with me that you would be beyond using such underhanded methods. Then, you take me to bed and....."

She pauses, and all I can do is watch her with my jaw dropped as her chest heaves from her impassioned speech. I can feel the heat of anger, desire, and embarrassment wafting off her, and it in turn fills me with shame over my actions.

"And then you leave me, alone, in a foreign tavern to face the morning without you. You leave me to do so for days afterwards with no idea whether you simply found the act of taking me to bed so vile you couldn't remain, or a triumphant hunt that quickly bored you." Her voice had softened to almost a whisper by her last words, and her eyes shone with tears that were one breath away from raining down her flushed skin.

What words could I offer to erase what I'd done? What type of apology would be good enough to soothe the wounds I'd never meant to inflict? She was right. I hadn't even considered her past when I'd given her the wine or drugged her. I hadn't even thought about how it would affect her until after I'd taken her roughly.

But to leave her.... that was unforgivable. No matter the shame I'd felt, leaving her had flared every insecurity she had. She had every right to hate me. And may the forces of nature forgive me, because she was going to hate me even more before we were through. No matter how either of us felt, I was still on an imminent deadline to save my kingdom from the darkness running through my veins.

"There are no words I can give you to make up for my behavior," I said finally. "You are most definitely not some hunt, and trust me, I fully enjoyed what we did." I paused as she glanced away in embarrassment, wishing things were different. That I was different.

"But I also don't regret testing you, because it is my duty as Prince of Forest to ensure the safety of Alyvia, but wish I'd done so in a different way. I do regret leaving you in pain. That was not my intention and I sincerely apologize. But know that I will do whatever it takes to save my people."

I stood to my feet, my gut twisting. Ember stared up at me, at a lost for words as anger and hurt battled in her hazel eyes. I turned away so I didn't see the questions in them. Questions I couldn't answer even as the tattoo over my heart burned.

"I'm going after the foreigners stalking my kingdom and you're coming with me." I could feel her confused gaze on me.

"What do you mean?"

"It's time I went on the offensive. I keep just missing them, and it's time that came to an end." I turned to eye her again. She watched me back with heavy contemplation. I wondered distantly what she saw.

"If they are after you, then you can draw them to me."

"And when you find them?" she asked carefully, ignoring my admission of using her as bait. There was a warning in her gaze.

"Then I'll return them to nature where they belong."

"And if I refuse?" I smiled mockingly at her, hating what I was about to do, but knowing it was the reason I'd made the deal in the first place.

"You won't," I snorted without mirth. Ember's eyes narrowed as she stood, her hands fisting as she bristled.

"And why is that Prince?" she spat, but I only gave her a dark smile.

"Because you owe me a favor."

Chapter 36

Ember

Bait. He was using me as bait for a group that had gone around destroying resources and people in his kingdom just to start a rumor. Dread twisted my stomach, reminding me of what his older brother had mentioned. Was this because he still thought I was some trap laid out to end him? Or was he still against the idea of me being the cure the king and queen desperately hoped I was?

Regardless, I felt like I was standing on the edge of a cliff waiting for the ground to crumble underneath me. I couldn't shake the feeling that there was something more to this situation than I knew. It felt like we were hurtling straight for disaster, or a trap of our own. I needed to get a handle on these fire abilities as soon as possible. It may be the only thing that saved me in the end. I couldn't count on the Prince of Forest to do so when he thought I was partly to blame for the battle we were likely heading into.

So, here I was again, standing in front of our campfire, trying to will it to do as I desired as the forest did Thatch. I wish I could say it was going well. It wasn't. I'd set fire to the forest at least ten times today and every time, he'd had to smother it. So not only could I not control the fire, but

I couldn't even put it out when I did lose control. Weeks of practice and nothing to show for it. What good was fire powers I couldn't use?

The only time the dancing flames did remotely close to what I wanted was when Thatch himself guided me. I detested how having his strong body pressed against me, or his deep, wicked voice in my ear was the only time I had control. Detested it and loved it at the same time. Was it wrong to be as attracted as I was when I should be angry with the dark prince?

My body didn't think so. And apparently, my abilities didn't either. Despite the logical side of me that said I really, really shouldn't, I couldn't help craving his touch. Crave the way he'd taken me. Roughly. Thoroughly. Like he owned me. I shivered, afraid to look too closely at my inner psyche just in case I enjoyed the thought instead of being disgusted by it. And I should be disgusted. I'd spent my entire life around abusive males. You would think I'd want nothing to do with this one. Especially after how he'd treated me.

But even though anger still washed through me, I knew Thatch wasn't like the males of my past. First of all, he was a full blooded warrior, Fae male who had already lived several lifetimes before I was even an idea. Secondly, he was an honorable prince who loved his people and who stood to rule an entire kingdom soon. He'd explained to me on one of his "good days" that his parents were waiting for the curse to lift before handing off the four nature kingdoms to the princes to rule. He'd snorted when he told me.

"Guess they'll be ruling forever then," he'd said mockingly, but I could see the sadness in his eyes. Thatch actually wanted to rule Alyvia and I couldn't help thinking after the glimpses of the life within him, that he would make a great ruler.

"You say that as if you still don't believe it's possible even after seeing I have power I shouldn't," I'd pointed out. He'd gazed at me with a look so deeply forlorn and full of longing that my heart bled for him and his brothers.

"What did we say about dreams Princess?" he'd said softly, and what was I to say to that? Neither one of us believed in those anymore. But if I could just get some amount of control over this power of mine, maybe...

"Grrr," I snapped, stomping my foot in frustration. Thatch lifted his gaze from where he was sharpening arrows. "Why can't I do this?" I gestured at him in annoyance.

"You won't always be there to guide me. I need to be able to do this on my own. What am I doing wrong!" I paced back and forth, muttering under my breath. I could feel his eyes on me, but I continued to rant in frustration.

"I have an idea," he said suddenly. I stopped and faced him. The grin on his face was dark and wolfish, but his eyes were a lighter green than when I'd first met him. I frowned. Was it the curse or Thatch talking? I remember Wink saying the Prince of Forest had always been mischievous and a little dark. I'd seen plenty of that myself, and I wasn't inclined to trust him right now.

"Do I want to know what you're thinking?" I asked hesitantly. His grin grew broadly. Yeah, that was a definite no.

"Have you lost your everlasting mind!" I screeched, staring down at the small volcano bubbling away. Silly me for thinking he was simply making us climb yet another mountain.

"Maybe," Thatch said with a shrug. "Or maybe I'm a genius." I stared at him in utter disbelief.

"I'm not going down there!" His eyes darkened, and he took a menacing step towards me. "What...what are you doing?" Thatch didn't say anything as he herded me towards the edge. I glanced back nervously as the ground crumbled beneath my foot. The center of the volcano was not that far away. It really was small compared to some volcanoes I'd heard about. Considering we'd used some type of portal to travel *through a tree* that had left me nauseous and with a severe case of vertigo, I should have known the cursed prince was up to no good. But whether this was a small or large volcano, any fall into its depths would kill me.

Please, Thatch," I begged, tears flooding my eyes as terror saturated my veins. "Please don't do this."

"It's the only way Ember," he stated, gesturing at the lava below. "You are the Princess of Fire. It's time to embrace your birthright."

"But we're not even sure I'm truly her!" I exclaimed, trying to reason with him. He tilted his head contemplatively, and for a second I thought he would reconsider. Then he shrugged.

"Guess we're about to find out."

"Wait, what? AHHH!!" *He. Pushed Me.* He actually pushed me. Time slowed as I stared up at him watching me as the heat at my back grew. Then, everything was red and orange, my body was on fire, and I was screaming and screaming and swimming.

Wait. I was *swimming. In lava.*

With a gasp, I surfaced from the volcano's depth to find myself treading in what honestly just felt like hot water. Unable to believe my eyes, I trailed my fingers through its thickness, marveling at how even my clothes were intact. Feeling unsteady with this change in events, I quickly swam to the edge and hoisted myself out of the volcano to meet a very smug prince.

"*See,* Princess of Fire. Now that you understand that it cannot hurt you, that it's a part of you, you can control it." Thatch said it matter of fact, but I could see the wonder in his eyes. Some part of him hadn't expected me to survive, and that made the rage in me grow to epic proportions until I felt like I was the volcano itself.

"I could have died," I snarled at him, my fists balling. He shrugged.

"But did you die though?" With an enraged shriek I shot ball after ball of fire at him. He blocked each one with a plant or another, but I didn't stop. I screamed until my throat was sore, until my arms were imploring me to stop, and I still didn't until suddenly faster than I could see, Thatch was behind me, pinning my arms to my body.

"Easy now Wildfire," he crooned in my ear. "Easy, I got you. You're okay, Ember. You're in shock, but you're okay." I hadn't even realized how badly I was shaking. I couldn't even see the ground in front of me past the film of my tears. I barely registered traveling back through a portal to our campsite again. Thatch was still whispering comforts in my ear. How dare he? How dare he try to comfort me when he was the one who tried to break me?

Furious, I wrenched myself from his arms and glared at him through my tears. "Don't you ever touch me again!" I growled. "You may be cursed and ready to die, but that doesn't give you the right to play with others' lives." He said nothing but held his hands up in surrender as he stepped towards me.

"Stop!" He did, remorse flashing through his still hunter green eyes. Well, it was way too late for that. "You're right, I can feel the control over the flames now, but I will not thank you. There is always another way, and you chose the one that had a fifty-fifty chance of ending in disaster.

"I understand now that you will always do what is best for your kingdom no matter the detriment to me. You will always allow the curse to twist your actions into a darker more malicious form. I don't trust you. I don't like you. And if you touch me again, I will burn you to the ground until you rejoin the nature you love so much."

Maybe that was below the belt, but I was still reeling from feeling the connection to the flames, from the terror of my impending death. He was worried about betrayal, but *he'd* betrayed *me* when he'd tossed me into a gods damned volcano.

Unable to face him any longer, I turned away and stalked off. "I'm going for a walk, and don't even *think* of following," I growled over my shoulder. His regret was palpable in the air, and I could have sworn I felt his apology in that weird warmth around my heart, but Thatch said nothing and let me walk away.

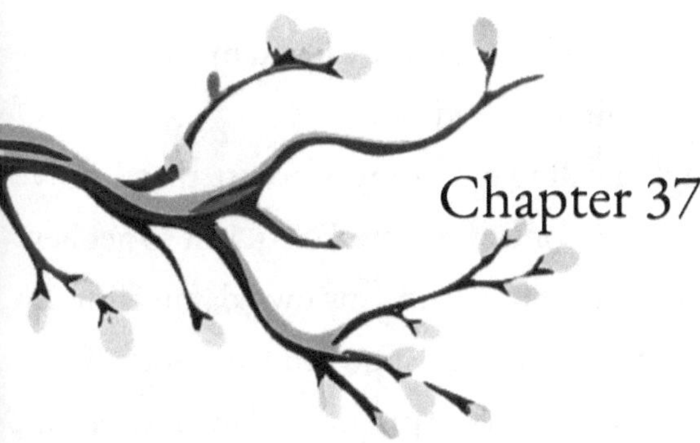

Chapter 37

Thatch

She was furious with me. She loathed me. And I couldn't even blame her. I knew she needed something drastic to accept her power, and I'd been confident she'd come out of the volcano unscathed. My father had done something similar to each of my brothers and me. Torm was flown thousands of feet high on a dragon and pushed off...it was how he'd gained his wings. Theseus was left in the middle of a turbulent ocean for days. Therek was basically buried alive. And I was tossed into the Feral Forest between Alyvia and the western seas to fend off the carnivorous plants and ferocious animals there.

All of us had experienced that moment of terror where we were sure we would die, before deciding that we didn't want to. That realization that the things we were afraid of couldn't hurt us because they were a part of us. So, yeah. I'd done the same to her. Even used the special ability of portal hopping that allowed my brothers and I to travel through our element to each other's kingdoms in an emergency.

Was it cruel? Did the curse enjoy her terror a little too much? Yes and yes, but she'd shown amazing control of her fireballs when she'd attacked me. And now the Fire Princess in all her fiery glory hated me. And for a reason I was still reluctant to admit, it gutted me.

So here I was, painstakingly healing a section of forest that I only remotely remembered destroying in one of my blackouts, just to get her expression to turn even slightly approving. It was my own damn fault. If that wasn't bad enough, now if I so much as appeared like I was about to touch her, she flinched away, erasing all the progress I'd made over the last few months.

I growled in frustration. At her. At the curse. Myself. The entire forest. To make matters worse, the tattoo was shooting flaming pain through my chest again. I'd discreetly checked it this morning to find the flames inside the tree had grown this time. Tendrils of it weaved into the intricate grooves of the trunk and spread out into each of the branches. It was beautiful, but its presence was sending cold fury and fear flooding down my veins as I realized the bond I wanted to deny was growing stronger.

If I focused, I could sense it waiting, whether for me, Ember, or both of us to acknowledge it, I wasn't sure. There was this warm heat behind it that caused my natural power to stretch towards it like a plant to the sun.

So distracted by the bond warring with the darkness within me, I didn't feel the shift in the forest until Ember gasped in alarm from behind me. My head shot up....and my very being froze.

The forest was...infected. I didn't know how else to describe the blackness seeping from the ground and plants around us. The area smelled of death and rot, and I fought the rolling of my stomach as I gagged. There was no green as far as the eye could see, and the ground felt either crunchy or slimy from whatever substance the land was infected with.

I dismounted Cerberus as Ember watched on from atop her roan mare. Squatting, I laid a hand onto the ground, trying to feel for any life left in this place, in this strip of land that was so close to the spring arc. It should be covered in a fresh blanket of snow. The trees should be bearing tiny sprouts, forever stuck in between seasons. Instead, it was deader than winter should ever be. Winter meant rest, not this unrecoverable death.

"What...what happened here?" Ember whispered, her hand wrapped around her throat as she scanned the forest with wide eyes. I was too ashamed to answer her. We both knew what had happened. This was the true representation of the curse. This was what would eventually happen to the entire Forest Kingdom if I didn't leave.

"Did you...did you do this?" The hesitation instead of accusation in her voice had me raising my head to meet her gaze. There was no judgment in them. Simply a sad understanding as she finally saw the extent of the destruction I was capable of.

"Yes," I told her. What use did it do to deny it? The Prince of Life was now the Prince of Death. Here was the evidence. Here was my legacy. I would never rule, because by the time I was given the throne, there would be no kingdom left to rule.

"Why?" Why what? Why hadn't I fixed it? Why couldn't I stop the urge to bury the guilt and grief under the darkness eating me alive? I had no answer for her, so I said nothing. She dismounted and strolled towards something that had caught her eye. Another sharp gasp fell from her as she covered her mouth and tear after tear skimmed down her cheeks. A deer skeleton lay on the ground undisturbed as if the rest of the animals had feared touching it.

My gut clenched as the presence in my chest yearned to comfort her. She would not take my embrace though, and with my history, I'd likely kill whatever fire roared within her anyway. I blinked and that warmth in my chest increased as if trying to tell me something. At the same time,

I felt a tiny thrum beneath my hand. There was life deep below the curse bleeding from the land.

I jerked my eyes to Ember. Fire. It was an element one would think would be the ultimate enemy of the forest, but on the contrary. Fire was cleansing, it wiped out the unnecessary so that new life could breathe and grow. Wildfires were always allowed to flow, our cities protected by water barriers whenever they grew too close, but overall they were left to move as nature intended. The disasters were considered so due to their destructive nature, but one could not have the good of nature without the destruction to balance it out. I finally understood what needed to be done.

"You need to burn it!" I exclaimed, jumping to my feet. Ember spun to face me, a frown on her face.

"What?" I gestured at the land around us.

"I need you to use your fire to burn it."

"What? *Why?* I could destroy the entire forest!" Ember protested, but I shook my head.

"No, you would save it. It's the only thing that can wipe the land clean so that new growth can blossom. It is the way of nature for a reason. *We* are the way we are for a reason." Her nose scrunched up, and I knew she didn't like that her birthright labeled her a disaster.

"There can be no forest without fire," I told her, moving towards her. "Fire holds it in check so some plants don't overgrow and choke out others. It renews nutrients in the soil so life can flourish. Yes, it looks like devastation at first. Like death." Ember tensed and gazed forlornly around us.

"But..." she glanced back at me. "Like in winter, new life rises from the ashes. Not gone. Just asleep." I moved closer so we were only a few feet apart.

"Ember, I need you to try," I implored her.

"I can't!" she exclaimed, shaking her head violently. Tears poured from her eyes again. "If I can't control it...if it keeps going." She choked on a sob. "I couldn't even..."

She hadn't been able to save herself for so long, and, eventually, she'd burned her home down in retaliation of what had been done to her. What she didn't understand was that I didn't fault her for it. In fact, I agreed with her actions. In the end, she *had* found the strength to break the chains confining her. That in itself spoke of her inner power and resilience. And I'd seen that strength grow the longer she stayed in Iyris. She may not have noticed yet, but she was no longer that fearful human girl trapped by her scars and memories. No, she was so much more.

"You cleansed the land, the memories, even then," I told her softly. "You can do so again. Don't let your fear keep you from seeing how powerful you really are." She shook her head again, glaring at the ground, squeezing herself tightly with wrapped arms as terror took over. She wouldn't let me touch her, but this was too important. I crossed the remaining distance between us and lifted her chin.

"I'm calling in a favor." Ember froze and stared at me with panic filled eyes.

"You wouldn't," she whispered. I nodded resolutely.

"I would."

"Have you lost your mind? You would use your last favor for something like this?" I knew why she asked. I'd weaseled my way out of using it when I kissed her the first time, and the next time when I'd coerced her into being intimate, but she didn't know that.

"I still have one more." She frowned, and then her eyes widened as she realized. I nodded, shame making me glance away. "I never directly told you it was a favor. I manipulated you...and I'm sorry." Just something else for her to loathe me for, but this was different. This was hope blossoming under a hard ground.

"You're not kidding?" she whispered. Her hands were clenched and her eyes were hard as she glared at me, but I could see her worry.

"I'm not. Burn it Wildfire." Ember gritted her teeth, but she spun to face the dead land. I watched as she closed her eyes and took a deep breath.

"Please, please don't destroy the entire forest," she whispered, and then the heat rose all around us as suddenly everything caught on fire. I stepped closer to her, unafraid of the dancing flames around my feet.

"Focus your energy so that your fire only eats away at what doesn't belong. You can feel the wrongness in the trees, the earth. Guide your flames so you can remove it." Ember nodded and concentrated as piece by agonizing piece she burned away the sickness. Sweat was raining down her forehead and neck, and her body was shaking by the time she was done.

With an exhale, the flames went out, leaving only charred land all around us. I watched her closely just in case she started to collapse, but she managed to stay on her feet as she glanced around, panting.

"What now?" she asked me. I took a deep breath of my own.

"Now, it's my turn." I closed my eyes and called to the land as I did the trees back in Sorlic.

"Forest, hear my plea. I have wronged you. I have allowed the curse to use me to harm thee, and for that I am sorry. But I am here, and if you would allow me, I will heal that which I have destroyed. Let me use the gift the forces of nature have bestowed upon me, to walk in the title of my birth. Forest, I beseech thee. Let me heal thee." And then I began to sing a song of life, of hope, of nature.

With every verse, I felt the land respond, felt it hesitate as I coaxed it to raise its head. Assured it that I was here to protect, not harm. Then I felt it stretch its arms and grow. And as it did, the small piece of me I thought long gone, started to sprout. The heat in my chest prevented the curse from overtaking it again as the fire had done the land around me.

When I opened my eyes and met the fiery eyes of the female before me, I didn't have to look around to know the forest was lush with growth and life. That I'd unintentionally placed a batch of spring in the winter arc until things balanced out again. I could feel it within me. Every leaf, blade of grass, drop of dew on every plant and rock. And I knew.

I knew who she was to me and would always be to me. I didn't deserve her. There was also the matter of what had occurred to the last female I'd let near my heart. But even though I knew I shouldn't, I wondered how, when all this ended, I would survive letting her go.

Chapter 38

Ember

He'd healed the land and turned it into a lush forest. It was beautiful and I couldn't help being in awe, but he'd used a favor to convince me to burn the forest...after tricking me into doing what he wanted twice before, reminding me that the Fae male was not to be trusted. He'd thrown me into a volcano for crying out loud. Who did that?

He'd tricked me into dancing the night away with him and drinking that sparkly drink that had removed every inhibition I ever had about him. I paused, feeling my cheeks warm and butterflies flutter uncontrollably in my gut. Okay, so maybe I'd enjoyed every aspect of that night, but still! He'd tricked me. Faked a favor to convince me to drink something I'd never would have before.... convinced me to allow him to touch me in ways I really shouldn't want him to do again.

I huffed in irritation. I swear I was back and forth when it came to the dark prince. One minute I was rooting for him to succeed against his curse. The next I couldn't wait to just be done with this journey so I'd never have to see him again. The knot in my chest tightened. Lies.

Despite the fact he'd thrown me into a volcano. Despite the other questionable things he'd done. The last favor he'd asked was for his kingdom. If I was honest, using the one before that to make me bait was for his kingdom in the long run as well. And maybe...maybe I didn't actually want to never see Thatch again.

Rustling to my right had me jerking my head up. My eyes widened as I realized that once again Thatch had disappeared while I wasn't looking. Yet, I wasn't alone, not if the figures surrounding me were any indicator. They were in dark gray that blended well with the hickory and ash trees around me. They smiled deviously at me as they drew their daggers, and I knew I was in trouble.

"Pretty princess. Where's your prince?" one of them crooned. I spun to face his twisted smile, the horns upon his head and goat feet telling me he was a faun. The others were a toro, and two Fae. All appeared to be more than simple thieves. All bore the symbol of twin iron hammers on their chests.

"Great. More assassins," I muttered, feeling my fire rise up. Ever since the volcano, it came readily when I called, rousing whenever it felt my emotions spike. I reached for the leaf dagger Thatch had gifted me, wishing for the millionth time that I'd asked him to teach me how to handle a sword. Then again, considering how my fire lessons had gone, maybe not.

"Come now Fire Princess. We mean you no harm," one of the Fae cooed. His eyes were blood red and stood out with his dark skin and jet black hair pulled back in dreads. When he grinned, revealing sharp canines, I shivered at how much he reminded me of vampires. As far as I knew, those didn't exist here. I hoped... especially as he licked his lips.

"We only want the prince," yet another said. "But you'll do nicely as well." Yeah, no thanks. I didn't even hesitate. When the toro shifted towards me, I struck, sending my flames shooting out. Curses flew as they realized I wasn't going quietly this time.

"I am sick and tired of you all trying to hunt me down," I growled. "What the hell do you want?" The red-eyed Fae smiled and shrugged.

"The King of Iron and Steel wants the forest and the forest he will get. And there is nothing the cursed Prince of Forest can do about it." Then they were upon me, attacking from all sides. Only my fire kept me from being overrun, but I had no training in fighting with fire. I barely knew how to fight at all and I was tiring quickly. I barely dodged one dagger, only to get sliced on my upper arm by another. I didn't even see the iron-dipped whip until it was too late. I screamed and shut my eyes as I threw my hands up. The whip never landed.

I opened my eyes to see Thatch staring down the males with the whip wrapped around his arm from where he'd caught it. He was growling as he tugged on it and the assassins all hesitated, uncertainty passing through them.

"Heard you were looking for me," Thatch growled, and then his face split into a wicked smile. "Looks like you found me." And then there were screams anew as dark vines whipped from the trees and wrapped around each male, squeezing them tightly. But instead of killing them, Thatch stalked to where they hovered a few feet above the ground, blood dripping onto the ground from the thorns piercing their skin.

"This is your last warning," he snarled. "Tell your king that if he or any of his assassins set foot in my kingdom again, I will bury you all alive and feed you to the forest." The males shook, their eyes wide behind the vines covering everything but their eyes.

"Now, be gone," he growled and muffled screams followed the assassins as the vines took them deep into the forest and likely out of the kingdom itself. I stared in wonder, awed by the power of the male before me. If he could do that, then he likely knew when they'd approached in the first place.

Wait.

I spun to face him. "You used me as bait!" It took several seconds for his eyes to meet mine, and then they tracked over me from head to toe. Looking for injuries? His eyes grew hard as he noticed the cut on my arm. He was at my side in a second, examining it. He gripped my arm closer, but I yanked it out of his grasp.

"Answer me!" I snapped.

"Yes, I told you I would. It's what you're here for, no? To help save my kingdom? Well, you can do so by drawing out all the assassins hunting us down. If we're lucky, I won't have to kill any more of them." He turned away without another word as if he hadn't just said he would risk my life...again. I gritted my teeth as he dug around my bag and came back with bandages.

"Hold still Princess."

"I don't need your help," I growled. Emerald green eyes drilled into me and I jolted. Were they getting even lighter?

"Considering that blade was poisoned, I'll say you do." Gasping, I glanced down at the cut on my arm and frowned. I didn't feel any different. Thatch sighed.

"Can you feel your power?" I froze and then realized he was right. I couldn't feel the flames at all, and the constant warmth that normally filled me was absent. I shivered despite my coat.

He nodded. "It'll fade eventually, but I still need to clean out the wound. It's a poison made from the sea lilies in the Sea Kingdom, although it didn't use to be seen so commonly."

Another side effect of the curse no doubt. This time from his brother Theseus. I said nothing else as he cleaned and wrapped it, but I couldn't help studying him as he did. When he finished, he lingered for a few seconds, simply holding my arm.

"I could have died," I pointed out, just to see his reaction. His eyes darkened, but Thatch said nothing as he walked away and picked up his pack again. I couldn't stand it anymore.

"What happened to you?!" I snapped, needing to know what truly caused Thatch to give up. To treat me the way he did. It had to be something more than the darkness leaking through his veins. No, there had to be an event that tipped him over the edge into despair. To turn him into this person who would sacrifice a female he called a princess just because he could. To deny I could help break his curse while demanding I use a favor to burn the forest to heal it. He was a walking contradiction, and I couldn't stand it anymore. I needed to know why.

"You know what happened," Thatch growled softly "I am cursed. A curse my parents still refuse to explain despite centuries." There was such pain reflected in his eyes when he glared at me. Such anger and darkness. But...but their hue was a lighter green than when I'd first met him. So even though I still didn't trust him, I needed to push for his people's sake.... and our own.

"No. I mean what happened to make you stop fighting the curse? Something changed. After everything, don't you think I deserve to know?" Thatch looked away, his body tense, waves of his power permeating the air. I could feel his hesitation, but I stepped closer to him.

"Thatch?" His eyes met mine and that's when I saw the guilt. He was riddled with it, and I knew it had to be much worse than I thought. "What did you do?" I whispered, and then I watched the Prince of Forest crumble. Tears flooded his eyes but didn't fall. The land around us seemed to mourn with him, the trees leaning in to enclose us in our own bubble. The wind brushed against our skin as if trying to soothe the grieving prince.

"Thatch?" I whispered again, wanting to reach out to comfort him, but not able to close the remaining feet between us. He noticed my hesitation, and he withdrew within himself as he looked away again. If it wasn't for the wind, I would have never heard his next words as he turned to walk away.

"The last one I loved died by my hand." I stood frozen as he disappeared into the trees. That insistent humming within me begged me to go after him even as I stood rooted to the ground watching him leave. Maybe I should have. Maybe I should have asked more questions. But I couldn't get his words out of my head.

"The last one I loved..." What did that mean? Was he saying? No, I wouldn't dare believe such a thing. That was for dreamers, not realists like us. But as the wind ruffled my hair, I could almost hear the forest defending its prince. Imploring me to be the one to burn away the darkness still fogging his soul. To free the lost heart of the forest.

Chapter 39

Thatch

They'd poisoned her. *Again.* Rage ran rampant alongside the darkness in my veins at the memory as I considered how long it would take for her fire to return. It had been a strategic move, and I'd considered hunting the assassins down and disposing of them multiple times over the last week. I had little hope that my warning would be enough to dissuade the invading king, but I had to try.

I could feel Ember watching me as we made our way to the last city of this arc before we entered Spring. Our journey was coming to an end, and although I had a name for the person responsible for the attacks on my forest, I was no closer to stopping him. King of Iron and Steel. The opposite of nature, his very name the poison we could not bear.

Why did the Metal Kingdom's king suddenly decide that the Nature Kingdoms were something he desired? Who else had he sent out to do his bidding? Had he produced heirs since I last heard of him?

I needed to contact my brothers. Did this all have to do with the curse? Maybe the death and destruction my brothers and I were causing in our kingdoms were cultivating an environment perfect for this other king to take over. I couldn't let him. Not if I wanted my people to survive. If he continued to invade, we may have no choice but to bring the fight to him.

I sighed. But with the end of my journey through the kingdom, came an end to my time here...and with her. Except, I no longer wanted to reach the end. I no longer wanted to flee my land. No, I wanted to stay and fight to keep it with her by my side. I wanted to watch her auburn hair flow in the wind. I wanted to feel the warmth she expelled with every step. I wanted to get lost in the life in her fierce eyes. I wanted her to burn away the darkness within me. And...and I wanted her to want to stay.... with me. To forgive me.

And maybe...maybe I could. Maybe I could have both, my kingdom saved and a fiery hearted princess. Maybe despite what I've done, those I've failed, the one I....

I tensed, remembering the last time I dared to dream, to hope. To think that maybe I could have something despite the curse's dark tendrils around my heart. I'd been foolish then, thinking that love was all I needed to wash the darkness from my soul. I'd been wrong, so horribly wrong. I couldn't risk being so again. I wouldn't survive it. *She* wouldn't survive it. And despite everything, despite my forest dying and my brothers believing Ember would betray me, I couldn't stand the thought of her fire being extinguished forever.

For the female who had stood up for my people when I cared not. For the female who'd feared me but fought despite her pain. For the female who had given herself to me when I had no gentleness left. For her...for her, I would try one last time before I gave up fully to save my kingdom. Because if she could face her darkness, her nightmares, then surely so could I.

It was crowded in Wolvern when we finally arrived late in the evening two days later. People danced and ate around a bonfire. Many had come from far and wide due to lost homes or attacks from the Iron King... and my own destruction. Their movements were subdued, the moods somber, and yet they danced. They wore their fears and exhaustion like cloaks, and yet they still greeted me like I deserved it.

I chatted with them, trying to boost their spirits as if I wasn't the one who'd caused their suffering in the first place. That didn't stop the children from wrapping their arms around my legs or begging to be lifted for a hug. And while some parents seemed reluctant, they would study me for a moment before giving a small smile and allowing their children to run to me. I was too occupied with catching the little ones and watching Ember play with her own set to take offense. Her laughter made my heart skip and beat faster as the tattoo warmed. She was a wild flame as she danced with the young ones, her head back and arms outstretched as she spun with them.

I couldn't take my eyes off her. Not as she laughed again and the flames jumped and danced with her. The children shrieked with joy, too young to understand how much fire was to be respected. Or maybe they simply knew that they were safe with the Fire Princess there with them.

"Many fear fire because of its destruction, but without death how can there be life?" I turned to gaze down at the elder next to me. She had to be many, many centuries for the wrinkles to be prominent on her silvery skin, despite the still lush flow of her long, black hair. She leaned heavily on her walking stick as she watched Ember.

"That's a horrible burden to place on someone," I told her. "No one wants to represent death." Wise, silver eyes met mine.

"Oh? Because winter does not like the appearance of its dead, looking trees and freezing temperatures, does it make it any less important?" I frowned.

"Of course not. Winter provides rest. A time for plants to take a break so that new growth may occur." She nodded.

"Yes, but if you only focus on the surface, will you see that? Will you see the flowers curled in their brown buds? The new branches waiting to sprout underneath coarse, dry bark?" I tilted my head, trying to understand.

"I don't think I fully grasp what you are trying to tell me," I admitted. The elder gestured at Ember who was still dancing with the children.

"You carried disaster within you for centuries My Prince, and you destroyed. She carries disaster within her and she restores. It is not the power, but who wields it. You were never meant to carry both alone. Only to hold it until someone could restore the life in you."

I turned to her surprised, ready to refute her, but she held up her hand.

"Did you know that your eyes are reverting to the green of your birth? Did you notice how the children of Fae and creature alike no longer shy from you, or how the forest has begun to speak to you again?" I stared stunned.

"She heals you even now My Prince. You fear that she is here to betray you. That you will be lost to the darkness wrapped around your heart, but I tell you that there lies your torch to lead you back to the light. Why hide behind a curse, your guilt, and your wounded pride? Claim your mate."

The tattoo flared, and I knew it had grown as if to confirm all that I'd been told. I could feel the steady warmth it emitted, burning away the thorny vines around my heart.

"I'm afraid," I admitted with a whisper, my eyes following the fiery female before me.

"Good," the elder chuckled. "That means you have something to lose, and that you care enough to notice." She laid a hand on my arm, but I couldn't look away from the scene before me, and she chuckled again. "Follow the light My Prince. Follow your heart."

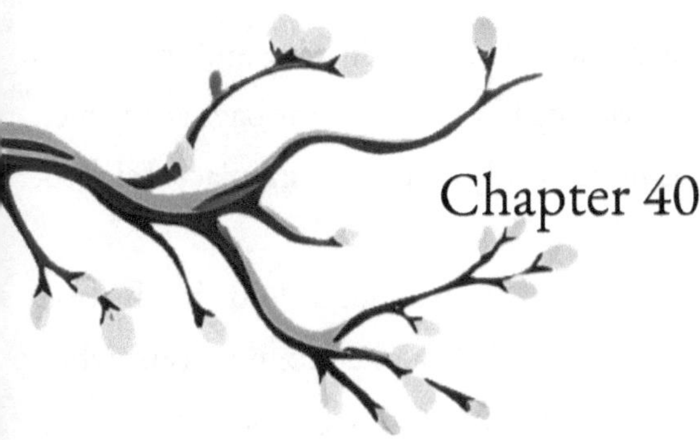

Chapter 40

Thatch

It was late when we finally decided to turn in for the night. There was only one room available with my normal house being used for the influx of people, and the innkeeper apologized repeatedly. I waved him off, telling him that I understood and that what he had was more than enough. He didn't seem convinced and had the cooks provide me with extra sweetbread to compensate.

Never one to turn down sweets, I'd graciously accepted. Now standing in the room next to the female who still didn't trust me, I realized I should have asked for more information. There was only one bed, something I knew Ember noticed immediately. When she whirled on me, I lifted my hands in surrender.

"It's all they had left," I protested. I didn't mention how the tavern owner had offered to kick the residents out of the much larger suites, but I'd refused him. What right did I have to the best rooms when I hadn't even treated my people with the care worthy of such? Ember glanced at the bed again, her hands rubbing up and down her arms as she warded off the chill. Her power was slow to return to its full potential.

Taking a quick glance around I noticed the small table and two chairs next to a slanted window and nothing else. Besides our bags at my feet, the room was bare. And that unfortunately included a fireplace. I sighed. It was going to be a long night.

Ember didn't say a word as I sat at the small table, and she the bed, to finish our dinner. Then again, she hadn't spoken to me except when necessary for days now. I knew she blamed me for a good many things including using her as bait for the assassins, but I'd known she could handle herself long enough for me to catch them unawares. And I wouldn't have let them harm her. Okay, so maybe that hadn't been true at the beginning of this journey. I froze, considering. Maybe the elder was right.

When there was nothing left to do but go to bed I spoke up. "I would offer to sleep on the floor but there's barely any room in here, and we may need to keep each other warm if the temperature drops anymore tonight." Ember shot me a dirty look.

"We are not sleeping in the same bed Thatch," she snapped. I raised a brow.

"It's either the bed or outside in the snow. You pick." She scowled for several seconds and then began readying for bed. I turned away, giving her enough privacy to wash up slightly and change out of her road clothes. I would have to have a bath brought in the morning. It would be a luxury after days on the trail.

When I'd finally heard her slip underneath the blankets, I began stripping my quill and jacket. I fought a smile at the sharp intake of breath as I pulled off my shirt, but when I went for my pants, I heard her sit up abruptly.

"What are you doing?" I shot her a questioning look over my shoulder.

"Getting ready for bed."

"You aren't planning on climbing into bed naked are you?" she snapped, obviously flustered. I lifted a brow.

"Is that a problem?" She scowled.

"Uh, yeah, that's a problem. It's bad enough we have to share a bed. I don't want to be in bed naked with you." I turned to face her and smirked as I saw her eyes drift down before shooting back to mine.

"Well, I'm not sleeping in dirty clothes so you'll have to get over it. Plus, it's not like you're naked, or like you haven't seen it all before." She sputtered, trying to come up with a response and my grin grew. "Relax Wildfire. I'll keep my undershorts on."

"Fine," she grumbled as she rolled over so her back was to me. "And stop calling me that." I chuckled softly to myself as I finished pulling off my pants. Yeah, not a chance.

As I climbed into bed, I felt and saw her tense. "Just don't get any ideas," she warned. "And no touching." I fought a sigh. I deserved it after all, so I made sure I laid as far from her as the small bed allowed.

"You have my word," I promised her, wishing I didn't have to.

I woke to her shivering violently across from me. The temperature had dropped drastically in the middle of the night, and she was almost in the fetal position in her search for warmth. I sighed. Despite my vow not to touch her, I shifted closer and tucked an arm around her waist before pulling her into me until her back was flush with my chest.

"Wh...what are you doing?" she stuttered as she shivered. Once again I felt a shot of anger rush through me at the thought of her being poisoned, especially since it had been a stronger dose than I'd ever seen used previously. Who knew when it would eventually fade, but until it did she couldn't produce her naturally higher temperature.

"Warming you up," I muttered back, slipping my leg over both of hers and my other arm underneath her head to wrap around her chest. I fought a shiver of my own at the feel of her icy skin against mine.

"I…I didn't ask you to do that," she complained, but she snuggled deeper into my warmth, and I grimaced. Gods she was cold.

"I know," I muttered.

"You…you promised not to touch me," she continued even as she gripped the arm wrapped around her waist.

"I know," I repeated. I leaned in until my lips were at her ear. "Sleep now Wildfire," I whispered teasingly. "You can always roast my ass in the morning."

She growled quietly, but slowly so slowly her shivers abetted until she sighed softly and relaxed in my arms. This felt right. It shouldn't, but I couldn't help the thought that this – her secured in my arms – was how things were meant to be. I glanced up into the mirror across from us, enjoying the view of our bodies intertwined. I startled then as I met eyes a much lighter color than they'd been in centuries.

In fact, they were only a couple of shades darker than my true green. It had to be her. The brave female in my arms who'd insisted on making me feel. Who the darkness recoiled from. What if it could remain this way? What if she truly could cure the curse and I could stay in my kingdom? What if I really could convince her to stay with me? I held her closer and for the first time in a long time, I let myself hope.

I could feel her eyes on me as I slowly woke. Her hand was on my chest, my arms still wrapped securely around her, and it felt just as good as it had when I fell asleep. Opening my eyes slowly, my gaze met hers. She was watching me, a look on her face that I couldn't identify. What was she thinking about so early in the morning? It cleared as she noticed I watched her back, and although I expected her to attempt to escape my embrace she remained still.

"Are you okay?" I whispered, hesitate to break the silence lest she ask me to let her go. Ember shrugged.

"I haven't been truly okay in a long time," she admitted. I stiffened and tightened my arms around her.

"I'm sorry." Her eyes widened in surprise with a hint of skepticism and I sighed. "For a lot of things."

"Like what?" she asked, studying me.

"For how I've treated you. For throwing you in the volcano." She tensed but didn't pull away. "I did it because that was how my father had taught my brothers and I to face our power, but I should have warned you. I should have asked." She continued to gaze at me with a look I couldn't decipher.

"And...and I'm sorry for being like the males who hurt you." She froze. She was quiet for so long, I started to pull away.

"You're not like them," she whispered finally. I paused. "They never made me feel like you do."

"How do I make you feel?" We were close, our lips almost touching, but I didn't take my eyes off hers.

"Warm. Alive. *Safe*. With you.... with you I almost dare to hope."

"Hope for what?" We'd inched closer together somehow, lost in whatever confession fell from her lips.

"A better future. The freedom to dream."

"And what do you dream of Princess of Fire?" I whispered, my heart clenching as I held my breath. Ember was quiet, and then she whispered shyly.

"You."

And I couldn't help myself. I leaned towards her slowly, giving her a chance to stop me, but she didn't. She remained still as I pressed my lips to hers, sucking in a breath at how soft they were, like a bed of flower petals. It was a gentle caress as I waited for her reaction. When she still didn't pull away, I leaned closer and pressed more firmly, tracing my tongue along the seam of her lips. I needed to taste her like I needed my next breath.

Open for me, I implored her silently, and as if hearing my plea she finally melted into me, her lips parting in a sigh as she kissed me back. I speared my tongue into her warmth, moaning at the feel of hers on mine. My grip tightened as I pushed her onto her back and tilted my head to delve deeper. This kiss was nothing like the last one. There was frenzied hunger roaring in my veins I couldn't deny. I couldn't feel the darkness, only her warmth, only the light flowing through her and awakening me. I could feel her fire filling her veins again and subsequently me.

She moaned into my mouth as her hands drifted up my chest and into my hair. I groaned in pleasure. Fuck, that felt good. She tugged at the strands, pulling me closer to her as if she too felt this need to meld into each other and become one. I shouldn't. There were a million reasons why this wasn't a good idea. The rough way I'd taken her last time, being one of them, but it didn't stop my hands from drifting down her body to the spot between us. Ember rubbed against me, making the bulge in my shorts grow and I bit back a growl.

And then I was pulling her gown up and pulling her underwear to the side so I could sink two fingers into her tight heat. She pulled her lips from mine to moan deep and breathy. Gods, I loved that sound. I pumped my fingers in a steady, hard rhythm, watching her face twist in pleasure. It wasn't enough. I needed to feel her coming apart around me. Quickly withdrawing my fingers, I kissed away her protests as I pulled off her panties, yanked down my shorts, and fisted my length in my hand. I wrapped her legs around my hips, and I shifted between her thighs, my length positioned right at her opening.

"Say yes," I panted onto her lips. Pleasure clouded, hazel eyes gazed back at me, her gorgeous auburn and black hair sprawled across the pillow like the sun. "Say yes," I said again, pressing slightly, my entire body shaking with the need to take her, but needing her explicit permission this time.

Ember arched her body into me, her eyes not leaving mine as she breathed, "Yes." With one long thrust, I bottomed out in her, watching as her eyes widened.

"Fuck!" I growled, feeling her clench around me as I waited for her to adjust. Only when her nails dug into my back, and her hips rolled to meet mine did I start to move. My eyes rolled to the back of my head as I continued to pound into her with long, slow thrusts, trying to get as deep as I could with every stroke. Her nails dug into my skin almost to the point of pain but I didn't care. I wanted her to mark me. I wanted to have something to remember her by if at the end of this she was gone.

The thought sent a wave of pain through me, and I picked up the pace until the sounds of our pants and moans were louder than the pain of the thoughts in my head. It wasn't long before I could feel her tightening around me. I went faster, pounded harder, determined for us to come together.

"Thatch!" she called out, her body arching toward me. "Oh...ohh." I gritted my teeth against the feelings rising in me. It was growing between us. I could feel it. Like a hum that grew louder and louder, reverberating through my chest, my core. And then her hand slapped over my heart at the same time her other gripped the nape of my neck. And like that I was coming, roaring my release to the world as she screamed my name.

Slowly, so slowly I came back to the world, managing to shift us so she once again lay in my arms, but with her head against my chest. She quickly drifted off to sleep, but my chest was still burning as if she'd summoned fire. I glanced down and felt everything in me freeze. The tree across my heart was larger, little buds of green on its branches. But what made my heart beat faster in fear and longing, was what was happening in the middle. The fire within had come alive and now flickered with internal flames. And in my core, I felt the hum, the steady beat of another soul tied to my own. The bond had finally snapped into place.

I feel it.
The darkness slipping,
giving way to this kernel of light
I can't contain.

I feel it.
The budding of hope.
Of new life.

I feel you.
Filling in these jagged cracks.
Warming this cold heart.

I feel you.
Holding my hand.
Standing at my side,
even as I waver.

And for the first time...
I am not alone.

So maybe I will dare...
To dream
To walk in this spring.

Spring

Chapter 41

Ember

Things were different between Thatch and I as we went about our day. I felt closer to him somehow, like he had become a part of me. At first, I avoided meeting his gaze, afraid it would become awkward, but then his hand trailed down my arm to take my hand as we traveled through Wolven. My gaze shot to his, and he gave me a secret smile as he led me down the packed dirt path. Unlike most cities we'd traveled through, Wolven was on the ground, the homes built into the tree trunks themselves or under an arch of tree branches. The streets were just as lively and lit by glowworm lanterns by night, but I could smell flowers in the air.

When he caught me sniffing the air for the fifth time Thatch chuckled. "It's the smell of spring," he explained. "We're right on the border of winter and spring so Wolven is half in both. Here, I'll show you."

I followed alongside him as we traveled to the other side of the city. He stopped to speak to his people as we went, only letting go of my hand long enough to get us both powdered sweetcakes that reminded me of doughnuts before grasping it again.

I watched the city around me in awe. The subtle shifts to spring from the tiny buds to little green shoots springing from the snow, to the smell of coming life in the air reminded me of the male at my side. At first, I'd doubted what my eyes and heart had been telling me, but now I could see it. His eyes were a deep, rich forest green that was slightly lighter than the hunter green clothes I wore. Considering Wink had dressed me in Thatch's color, I had to wonder if it was his true hue.

He still wore dark green to almost black pants and shirts with his dark jacket, but they didn't give me the same ominous vibe they used to. He wasn't overly kind, but then I had a feeling Thatch had never been, making the moments he was like a burst of new growth. He was still snarky and mischievous, except the smile he gave with it didn't make my blood run cold with fear. Even his aura ran closer to a deep grass green these days with dark streaks along the edges.

But it was this feeling in my chest that had spread each day and seemed to burst overnight. A feeling that had flared when I'd touched the most elaborate tree tattoo I'd ever seen. I was sure no other person had ever had a tattoo like Thatch's before because even though I'd never seen him add to it, it grew. It was three times larger than when I'd first seen it months ago. If I wasn't in a world of mythical beings I would say I was imagining things, but not only did it grow, it seemed to be alive in the way the fire within flowed through the trunk into the branches. With a living tattoo growing over his chest, I couldn't help wondering if it symbolized what I thought it did.

And this feeling within me. The queen had mentioned a bond. Said it would snap into place after being put to the test. Well, we'd been through a lot together in the last few months, and despite the questionable things he'd done, I couldn't help feeling like Thatch and I were on the cusp of everything changing for good. A part of me wanted to run for the hills, to not even risk walking to the edge of the cliff to see what awaited there. The other...the other gripped the Prince of Forest's hand firmly and wished for the first time in a very long time, that whatever this was between us would last.

"Wildfire." I glanced up at Thatch, realizing I'd been deep in thought for a while now. He smiled down at me, some emotion I couldn't read flashing in his eyes. "Look."

I frowned and then turned to stare in front of us. I gasped, tears rushing to my eyes as I took in the most beautiful orchard I'd ever seen. It was a sea of cherry blossom trees, each with a patch of blue and brown irises growing around them. Not even realizing I did so, I wandered deeper among them, content to breathe in the heady scent of flowers and life. I crouched down to lift one of the beautiful irises closer to my nose and sighed.

"They remind me of you." Startled, I glanced at Thatch, but he was studying the flowers. "You smell just like the cherry blossoms, and I remember thinking that your skin reminded me of the deep golden tan of the iris. Most people prefer the blue or the purple and white, and they may be beautiful, but sometimes beauty is subtle...until it isn't. Sometimes it's lost in a sea of others until its heart burns brighter than them all. Just because someone else is unable to see its worth doesn't mean it's not priceless."

I stood slowly to my feet, gazing at the flowers all around me with new eyes. There were far fewer brown irises than blue, and even I had gone for the brightest first. But if I truly looked, the golden brown stood out simply because it was unique.

"You are a brown iris Ember." I turned to him as he slowly made his way to my side again and took my hand in his. He raised it to his lips and kissed the underside of my wrist. "And I'm only just realizing what that means." I swallowed, not daring to look away from him just in case the spell would break.

"And what does it mean?" I asked softly. Thatch moved closer and laid his forehead upon mine. Both our eyes drifted closed and for several seconds we just stood there together, breathing in the new life around us, letting it wash away the scent of death that had followed us both for far too long.

"That spring is my favorite season." I opened my eyes to find him already watching me. He opened his mouth to say something else, but then a group of giggling Fae children chased each other through the orchard. They squealed in delight at the sight of Thatch, and I stepped back to watch him with them as he tossed them in the air or lifted them on his shoulders so they could reach the cherry blossoms. They each begged for his attention, and he supplied it with a smile and never ending patience. He would make a great father one day and an even greater king.

I smiled and hugged myself tight, feeling more at peace than I'd ever had in all my life. Maybe spring was still my favorite season. And maybe a Princess of Disaster was meant to help a Prince of Nature break an ancient curse. And maybe, just maybe they were meant to be so much more. A warm hum filled my chest in answer.

Chapter 42

Ember

We were in the last leg of our journey and while I should be excited that we could soon return to the castle, I found myself hesitant to do so. I wasn't ready to leave until it was clear where Thatch and I stood. Would he want me to stay? Did I want to stay? There was nothing left for me back home, and I have grown to love Alyvia and its people.

Maybe I would stay for a while even after this journey ended. At some point between one city and another, I'd found myself forgiving Thatch. If he and I haven't come to an understanding by the end of this, I could always visit the other nature kingdoms. I'd always wanted to travel, and now after months of it, I loved the freedom in it. But I also wanted a home. Could this be it?

I could tell Thatch was anticipating the end as well. He was tense as we stopped in Sorren, his expression tight and focused as he handed off our horses and led me through the city. This one also happened to be on the ground with a lovely spring bubbling through it. Thatch was silent though, only nodding briefly to those who greeted him as he led me to a tavern. Slowing so I walked beside him, he put a hand on my lower back.

"Stay close," he warned, and I nodded as we strolled in. He quickly led us to a corner in the back where two males I'd met already waited.

"Lurk. Wolf," Thatch greeted the warriors as we sat across from them.

"Thatch. Princess." They greeted in return. Wolf turned to grin at me.

"Good to see you're still in one piece Ember." I scoffed.

"Yeah, well, that hasn't stopped them from trying," I retorted. Lurk glanced at Thatch with a raised brow.

"You haven't taken them out yet?" Thatch scowled.

"That's why I called you both here. I *have* been taking them out. And I sent a warning to the Iron King, but they keep showing up despite the alternative routes I've been using."

I shivered, thinking of the ones that had ambushed us on the trail yesterday. I was grateful for my fire but using it to harm was still not something I relished. Wolf frowned, growing serious now.

"But how? Unless there's a spy in our midst." I appreciated how none of them glanced at me. They were quiet as a lovely faerie came by to fill their drinks and drop a nightgaze in front of Thatch and me. He took a deep swig before continuing the discussion.

"That's just it. If there was a spy, I would have spotted them by now," he said. My heart warmed as he shifted my nightgaze to his side and instead poured me a glass of water from the pitcher on the table. Lurk and Wolf glanced at my glass and then at each other before turning back to Thatch.

"The forest speaks?" Lurk asked, surprise plain on his face for multiple reasons. Thatch inclined his head, and both males grinned at him. I simply sipped my water.

"So…" Wolf began, but Thatch cut him off.

"No, the curse is still alive and well." We all grimaced at the pun. "But right now I'm more concerned about the King of Iron and Steel." Lurk glanced at me before shifting closer.

"Have you told King Hyperion and Queen Sequoia?" Thatch shook his head.

"No, and while I sent a message to my brothers to watch their lands, we still need to figure out how they're tracking Ember."

"What?" I spoke up for the first time, choking on the sip of the drink I'd taken. The males all turned to me. "What makes you so sure they're tracking me?" They glanced at each other, and I didn't like the way my stomach tightened at the sight.

"Ember, the attacks started almost exactly when you entered this world, and if they were tracking Thatch, honestly they would have attacked by now," Wolf explained.

"Plus, have any of the attacks actually been directed at Thatch, or mostly when he's not present?" Lurk added. My gut tightened further. "That's why he's been able to use you as bait at all." Okay, I wasn't going to touch that comment.

"But how?" I insisted. "Surely you don't believe I'm working with them or purposely leading them to Thatch." The silence went on for a second too long and my stomach dropped.

"No, of course not," Lurk assured me, but when I glanced at Thatch, he said nothing. My heart clenched. Surely he didn't still doubt me.

"It doesn't matter," he growled, leaning forward. "I can't return to Verdis until the threat has been removed from Alyvia."

"So we're going hunting," Wolf said, a ravenous grin on his face, that the other two males returned.

"We go hunting." I glanced between them, trying to ignore the ominous feeling building in my gut. This was either going to go well or really badly, and I had no interest in finding out which.

I knocked tentatively at his door, wondering if this was a good idea, but feeling the rightness of it all the same. Lurk opened it to peer down at me before lifting a brow in question.

"Um, hi. I was just wondering.... well..." Lurk's lips lifted in a knowing smile, but he said nothing. He was going to make me ask. I sighed and stood up taller. "Does your offer still stand?" His jagged scar shifted as his grin grew.

"Absolutely, Princess," he answered, moving out of the way to gesture me inside. I sat nervously in a chair, glancing around his cozy, if not masculine room. A small fire was simmering in the fireplace and his tattoo kit was already set up on the dining table. I turned back to him as he began assembling what he needed. When he turned back to me, I swallowed my nervousness and glanced up into his questioning eyes.

"Are you sure about this Ember? I meant what I said. This tattoo belongs to you no matter when you're ready for it." I nodded resolutely.

"I'm ready." Lurk gave me a pleased smile.

"Where would you like it?" I pulled up the sleeve of my right arm. He nodded. "Good choice." And then he went to work. I watched in awe as vines intertwined with flaming lilies, irises, and roses were etched from my shoulder, across my collarbone, and down my arm. When he was done, it reminded me so much of the intricate vines on Thatch's arm.

It was beautiful, the flames seeming to be alive as they flickered on my skin. The tattoo could be considered simple and yet represented all that I was. Fire brought new life and beginnings. And I would forever wear that reminder whether I remained in the Nature Kingdoms or returned to Earth.

"Thank you," I breathed, unable to take my eyes off the image reflected back at me in the mirror. I wiped a tear from my eyes. "You don't know how much this means to me."

Lurk smiled as he studied his work. "Trust me, Ember. I know very well." I jumped up and hugged him, and he gave me a knowing smile as I bid him goodnight.

Chapter 43

Ember

I was exhausted. The males had dragged me all over the spring arc following reports of the King of Iron and Steel's men to no avail. Their attacks had only increased as we traveled through Alyvia. We stopped along the way to heal any damage to the forest as my agreement with Thatch still demanded, along with a little help from my flames.

Right now, we were about a week out from the edge of the Forest Kingdom, and as we stopped in the city of Boric, I could feel the desperation and rage rolling off Thatch. I couldn't help but wonder if he was starting to believe that I was actually to blame for the fact the people we hunted always seemed to disappear right before we arrived.

Lurk and Wolf had taken off in opposite directions this morning to investigate two more reports, but I guess Thatch was taking pity on me because he checked us into the royal townhouse and sent me up to rest while he continued to question his people.

Too tired to argue and sick to my stomach with this growing apprehension, I quickly crawled into bed and fell asleep.

Something was wrong. Awareness returned to me all at once and I forced my body to pretend to be asleep like so many times before while I scanned the room with my senses. Someone was here, and I could tell that none of my males were anywhere near. I kept my breathing deep and steady as I puzzled out what to do. I didn't want to blindly shoot my fire and end up burning the inn and all the inhabitants down with it.

"No need to pretend Princess. We already know you're awake." Well okay then. I sat up slowly and scanned the room until I met the cruel eyes of the assassin. He had a long narrow blade in his hand as he watched me. Taking a deep breath, I readied my fire.

"I wouldn't do that if I were you." I froze and he smiled cruelly. "You really think we won't kill the prince and ensure the kingdom blames you for it?" My eyes widened slightly.

"You can't defeat Thatch," I scoffed, trying to project more confidence than I felt. The assassin laughed.

"The Prince of Forest is cursed and Alyvia is dying. Thanks to the King of Iron and Steel and you, it's just progressing quicker." I frowned. That couldn't be true, could it? I thought I was helping.

"Ah, I see. You thought you were the cure to his curse? No, you are the catalyst. Thatch will fall, and the forest with him sooner rather than later." He grinned wickedly. "Especially once the poison he ingested tonight takes effect." My blood ran cold, and I froze.

"What?" I whispered, and he grinned.

"Took forever to get you separated in a situation that allowed us to trap the prince, but fear is a great motivator. And let's just say that not all Thatch's people are feeling forgiving towards him."

My gut twisted with dread. Surely he wasn't saying what I thought he was. Had one of the cooks or barkeeps snuck something into Thatch's food? Is that why he hadn't come back yet?

"Don't fret Princess. I'm willing to make a deal with you. Our king wants to meet you, and in return, I'll leave the antidote for your prince. I'll even have my comrade outside deliver it personally to Thatch himself. Once you leave the kingdom, the curse will slow again, allowing time for the real cure to be found."

He cocked his head. "Or not, but either way, unless you leave with me willingly, your precious prince will die tonight."

"How do I know you're telling the truth," I managed past the lump in my throat. The assassin grinned wickedly.

"You don't."

I couldn't tell whether to believe him or not. I couldn't right? But it wasn't like I could go find Thatch and figure out if he was lying or not. It could be too late by then. And we'd been a step behind these assassins for weeks now. No, I had to take the risk. Maybe I could use this as an opportunity to get the information necessary for Thatch to catch this king. For the sake of the prince and his people, I had to go with the enemy. Hopefully, Thatch would find me in time as he did in the past. I had to believe he would. That what I was about to do wasn't in vain.

"Fine. I'll go." The assassin grinned again.

"Good answer."

Chapter 44

Thatch

I was frustrated and exhausted, and yet I felt more alive than I had in centuries. I was connected to the forest and my power again, and that feeling was like a breath of fresh air. There was only one person I could thank for this. The female bonded to me....my fiery hearted mate... and if she truly was, I owed her everything. She'd stuck with me through darkness and despair and now that I felt that darkness lightening, I knew it had to be her, reminding me what living was.

I wasn't ready for this journey to end because despite how I felt about her, I wasn't sure how she felt. She had no reason to trust me, to want to remain by my side, and yet I desperately wanted her to. I wanted to wake up with her in my arms every morning. I wanted the first thing I saw to be her passionate eyes staring back at me, her fall colored hair fanned across our pillows. I wanted her to lead my people into the coming age with me. I wanted her to be my queen. Even the beautiful tattoo now engraved across her shoulder and arm was the twin to my own, and I was drawn to it every time I saw her.

But I had hurt her. And there were still these assassins after her. Ones that I still haven't managed to find much to my immense irritation. I felt like there was something I was missing, but too exhausted to think any further tonight, I dragged my weary body towards the townhouse, only to stop dead in my tracks. Was that? *No.*

"Ember?" The figure that was following alongside a warrior most definitely not from my kingdom, turned briefly, flashing those hazel eyes. She didn't see me and quickly disappeared out the city gates and into the forest as I followed from a distance. I stopped once the trees absorbed them, unable to believe what my eyes were seeing.

"No," I said again. "She wouldn't. She couldn't be." Was Therek right?

I hadn't felt this level of betrayal since.... gods I didn't want to think about it, but my heart started pounding painfully, the darkness flaring, and I was thrown back to one of the worst nights of my life.

I hugged the female to my side as I sighed in contentment, but she was tense despite the intimacy we'd just shared. I frowned. Was she still worried about the curse developing? She didn't need to, it only flared occasionally. It wasn't anything to be concerned with. My brothers had gone much longer than I had before it became an issue.

But I couldn't shake the feeling that something bad was going to happen. Before I could even consider why that was, I noticed movement in the shadows. Jerking upright, I barely dodged the arrow to my chest. Briar screamed and fell from the bed as the arrow lodged where I had been lying. Jumping to my feet, I dodged the dagger thrown at me next and then met the assassin head on. Eyeing my gear on the other side of the room behind him, I had no choice but to dodge, twist the dagger out of the attacker's hand, and use it against him.

Another scream had me glancing to my side where Briar was held at knife point by another assassin. My eyes widened in horror, but something still felt off. Why wasn't she scared? She'd screamed, but her body showed anticipation, not terror. I frowned in confusion. My suspicions were con-

firmed when her eyes flickered to the assassin I'd forgotten about. It held an order. My eyes widened as I spun too late to stop the dagger to my side. A distraction. She was a distraction.

I fell to my knee, my hand pressed over the gushing wound, but my brain couldn't process what my eyes were seeing. I looked up to the female I was engaged to. She now stood with the assassins flanking her as she faced me.

"Briar," I groaned, my heart clenching in my chest. I could feel a darkness growing as the dagger's poison seeped into my bloodstream, but I fought it back. I couldn't afford to lose control of the curse now. "Briar, why?" She scoffed.

"Why? Because you were becoming a liability. Did you think I would want to be associated with the prince who will destroy Alyvia?" She shook her head. "No, it is my duty to ensure the safety of the kingdom, even from you."

"I would never have hurt the kingdom," I gritted out, the pain and darkness growing. "I would never have hurt you." She rolled her eyes.

"You're a disaster walking. I only agreed to this engagement for the status, not to watch my home be destroyed. You said so yourself, you wake up without knowing what you've done. I couldn't risk it."

I couldn't believe what I was hearing. I could barely think straight, not as she gestured to the assassins. "Finish him off. I have a fiancé to grieve. Too bad this couldn't have waited until we were married, but for the love of the kingdom."

"But not love of me, right," I said darkly, a haze beginning to leak into my vision. She snorted.

"Oh my sweet prince. What we had was not love. What would a dark prince know of love?" My eyes narrowed, and I stood to my feet, gritting my teeth. The darkness grew and grew until I could feel the forest shudder, and the animals fleeing in terror.

Her eyes widened, now fear tinging them as she stepped back. She ges-
tured at the assassins, and they moved to face off against me. Bad choice.
The world blurred as I pawned the dagger in my hand and shifted into
position. I didn't even give them a chance to attack me before I was upon
them. For the first time, with the betrayal flowing through my veins, I em-
braced the darkness enveloping me. Before they knew what was happening
the assassins were in pieces on my floor, their screams dying as their lives
faded away.

Then I turned on the female who had sought my death. The one who
I'd thought returned my love. The reason I hadn't feared the curse, because
secretly I was convinced she loved me enough that she could cure it. The only
emotion I felt now was wrath. Unadulterated, dark rage.

"Wait, Thatch, please! This was just a misunderstanding." I didn't
respond. I blacked out. When I became aware of my surroundings again,
I could hear the royal guards shouting and smell the coppery scent of blood,
but all I could feel was my heart being crushed under the darkness I'd
embraced. All I could see was the broken body of the female I'd loved, her
sky blue eyes dull and staring off into oblivion. I felt the life in me dwindle
and die along with the life I'd just taken as guilt flooded me. I was no prince
of life. I was now death.

I shook my head violently, trying to breathe past the pain squeezing my
chest. Was I reliving the past? Was my mate working with the assassins
to set me up? What would happen if I showed up to save her? Would
I accidentally kill her as I had done to Briar? Would they try to kill
me? Thought after thought flashed through my mind and the darkness
roared, sending waves out that started to kill the plants around me.

But then a flare of heat spidered out from my chest, and I took a sharp
breath. No. Ember wasn't Briar. Briar hadn't triggered the tattoo over
my heart. She wasn't the Princess of Fire. She was just a selfish female

who'd thought she could secure her position in the court by using me. Ember had treated me when I was injured. She'd accosted me about my treatment of my people. People she didn't even know but cared for anyway. Even daring to make an agreement to heal the kingdom with no regard to the threat I was to her. She had not betrayed me. She wouldn't have.

Determination flowed through me, along with a possessive flare I was now ready to address. No, this was different and I wouldn't lose myself to the darkness this time. She deserved better than that. She deserved better than me, but I would save her. Save my land. And remind the world why I was the Prince of Forest.

Chapter 45

Ember

Assassins. If I never saw another one, it would be too soon. But it was either me or Thatch, and despite his curse, he was the obvious choice. His people needed him. I was dispensable.

I followed behind the evil male in front of me with samurai looking swords and tried not to look back at the matching one following behind me. He had appeared from the shadows after we'd left the city.

Yet the deeper into the forest we traveled, the more I realized I didn't want to die. Maybe I could still get out of this. I did have fire after all, and they'd left the antidote for Thatch.

Suddenly, they gripped my arms roughly. "What are you doing?" I screamed trying to wrestle my body back.

"We can't have you seeing where we're going," the male smiled wickedly. "Who knows if you have a way to tell that prince of yours where we are. We can't have that." His smile grew and my eyes widened in horror.

"Wait! No! I..." A hard object slammed into my head and the world was black. When I came to, I found myself bound to a tree, the iron chains cutting in so tightly, I could barely breath, and my power was gone. My arms were still sore from their grasps and would likely be bruised later. If I was still alive.

"What can you tell me about the princes?" I jerked at the sound of a deep voice. I froze, my heart trying to leap out of my body as a figure clad in a long black assassin creed hood appeared in front of me. Glowing yellow eyes watched me from under them and I couldn't help but notice the daggers along his waist and in his hand. He wasn't the same one from earlier.

"What?" I asked, squirming. I glanced around, looking for help that wouldn't come. I was deep in the forest somewhere. No one would find me and no one was looking.

"The princes. Tell me about them." What about the princes? Why was he asking about all of them and not just Thatch?

"I don't know anything about the princes," I insisted.

"You were in the castle. You travel with the youngest one, the Prince of Forest. You know something." I shook my head franticly.

"I swear. All I know is their names. I don't know anything else about them," I swore. The figure moved closer menacingly, lifting the dagger in his hand. He trailed it down my arm before giving me a dark grin.

"Maybe you just need a reminder." Before I could blink, he had sliced my left arm right above the elbow. I sucked in a startled breath as the sting spread through me. I gasped in pain.

"How about now?" he asked, leaning in closer. I fought to hold back tears as I felt the blood draining down my arm.

"I don't know anything," I gasped out. He tsked me.

"Wrong answer." Another slice. This time on my other arm. I sucked in a breath, trying to hold it together.

"Please," I begged. "I don't know anything but their names." A tear escaped, but I fought to hold it together. Males like this reveled in shows of pain.

"What about the curse and the women meant to break it?" I froze, my eyes going wide. Oh god. Is that what this was about? I said nothing. I wouldn't reveal their secrets. Plus, if I told this male that I was supposedly the cure for the Prince of Forest's curse, I had no doubt he'd killed me. Who was I kidding? He was probably going to kill me anyway. That didn't mean I was going to drag the princes down with me though. Thatch may act dark and broody sometimes, but I wouldn't hurt him and his brothers like that.

"Hmm, maybe you need a greater incentive." He smiled maliciously and then ripped my shirt open. I gasped, fighting desperately to cover myself, but he only ripped it open until my entire chest and stomach were revealed. I saw him eye me hungrily, his eyes catching on my breasts.

"Mmm. On second thought, keep refusing to answer. I'll just have some fun in the meantime." I froze, suddenly thrown back to the night at the dinner table where the sheriff eyed me like I was dinner. I felt dirty then, and I felt even dirtier now. I was so focused on my shame that I didn't realize he had lifted the dagger again.

"No, no. Please no," I begged hoarsely.

"Shall we continue?" he asked sweetly and then sliced me three times in succession. Crisscrossed lines now covered my stomach and I screamed. "Still no? Let's continue then." I zoned out then. Distantly I could hear screams, and I could smell the coppery scent of blood. I could feel the trails trickling down my arms and stomach, but I was no longer there. It was how I survived my dad's attacks. This time, I hoped I would be dead before I was forced to reenter reality. That would be better than this. Anything was better than this.

"Maybe we should try something different." I lifted my head, dazed as another figure appeared. "Say hello Princess. He's missed you." I frowned, confused why I would know the hooded figure. And then they lifted the hood away and I froze in terror. Burns marred half his face and down his neck, but the scowl was the same. Those cruel, evil eyes were the same.

"Dad?" I whispered. He snorted in disgust.

"You were never a daughter of mine," he spat.

"I...I don't understand." I glanced between the yellow-eyed assassin and the male who starred in all my nightmares.

"Oh Ember, you poor thing," yellow eyes crooned. "Don't you know you were a pawn from the start? You were never meant to arrive in this land. As soon as you showed any signs of power, Daddy dearest was supposed to end you. How do you think we've been able to track you all this time? Years of you ingesting our special powder made it easy. Unfortunately, that fire of yours has made it quite challenging with it slowly burning the traces away. Didn't matter in the end though, did it?"

If I wasn't already in so much pain, his words would have been a dagger to the gut. And now I knew how I kept leading the danger to us this entire time. "Why?" I croaked. Yellow eyes cocked his head with a wicked grin.

"You can't be allowed to remove the curse. The king wants what was stolen from him and soon he'll have it. Of course, we still need to find the other three daughters of disaster and ensure they too fail to save the other princes. And to do that, we need to better understand the cursed abilities of the princes and the natural ones. See if they've already tracked down their mates."

But why hadn't they just killed me at birth? Reading the question in my eyes, he continued. "We had to make sure we had the correct daughter you see. So we needed to wait until your power manifested." In other words, they had too much fun torturing me. How I wasn't unconscious currently I didn't know.

"What are you going to do now?" I gritted out. I was too exhausted to use my power, and the iron around my arms prevented me from doing so anyway.

"Now, I let Daddy dearest take his fury out on your body. And since you have no valuable information to yield, then, Princess, you die." My eyes widened in horror as the only father I'd ever known took the dagger and stalked towards me. Yellow eyes chuckled as he turned away.

"Goodbye Princess of Fire. Don't worry, your prince will see you again in the afterworld." Sobs shook my body as I watched in defeat as my dad held the cold metal against my skin.

"You don't know how long I've waited for this moment," he sneered. Tears poured down my face as I stared into the devil's face.

"Please Dad. Please don't do this."

"I'm not your father!" he snapped. "That stupid King of Disasters is, but where is he now hmm?" He grinned then. "He abandoned you just like your good for nothing mother and brother. Just like your prince will when he finds out you betrayed him." I shook my head in denial, but then he was cutting me again and blood was flowing like rain from too many cuts to count.

I couldn't hear my own screams anymore. Couldn't hear his chuckles of delight. I was dying and my one regret was that I wouldn't have more time with Thatch. That I hadn't told him how I felt. Now it was too late.

It took me a while to notice the movement of vines behind the male that was laughing and slicing me gleefully in between still mocking me. The vines had six inch long thorns along them, and they steadily crept closer toward us. Maybe this was how I would end. Get eaten by a plant like Little Shop of Horrors.

But then the vines started creeping up my father until suddenly they were squeezing him. He shouted in surprise, only now realizing the danger he was in. He cut at the vines, but they multiplied until they were completely wrapped around him, and then... he stopped moving.

It was silent again. My vision was fading now, but I stared at my abuser as he bled out from the puncture wounds all over his body. *What a way to die*, I thought. Then, I watched the vines retreat at the command of the black clad male with forest green eyes. Thatch. His name was Thatch. My last thought was one of confusion because I could have sworn his lips were begging me to stay. That he had mouthed he loved me, but then the world was blissfully dark and I knew no more.

Chapter 46

Thatch

I was barely holding it together. I wished the assassins and her father were still alive just so I could kill them again, but slower. Seeing her bound to the tree, bleeding from multiple wounds, her clothes shredded as the male who was supposed to keep her safe spat disgusting comments at her, I'd lost it. I'd meant to question him.

That's not true. My first reaction had been unrelenting wrath and the need to end and avenge her pain. It was only after I'd considered that I should have held him for questioning. Oh well.

Now, as I dressed her wounds, spreading my mother's special healing salve that would prevent any of the vicious marks from scarring, I fought the simmering rage that threatened to crest again. She was covered in scars. Old ones and newer ones. They were on her chest, stomach, and back as if whoever abused her wanted to make sure the wounds could be hidden but not forgotten.

I wanted to avenge her all over again. Wonder why she had been so afraid whenever my temper flared, or I cornered her. Wonder why she looked at every male with distrust and fear. I never wanted her to look at me that way again. It had already started to twist my stomach a long time ago when she did, but now. Now, the thought made me nauseated and ashamed. I was not the male who did this to her. Even under the curse's darkness. And if I could help it, I would ensure no one else ever hurt her like this again.

I finished wrapping her stomach and arms and then pulled a new tunic from her bag, I carefully covered her again, discarding the destroyed shirt. Gritting my teeth, I tried not to take in the amount of blood covering it or tinting the bowl of water next to me red. Instead, I stood to my feet and covered her carefully with a blanket. She was lying in my bed, and for the remainder of our lives, that was where she would stay. No more separate rooms. If there were assassins still after us, I needed to keep her close anyway. I had given my word to bring her back alive. Now I gave my vow to protect her for as long as I lived.

I gingerly climbed in beside her, taking the side closest to the door. She was my mate, my other half, and although I had doubted her and let her down, I would never do so again. The anger at her current and past treatment was still rolling through my veins as I turned my head to study her. Her eyes had been vacant before she'd succumbed to the blood loss. They'd held resignation as if she'd finally given up. I loathed that. I wanted to be a male she could trust. One she could turn to. I wanted to be the one male she knew would never harm her. The one person she knew would always show up and stay by her side. That meant I needed to do better. I needed to cleanse this darkness from my veins, and my kingdom, once and for all.

I woke just as the sun rose the next day. I found her still sleeping next to me. I'd wait a few hours before redressing her wounds. In the meantime, I left to grab breakfast from downstairs, but not before ensuring a curtain of thorny vines prevented anyone from entering the room by the door or window. I lowered the curtain once I returned.

I was just sitting the food down when she suddenly jerked awake. She took one look at me and screamed. I was across the room in an instant, wrapping my arms around her. She fought me, her fingers clawing at my arms, her eyes frantic but distant. She wasn't seeing me. She was reliving last night.

"Ember!" I called, enveloping her in my arms. "Ember, it's me. You're safe Princess, my Wildfire. You're safe." I gripped and massaged the nape of her neck as she calmed. "He's gone. I've got you, my love. He's gone."

Gradually, she relaxed in my arms. She still gripped my tunic desperately in her hands as if afraid I was just a dream. She took deep breaths, taking in my scent. It must have grounded her because she relaxed some more until her head rested against me.

"I've got you," I whispered, my arms now wrapped around her back. "I will always have you." We stayed like that for a long while until she finally lifted her head to look at me. She swallowed as she stared into my eyes.

"Thatch," she whispered hoarsely.

"I'm here," I assured her.

"The assassins...my father..."

"Dead," I bit out, trying to keep my anger restrained. She was still staring at me as if she couldn't believe I was real. She shook her head.

"He wanted to know about you and your brothers' abilities." She swallowed. "He wanted to know about the curse and whether the princesses were the actual cure. He said they were going to kill my sisters anyway just in case. That's what my dad was waiting for. To see if I would develop power so he could kill me."

I tensed. There had been no need to torture her all her life. They could have done it the day she was born. Instead, they'd made her life a living hell. Gods, I wished the male was still alive so I could kill him slower. How had they even found her?

"I didn't tell him anything," she whispered, her eyes pleading with me to believe her, likely thinking the rage in my eyes was directed at her. "I swear Thatch. He asked and asked, but I still didn't tell him." My heart constricted and I pulled her into me again.

"Shhh," I told her as she continued to mumble in soft sobs. "I believe you Princess. You did good. You did good." She clung to me until the sobs had passed, and I was able to convince her to eat a little. She let me change her bandages but refused to watch as I did so. I didn't blame her, but I did explain that the salve would ensure she didn't have to live with the reminder of the attack. I wanted to ask her about the other scars, but I refrained. That was a discussion for another time.

"He tried to kill me," Ember whispered against my chest. I frowned and she raised her head to show me her watery gaze. "The only father I've ever known tried to kill me. Tortured me for.... for years." She shook again as the tears fell.

"Why did they leave me? Why didn't they save me Thatch?"

I knew she meant her mother and brother, but I had no answer that would bring her peace.

"Why didn't *he*?" she whispered in defeat. The fiery princess was still too cold in my arms, and I hugged her closer to me.

"It is common," I told her. "For the gods to come to mate with the common folk." Ember snorted in disgust, getting the reference.

"So they do the dirty then leave the child and mother alone to face the world?" she sneered, the hurt tinging her voice. I sighed.

"I cannot begin to understand their ways, and I cannot tell you what the King of Disasters was thinking, but I can tell you something about your mother that you may not be ready to hear." Ember pulled away from me again, eyes wide.

"You know where she is?" The confusion, hurt, and hope in her voice made my gut clench, but I nodded.

"I had Lurk and Wolf look into it a while ago." She gasped.

"And?" I swallowed.

"There was a female matching her appearance who appeared in this world around the time you said she left you. She didn't stay long in Alyvia and instead was said to leave it for the kingdom to the west of us. One where disasters run rampant."

I let the words and the implication settle. I saw the moment she realized what happened.

"She left me. And went back to the king." She blinked. "And to cross the border...she's part Fae." I gritted my teeth, angry on her behalf.

"She likely didn't believe it safe to bring you here without your power manifesting, but she herself couldn't stay." I didn't mention how disgusted I was at the idea that my mate's mother was too weak to protect her until she could protect herself. No, she'd allowed not one, but two children to remain in a home with a known abuser.

Ember was quiet for a long time, and I wished I knew what was going on in her mind right now. I could taste her pain in the air, and the power in me wanted to destroy, but there was no one else here to hurt but her.

"I want to find her and my brother one day," she whispered. "And...and my real father." She eyed me, strength growing in her voice as she sat up straight. "I want to see both my parents and have them tell me in their own words why they thought leaving two Fae children in the human world was wise." Her voice ended on a growl.

I hadn't even considered that her brother was of this world too. I inclined my head. "By the forces of nature, I will make it so," I promised her. She nodded and then bit her lip.

"What about us?" We were on a cliff. I could feel our lives hanging in the balance. A decision had to be made, but was it hers or mine? Before I could answer, a crash had me spinning to the door.

"Hey Thatch! It's us. You're going to want to see this." Ember and I exchanged curious glances before I strode downstairs to let my best friends in. Lurk and Wolf entered with cruel grins on their faces and an unconscious body between them. The Fae male was covered in cuts and blood like someone had taken claws and dragged them down his body. I shot Wolf a questioning look, and he shrugged.

"He struggled. I reacted." I snorted a laugh. As if the male shifted to his namesake only when provoked. If that was the case, all the times he'd gone dyrewolf on me should be discussed. As if reading my mind, Wolf shrugged again.

"Don't act like you didn't ask for it on multiple occasions Thatch. You can be a real bastard when you want to be." I snorted again, but he wasn't wrong.

"Okay, but why is this male in my house?" I nodded toward the still inert male. Ember who'd followed me downstairs stood by my side eyeing the cut up male warily.

"You'll be interested to know that this particular male was bragging in a tavern a town over about how his king had captured a Daughter of Disaster and was torturing her for information about the princes. Sound familiar?" Lurk answered.

I frowned. "Yeah, sounds like a trap to me," I growled. Lurk and Wolf both nodded.

"See, that's what I thought too," Wolf said. "So we decided to capture this one and use him to lead us to their camp. No one else was present."

"I took care of all the assassins sent to the kingdom when I went to rescue Ember. There shouldn't be any in the camp left to find."

"There was one more, but he left." We spun to face my mate. She stood with her arms wrapped around herself.

"What?" I asked, and she lifted troubled eyes to mine.

"The one with yellow eyes that tortured me first. He..." she shivered and swallowed. I fisted my hands waiting for her to continue. I'd missed one of her abusers. Something I would rectify soon enough. He must have been who she'd been referring to earlier and not her father as I'd thought.

"He gave the dagger to...my father...and then left right before you came. He went to hunt the other daughters." Meaning he was likely already long gone from my kingdom and into one of my brother's. Rage flooded my veins again as she seemed to sink into herself.

"We'll get him Princess," Lurk promised, making her glance at him in surprise. Wolf nodded in agreement.

"Right. Anyone who harms the princess of this kingdom will meet a bloody end." I hid my smile as she glanced between them in surprise.

"Wait...you don't think that I'm..." Ember stopped.

"What? Sent to betray our prince?" Wolf scoffed. "Naa. I'm pretty sure the bond prevents that." I scowled, not ready to have that discussion as of yet, but knowing it was time.

"Leave us," I told them. "Do one final sweep and then head home. I'll join you there soon." Wolf and Lurk glanced at each other, then Ember and me. They inclined their heads.

"We look forward to seeing you at home," Lurk said softly. With a hug to them both, and a thank you that brought smirks to both their faces, they were gone, dragging the nearly dead male with them. I took a deep steadying breath and then turned to my mate. She stood waiting, her eyes trusting as she watched me. I swallowed. Was I about to break that tentative trust?

"Ember. We need to talk."

Chapter 47

Ember

We need to talk.

Worse words had never been spoken. My gut fluttered with butter-flies as he pulled me to sit on the sofa but elected to sit in the chair in front of me. He leaned over his knees and stared at his hands for a long moment before he began to speak.

"I...I need to tell you something. About my past." I frowned, unsure what was causing him such discomfort. "It may change how you see me, but I need to tell you before we discuss what this tattoo over my heart means." Beyond curious, I nodded.

"Okay," I encouraged. "Whatever you need to tell me Thatch, I doubt it'll change how I see you. I've already seen you at your worst."

"Have you?" he mumbled and then sighed. "Just listen, okay." I nodded and listened intently as he told me about a female named Briar, his first love. I clenched my hands in my lap as he continued, and when he got to what caused the guilt and anguish marring his face, my heart broke for him. When he stopped speaking, I couldn't say anything for several seconds.

"I know you see me as a monster now. I've always been beyond love due to this curse, but I never realized it until it was too late." He glanced at me with pleading eyes. "You see now why I had to tell you. This tattoo, it represents our bond. It tells me who you are to me, but I could never ask that of you. For you to pretend to love a monster." I still said nothing, and he stood with a growl and prowled to the fireplace.

"We reach the end of the forest in a few days and I am still cursed. I will ensure you arrive back to Verdis safely, and I will protect you from afar as long as you remain in this world. That is my vow."

This was his ultimate shame. The catalyst for the curse gaining such a foothold on his life, and he thought I would hate him for it. I sighed. Apparently, my dark prince forgot that I knew what true darkness was. Thatch was anything but.

"Why do you feel like you are beyond being loved?" I asked him finally.

"Why do you?" Touché, but I stood and stepped closer to him before placing a hand over his heart. It beat faster at my touch.

"You told me once that someone else's inability to see my worth didn't mean I wasn't priceless." He swallowed but kept his eyes on mine. They were a lighter green today and I knew this was his true eye color.

"I'm telling you now, that her inability to see past the darkness to your still beautiful heart does not make the life in you any less vibrant. She betrayed you, but it's also she who lost because she missed out on being with the most passionate, caring male that I've ever met."

His hand came up to grip mine over his heart, but he still waited for me to walk away. "I see you Thatch. I feel you, here." I touched the center of my chest where the hum of the mating bond resided. "And here." I touched my heart. "We were bonded for a reason and now I must tell you something."

I smiled at him, feeling my heart overflowing with what I was starting to recognize as love. "I can see your aura, Prince of Forest." Thatch blinked, surprised.

"You can?" he whispered, hesitantly. I nodded. "What...what does it show you?" I smiled.

"You already know, but you are too afraid to believe it. I think it's been true for a while now. I saw it in your behavior. Your eyes. And now I'm telling you that your aura used to be black with tinges of green. Now it is the most vibrant green I've ever seen."

I felt his heart rate pick up as his eyes widened. I saw the moment it dawned on him, but I didn't know if he was ready to admit it.

"We should go. There are only a few days left and you promised to show me the edge of the kingdom." He swallowed, still staring at me with wonder.

"Aye, I did," he replied. I pulled away and headed for the stairs.

"I'll pack then." I didn't say anything else, and he didn't stop me, but as I packed for the last time, I prayed he realized everything I was trying to tell him. Because I'd learned something this trip too. I had a home here in this world, but I only wanted to stay if the male who had my heart wanted me to. I could not bear it otherwise and would leave before I spent the rest of my life pining for what I could not have. Not when I was finally learning to dream.

Chapter 48

Thatch

Was I foolish for believing the impossible? Maybe, but the closer we came to the edge of Alyvia the more I dreaded it. I'd spent the last few days searching every part of my soul, but only a tinge of darkness remained. I didn't even know when it had disappeared. It had to be some time after we made that deal to heal the land. The use of my power to grow had started to overtake the power to destroy, but I hadn't noticed that it had shrunk to the tiniest tendril deep within me.

As we rode, I felt myself reaching farther and farther across the kingdom feeling for sickness. I could tell the areas that I would need to heal. But the forest spoke to me. The animals greeted me. And I could once again feel every living thing from the tiny ant to the hawk flying overhead. Alyvia was healing, it was thriving. And I was its prince once more.

"Thatch?" I looked up at Ember's awed voice. We'd reached the end. Of this kingdom. Of this journey. And of my curse. As I looked out upon the vast mountain range that held my brother's domain, I did so with a lightness and hope. I turned to my salvation, dismounting my horse to stand by her side on the cliffs separating the kingdoms. I smiled to myself, knowing I was too selfish not to finish this, but willing to break our deal for her. Anything for her.

"I have one more favor to collect." Ember laughed and the bond and tattoo warmed at the sheer happiness in it. I wonder if she knew what I was about to ask for.

"Of course you do," she chuckled. What is it?" The question was asked tentatively, but a smile teased her lips. I lifted her hand to my lips and kissed her knuckles, causing her to turn to face me.

"Stay with me." Ember froze, her eyes going wide.

"Stay?" she whispered. Was that anticipation in her voice? Gods please be so.

"You are the fiery heart of the forest. My heart. We cannot live without you. Stay." I held my breath, afraid of what she'd say, but a smile lifted her lips as she lifted her other hand and laid it over my heart.

"You are what gives my fire life. With you, I can dream." Gods, my eyes were burning, but I couldn't help the hope building in my chest. "I love you Thatch. Of course, I'll stay." A tear fell then as I pulled her to me and kissed her. In that moment, I felt the last tendril of the curse fade, until all that was left was me.

I pulled away and laid my forehead against hers. "I love you Ember. With all the fire in my soul, I love you." Then I kissed her until only the need for air had her pulling away, a smile on her face, her eyes shiny with tears.

Together, we looked out upon the open mountain range, the open ocean far in the distance to the south of it, and the open sky above us. She glanced back at the recovering forest at our back.

"What now?" she whispered. I took her hand in mine and pulled her back into my arms.

"Now, we head home and heal the kingdom fully," I answered. She smiled and leaned up to kiss me. It wasn't going to be an easy endeavor. It would take a while for the forest to return to its original state, but with my mate by my side, I was no longer afraid that I'd fail.

"I'm already home," Ember replied, holding me tightly back. My answering smile was like sprouts breaking through the barren soil.

"As am I, my fire. As am I."

Chapter 49

One year later...

Thatch

"I have to admit. I didn't believe it was possible," Theseus said, shaking his head in disbelief.

We watched my mate laugh with several females of the court, her emerald dress adorned with golden veins flowing behind her. Mother had found her a golden diadem embedded with rubies and seeing it on her head filled me with pride. She'd come so far from the fearful, scarred female I'd met in the forest so long ago. Now she embodied every bit of the grace, confidence, and beauty she'd always possessed. The Princesses of Disaster were looked upon so negatively because of their name, but I never saw death when I looked at Ember. She was my guiding light, the fuel to my soul. I couldn't have asked for a better female to call mine.

"And I never thought I would see that," Torm added quietly. I turned to find my brothers all gazing at me. Torm's eyes carried a weary sadness, Theseus hopelessness, and Therek unrelenting fury.

"What?" I asked. Torm gestured between my princess and me.

"You look at her how Father looks at Mother." A small, rare smile appeared. "And when she doesn't think anyone is looking, she looks at you the same way." I should have felt embarrassed, but all I felt was the warmth of our bond and my tattoo.

"I love her," I told my brothers proudly. "Even if she wasn't a cure to my curse I would love her."

How could I not? She deserved the world, and I was determined to show her all the adoration and care she should have received all her life. I'd proposed to her a month before the one year anniversary of our journey across Alyvia, and to say I was overjoyed at her ecstatic yes would be an understatement. But seeing her walk down that aisle towards me in a gown representing the sun...I will never get over how beautiful she was, or over the fact that she was mine for eternity.

Therek growled next to me, his face twisted in a snarl. "Did you forget that there is no cure to this curse? Definitely not by a conniving female who led a king here to destroy Alyvia and you. She has you wrapped so tightly around her finger, you can't see the trap waiting to snap."

I growled back at him, my fists balled. "Careful brother. I love you, but if you continue to disrespect my mate this way I will draw your blood."

Therek shifted closer, a cruel grin on his face. "I dare you to try little brother."

"Enough," Torm snapped. "Thatch, put the dagger away and Therek you will respect the mate of your brother regardless of whether you like her." I glanced down, not even realizing I'd grabbed the dagger at all. I sheathed it, trying to calm my rage. Mother would kill us if we brawled in the middle of a ball.

"Plus Therek, although we may not believe that our cures are possible, you cannot deny that the curse no longer controls our youngest brother," Theseus added. He gestured at the windows to the land beyond. "You've seen it. You've felt it. The forest is healed and thriving. Our brother is free."

I glanced between my brothers sadly, seeing the resigned look I'd worn for centuries. Torm's worried me more than all of us. My brothers were giving up, and they'd suffered for far longer than I had, but I had to believe that they too would be saved. The alternative would be to lose them and their kingdoms, and I couldn't fathom that.

"I know it feels impossible, but if the cure was true for one of us, it has to be true for all of us." Therek huffed with disgust.

"I have no desire for a mate and especially not one known for destruction." I shook my head.

"If fate deems to give you one, you will not be able to fight it." I glanced at Ember, who gave me a questioning look. She'd likely felt my concern through the bond. I nodded at her to ensure her I was fine. With a smile, she turned back to her conversation.

"Don't get us wrong Thatch," Theseus said. "We are beyond happy for you. But forgive us for being doubtful." I sighed.

"We could talk for hours and still return to the same conclusions," Torm said with a flick of his hand. "Let us drop it for now. Thatch, go, enjoy your mate brother. If we cannot be cured, at least let us live precariously through you."

Therek snarled. "I need to go anyway. That yellow-eyed assassin of yours has been spotted in Amethyst and I must locate him before he causes the same trouble he did here."

We all wished him farewell, but I couldn't shake the feeling that the assassin's appearance in the Mountain Kingdom could only mean one thing. Whether my brother was ready or believed it or not, he was next to meet a Daughter of Disaster. I could only pray that she reached him before it was too late.

Chapter 50

Ember

I couldn't believe how much had changed since I'd come to Iyris over a year ago. I'd come here broken and bruised and risen a princess with a mate, a kingdom to protect, and a family. It was a dream like no other. A blessing that I cherished daily. There was only one thing I still wished I could do.

"My fire." I turned to see Thatch enter our rooms, a teasing smile on his face. I shook my head but returned his smile. My prince had proven in the last year that he was still the mischievous male he was infamous for, and I loved him for it, especially now that his pranks didn't entail me falling off mountains. I gazed deep into his forest green eyes as he pulled me to him and kissed me deeply. Our bond flared as I gripped his tunic to pull him closer.

"My heart," I greeted him breathlessly when he finally pulled away, my own heart almost bursting with happiness from what had become one of our common greetings.

"My soul," he finished before kissing me again. I could kiss him all day. The feeling of his embrace, loving instead of binding, made me feel safe and valued. Something I never thought I'd ever get a chance to feel. We'd spent the last eleven months traveling Alyvia, healing the forest, and simply getting to know its people and each other better. It had been the best time of my life. I finally felt like I had a place that felt like home. Wink, Lurk, and Wolf had joined us for a good portion of it, allowing me to get to know them more. I was grateful Thatch had such great friends in those two.

We'd been back in Verdis for the last month for the wedding preparations Queen Sequoia had secretly started months before. I was glad to see that none of the closeness had diminished between Thatch and I now that we were among the court and his parents. Although, I hadn't made much leeway with his brothers.

"Your brothers still hate me don't they?" I asked, thinking of their gazes during the ball last night. They'd been cordial at best during the wedding a couple of days ago, but they still seemed wary of my presence. Thatch sighed.

"No...well Therek probably does, but don't take it personally. He loathes everyone but his family and his people." I grimaced. The male was as unyielding as the mountains he ruled. Thatch gave a sad smile.

"I'm sorry," he said, but I shook my head.

"Don't be. I know they feel bittersweet about us."

"That's exactly how they feel. You remember how resigned I was?" I nodded remembering how he'd given up completely at one point. "They've suffered for far longer than I did. But I think that's about to change."

I lifted a brow questioningly and he explained about the assassin that had escaped being seen in the Mountain Kingdom. I sucked in a sharp breath.

"So some unknowing soul is about to come face to face with your wrathful brother with a heart of stone?" I shook my head with a grimace. "That poor girl doesn't know what she's in for."

Thatch chuckled but then turned serious. "But that's not what I came to talk to you about." I frowned. "I was wondering if you wanted...to meet your father today." I froze, my eyes wide.

"He answered your letter?" I whispered, excitement and nerves competing in my gut. Thatch had reached out to him months ago, and I'd started to wonder if we'd ever receive a reply.

Thatch nodded. "Are you ready to face the King of Disasters?" I gripped him closer to me and nodded firmly.

"Take me to him."

The Disaster Kingdoms were not what I thought they would be. Thatch explained that they were split much like the Nature Kingdoms were, but that they were ruled by one king. They were also not as beautiful or friendly as the Nature Kingdoms. Hurricanes and tsunamis were rampant along the coast, storms raged constantly in rotating precipitation in the north, earthquakes left giant crevices everywhere in the barren east, and the west was made of volcanoes. What plants did manage to grow across the kingdom were those built for living in extremes, but then, nature always managed to find a way.

"People live here?" I asked in amazement, staring at the harsh terrain. "How?"

"Believe it or not, some actually prefer the harshness of the Disaster Kingdoms, but there's a reason we don't interact much. The Fae here tend to be as ruthless as the land they live on," Thatch explained.

I grimaced and then faced the castle made of gray stone we were headed for. It was massive and oddly still beautiful. We'd traveled through a tree to get here, and although I was excited to meet my father, I didn't want to linger in this kingdom longer than necessary.

"Halt! Who goes there?" A guard dressed in maroon and black stopped us at the gate.

"I am Thatch, Prince of Forest of Alyvia. I have come seeking audience with King Zeus."

"What business do you have with our king?" the guard asked, studying us with heavy suspicion. I tried not to show my nervousness, but Thatch was undisturbed.

"I bring his daughter to meet him. The Princess of Fire. Your king has agreed to meet with me." The guard startled, and he must have noticed something when he studied me closer because he gestured for me to follow.

"Come. I will take you to the king." We traveled down several halls, all made of stone and marble, but I couldn't help thinking it felt cold somehow despite the obvious wealth. By the time we reached the throne room, butterflies had taken over my stomach. Thatch reached for my hand and lifted it to kiss my knuckles.

"It's going to be okay baby. No matter what he says, you will always have a family with me and mine." I smiled at him and gave him a quick peck on the lips.

"Thank you my love," I whispered back. Then I pulled away and nodded to the guard. We walked through the throne room to the massive male reclining on an obsidian throne. He wore a deep red tunic with black pants and a golden crown embedded with rubies upon his head. His eyes were golden and as hard as the land around him.

Thatch inclined his head as we stopped before the King of Disasters. "Your Majesty," he greeted.

"Prince of Forest." I shivered at his deep, gravelly voice. "Last I heard, you were rotting that forest of yours piece by piece." I felt Thatch tense beside me.

"Believe me, Alyvia is alive and well." Harsh, penetrating eyes considered my prince.

"So, it is done? You have found the first of my daughters and mated her?"

"I have." Zeus turned to me then. His appraising look gave nothing away, but I knew I looked the part in my high low sunset dress with a small diadem on my head. Queen Sequoia had insisted I wear it here.

"My youngest daughter. Princess of Fire. You are as beautiful as your mother." I stiffened.

"Thank you Your Majesty. But that beauty was hard to see underneath the bruising most days." I couldn't help the remark and narrowing of my eyes. This male had mated my mother and left her to fend for herself. Surely he hadn't been blind to her suffering.

"Ah, yes. It is unfortunate who your mother attached herself to in my absence," the king said with a dismissive wave.

"You mean who you allowed her to fall victim to after you abandoned her in the human world." I snapped.

"Easy," Thatch whispered a warning, but I was too busy glaring at the king who could have saved my mother, brother, and I.

"She was abused for years until she ran away and then I replaced her as the abused simply because I was your daughter. *Where were you?*"

Zeus gazed at me with such indifference it made my skin crawl. "It was necessary for you to reside in the human world until your power manifested. I could not interfere or else my enemies would find you before you could break the curse. It was the agreement we made. Your mother knew this. If you were abandoned, it was only by her, for you were to return to me once you were of age."

"They found me anyway!" I snapped. "Your enemies raised me."

"And as I said, that was your mother's doing not mine. And while you faced my enemies earlier than expected, you did survive."

"So you're telling me, my sisters and I were simply groomed to fight a curse we had nothing to do with? And embody powers of destruction we didn't want?"

"You may not like my methods, but fate will do as fate does, and it was done with you in mind. Your sisters shall claim their disasters as you have done, or the princes will fall. It matters not what they have endured to do so."

"And what about choice?" I snapped. He smiled.

"You did choose young one. You chose your prince, his people, and the curse was lifted. Would you rather the Forest Kingdom fell?"

No, of course not, but I still didn't like being bred to solve a problem caused by the kings and queens before the nature princes, my sisters and I were even born. *Wait.*

"You said you made an agreement," I said slowly. "With whom and for what?" Zeus was quiet and I growled. "I've made it this far. I deserve to know!"

He studied me for several seconds before inclining his head. "Very well, but I will have a vow of silence from both of you. The other princes must not know." I glanced at Thatch who snarled.

"I will not lie to my brothers," he snapped.

"You will if you desire their salvation." We both froze. I gave Thatch a questioning look. I wanted to know, but I would not risk his brothers' lives, nor would I force him to lie to them to sate my curiosity. Sighing, he nodded sullenly.

"We swear," I said turning back to the king. He lifted a brow at Thatch until he spoke his agreement.

"The King and Queen of Nature had my first wife and daughter killed." I gasped, eyes wide with disbelief.

"No!" Thatch exclaimed. "They wouldn't kill someone who was innocent!" Zeus eyed him coldly.

"And yet they did."

"But why?" I asked, not sure what to believe. Zeus glanced at me and I could see a tinge of pain in his eyes despite the centuries passed.

"A member of my court led an attack on Queen Sequoia's home city. Many were killed, including two of her close cousins, but it was not I, but the one you know as the King of Iron and Steel, who'd sent the attackers. King Hyperion, aiming to avenge his wife's pain sent men to attack a city of mine. My wife and child happened to be in the courtyard that day and were struck down alongside their guards." There was no doubting the truth of his words. I could feel it in the grief squeezing my heart.

Tears pooled in my eyes as I considered the destruction the King of Iron and Steele had created with just one command long before the princes were even born. A glance at Thatch found him grimacing with empathy, his own eyes watery.

"They never said..." he swallowed. Zeus inclined his head in acknowledgment.

"Such a crime cannot go unpunished and yet when I went to face them in battle, I could not strike the killing blow with the queen on her knees pleading for her mate's life. I spared him and as I went to walk away a seer appeared on the field, freezing the battle.

She declared that I would have four daughters and the King and Queen of Nature, four sons. They would be connected by life and death, and since they had sought to end life without hesitation, their sons would carry both. Balance could only be renewed when and if my daughters were to bond with the princes and love them, hence representing my stay of hand. And if they never bonded them, then the nature kingdom would fall with its prince."

Zeus glanced at me. "But the King of Iron and Steel is still a problem. He seeks to destroy both our lands, and if he were to find my daughters before the princes, the kingdoms would have no chance of surviving. My late daughter was to be mated to his son to bring a truce between our kingdoms, but despite having a hand in her demise, he still seeks retribution for a deal broken."

I stared at him in shock. "So, you hid us in the human world with the instructions for us to return once we came into our power?" He inclined his head.

"But the enemy infiltrated Ember's house," Thatch pointed out. "What if they've done the same to her sisters?"

Zeus sighed. "Then we hope they find their way to this world as the seer proclaimed." I didn't like it. It still didn't give a lot of choice to those involved, which was likely why he'd sworn us to secrecy.

"What happens now?" I asked, reaching for my mate at my side. I was desperately ready to go home. Thatch linked our hands without hesitation, his face pained as he likely considered his brothers' pending demise.

"The heart of stone must be freed." I blinked in confusion before remembering I'd made a similar comment about Therek. My father stood from the throne. "And now you must return. We'll meet again soon Daughter of Fire." With a wave of his hands, a portal back to our kingdom opened.

"And what of my mother?" I asked him. For the second time, I saw sadness scar my father's face as he sighed. Maybe he had cared for her after all.

"Your mother came to me sick, but I did not know until it was too late. I could not save her."

I sucked in a breath as tears filled my eyes, but I nodded. I turned towards the portal, but something had me stopping in my tracks. I turned back towards my father.

"And my brother? What happened to him?" The King of Disasters went wholly still.

"What?" his voice was the sound of a storm brewing. Thatch stiffened at my side.

"My brother. He ran away a few years after my mother." To see a male as powerful as this king blink in shock was almost comical.

"He wasn't the assassin's son?" he asked as if in a daze. "She'd said...but...he wasn't his?" I shook my head with a frown remembering a conversation long forgotten.

"No. I remember there being an argument where my...the assassin stated that Rye wasn't his," I told him. Zeus swallowed.

"What is his full name?" I paused, glancing at Thatch. My mate shrugged, his own eyes wide as if he'd reached an understanding I hadn't grasped yet. I glanced back at the king.

"Zyran, but I always called him Rye. We always thought it was weird that Mom named him that." The king collapsed onto his throne, his eyes closing as he groaned deep in his throat.

"I have a son," he said with grief and awe. A part of my gut tightened at the idea that he was more torn up at the existence of my brother than he was at mine. Zeus's eyes shot open and he pinned me with an almost frantic gaze.

"He must be found immediately!" He gestured at the guards who moved forward quickly.

"Wait? What? Why?" I stuttered, glancing back and forth at the guards now eyeing me and their king.

"Because it is no coincidence that your brother's name means storm. The very name I told your mother so long ago that I would name my son. He must be found because he is not only my son, but the heir to my throne."

I took a deep breath as we once again stood among the trees. I just stood there absorbing all that I learned. My brother was the heir to the Disaster Kingdom. And I knew even now my father searched for him after I'd given a detailed description of the brother I hadn't seen in seven years. He searched for him but had left me to my fate. Left my sisters to theirs. And my mother.... I choked on a sob before I let the tears fall.

"I'm sorry Ember," Thatch whispered, hugging me to him. He held me tight as I sobbed. I wasn't sure what hurt worse The fact that everyone I'd cared about hadn't cared enough to stay, or that my father was more excited at the prospect of a son he'd never met than the daughter he'd relinquished to a curse.

Thank the gods for Thatch, Lurk, Wolf, and Wink. Even King Hyperion and Queen Sequoia. They treated me like family even when my blood did not. Slowly the tears slowed so that I simply laid against my mate's chest. I sniffed and wiped my face before finally answering him.

"It's okay. She was gone long ago." He went to say something else but simply nodded. "I'm also sorry."

He sighed. "I can't say that it doesn't hurt knowing what my father did and the consequences we now bear because of it."

"So, heart of stone?" I commented, tilting my head to meet his gaze. He smiled sadly down at me.

"Sounds like it's Therek's turn to face the curse once and for all." I tensed.

"Will he....?" I hesitated. "He still doesn't trust me. How will he allow one of my sisters to save him?" Thatch smile grew.

"The same way you convinced me. By being your fiery self. My brother has lost all connection to any emotion besides stone cold rage and disdain. He feels nothing positive. It will be up to your sister to show him there's more than anger."

"Is it possible though?" I gripped his shirt tightly, afraid for this sister I'd never even met. The princes were not the easiest in their cursed form, and yet our father had groomed us to save them.

"If you'd asked me before I met you if it was possible to bring life back to a prince cursed with darkness, I would have said no. But then you revived the heart of the forest. I can do nothing but believe that your sister will break the stone around my brother's heart. For I wish for him to find what I've found."

I smirked at him. "And what did you find?" Thatch smiled.

"That you are the true heart of the forest. My heart. My mate. And soon my queen." Unable to fight the joy flooding my veins, I kissed him with every ounce of love burning through me.

"I love you Prince of Forest," I told him once we'd pulled away to catch our breaths.

"And I you Princess of Fire," he returned with another kiss. "From now until nature claims us again."

Support Indie Authors

Did you enjoy reading **<u>Heart of the Forest</u>**? Please leave a review and share. That is a great way for indie authors like me to reach other amazing readers!
Subscribe to my newsletter for updates on upcoming releases and give-aways: https://shaquillalunsford.com

Or follow me on Social Media!
Instagram/Facebook: @ShaquillaLunsford
Goodreads: Shaquilla Lunsford
TikTok: @authorshaquillalunsford
Pinterest: @shaquillalunsford

What to Read Next?

Read Therek's story in book 2 of **The Forces of Nature** series, **Heart of Stone**!

Haven't read the **Fall of the Dragon King Trilogy**? This New Adult Epic Fantasy is a must read for those who love: dragons, Fae warriors, enemies to lovers, love triangles, forced proximity, family secrets & betrayal, ancient prophesies, morally grey MMCs, and life or death journeys. Silivia's journey begins in **After the Fall of the Dragon King!** Turn the page for a sneak peek!

A case of mistaken identity. A family secret. A world she didn't know existed. A power she can't control and two polar opposite males. You know what they say, "Be careful what you wish for."

All Silivia wanted was to escape her father's paranoia and go off to college to do all the things normal seventeen year old's did. Then, a powerful organization appears, murders her parents, and kidnaps her sister instead of her. Now Silivia finds herself navigating the world of Fenriel where creatures she'd only read about in books abound, and everything - and everyone - wants her dead.

Caught between two Fae warriors, one sweet, burly male, and one the King of Shadows, she fights to master her new power. But will she be in time to save her sister?

-After the Fall of the Dragon King

Prologue

Silivia

I jolted awake, almost falling off my bed as I pushed back the hair covering my eyes. My heart was pounding hard as if I had just barely escaped from a nightmare, and I took a quick sweep of my room trying to figure out why. Nothing was out of place. A cool breeze caressed my heated skin, and a drop of sweat slipped down my brow. I frowned down at myself trying to steady my rushing heart. Somehow, my blankets had ended up at the bottom of the bed, and my window was open to the cool spring night, but I was still sweating like a pig.

I reluctantly crawled out of bed, catching sight of myself in the mirror as I did so. I looked like a terrified kid, eyes wide and hair a whirlwind around my head. I shook off the ominous feeling tickling my spine and continued to the window, attempting to pat down my hair as I went. I reached to close the big window, but something drew my eyes outside. I scanned the backyard, then the trees, and stopped on a black figure standing in the shadows looking up at my room. It had long, pointed ears and what looked like a tail. When it noticed my attention, its eyes glowed red, and it smiled, revealing sharp, jagged teeth.

I slammed the window shut and fell backward in my haste to get away. My heart was beating so hard against my chest at this point, I thought it would jump out and run. I could barely breathe past the lump forming in my throat.

"It was just my imagination," I thought franticly. "Get up, and you'll see you're just imagining things." Needing to believe this, I crawled carefully to the window and peeked outside. Nothing. The figure had disappeared as if he was never there. Feeling silly now, I closed my curtains and climbed back into bed, pulling my blanket up to my chin. I hadn't been this scared since I was ten and saw the man with the face of a bull in the woods beside our house. But he hadn't existed then, and this figure definitely didn't exist now.

"No more scary movies," I scolded myself shakily, slowly falling back to sleep. I failed to notice that the curtains blew slightly despite the closed window.

Chapter 1

Silivia

I woke up abruptly to my alarm screaming. Grumbling to myself, I climbed out of the bed and glared at the bathroom mirror as I tried to tame my black, curly hair. After several failed attempts despite wetting it, I quickly pulled it back into a ponytail. The strands were a quarter down my back even pulled up. I frowned. Maybe it was time to cut it.

"Yeah right. Like I'll ever get around to doing that," I muttered, quickly brushing my teeth, and grabbing my backpack before heading downstairs. Wisps of deer sausage and pancakes greeted me as I walked into the kitchen and sat at the island. It looked like Dad had gone hunting again with one of his friends.

"Morning Mom, Dad!"

Mom gave me her signature smile as she placed a steaming plate in front of me. Her smile always made you feel seen and loved, even when you felt at your lowest. Her dark skin went beautifully with blue eyes that always seemed deep in thought until they lit up with joy.

Dad nodded in answer as he continued reading the paper. He was always content to be the quiet one among the chaos in the morning.

My younger sister Daccy ran in then, jumping into her seat beside me. I rolled my eyes at her eagerness. Bouncy, dark brown curls fell freely down her back, held in place by a black bejeweled headband, accenting her already bright, blue eyes. She never had to fight to get *her* curly hair to lay like it was supposed to.

"Alright you two, eat and go catch the bus. Dalacia stop trying to steal your sister's food," Mom ordered as she handed my sister a plate while I fended her off mine. Mom shook her head as she pushed her own curly hair out of her face and poured a cup of coffee. She tried to hide a smile with her mug as she watched me and my sister bickering over her cooking.

"Mom, can I ride back with Jess today," I asked, snatching my sausage back.

"Only if you take Daccy with you."

"But Mom, we're both in high school. Why do I need to babysit her?"

"I don't need babysitting," my sister added, snatching a piece of my sausage again, and popping it in her mouth. I glared at her and then gave Mom my puppy eyes. Despite my sister being a year younger than me, my parents always acted as if she was still a child, and of course that meant I had to look after her constantly.

"You need to stick together," Dad cut in, looking up from his newspaper with a glare that dared us to argue. His eyes were a stormy grey under his unruly jet-black hair. My stomach dropped. Was something wrong? He seemed more tense than normal. I dared not argue the issue further even as my mind pushed for me to recall something. A bad dream perhaps?

Nodding, I quickly finished my breakfast. I peeked at him again after a couple of minutes, but he was focused on his paper again. I always wondered if my dad had been some type of drill sergeant in his past, but since that discussion was off limits, I would never know. Just like one, Dad reminded me we had training right after school, just as a horn honked outside. I groaned but kept my mouth shut as Daccy and I ran to catch the bus.

***

I waved to Jess as she dropped us off at home, wishing that I was headed to her house instead. We lived at the very end of our suburb, and our house stood a little distance from our neighbors with woods surrounding it on two sides. We had been banned from those trees after the so-called "bull man" incident, but it still stood over us, watching, as if it held secrets it desperately wanted us to know. I didn't know why, but an ominous feeling slithered down my spine as we walked down the sidewalk to the front door. I shivered and glanced at the woods, but of course, nothing was there.

"You good?" My sister stopped and glanced between me and the trees. I'd told her about the "bull man" when it first happened, and she was the only one who said she believed me. Even after our parents had said it was just a bad dream. Yet, I hesitated. Even if I could feel in my bones that something was wrong, it had to be nothing. Just Dad's paranoia rubbing off on me. Right?

Shaking my head to clear it, I continued walking. "Yeah, just thought I heard something." She didn't look convinced but fell into step beside me again. Did she have a bad feeling too?

We walked in to see Mom polishing the twin blades we kept in a giant mahogany wardrobe by the front door. They were thin and long, made of black metal with intricate swirls that led to golden hilts with a dragon wrapped around each. It usually hung right behind our coats.

She had the key stand's drawer open to show the few daggers that were kept there. "For 'safe keeping'," Dad had told us long ago, but I still never understood my parents' need to keep such weapons around the house. Normal people kept guns. My family kept axes, swords, and bows. We were to never mention the training or weaponry to our friends, but I was responsible for knowing where all the hidden ones were located throughout the house.

On more than one occasion I'd asked why Daccy was exempt from the training. Although, she didn't mind. She'd rather work on her art than train anyway. I hated it and found it pointless, but Dad had just told me that I must learn to protect myself and my sister. That it was my responsibility as the oldest.

"Just think of it as a PE class," he'd said, and I had complained profusely before he'd given me "the glare" and I relented. Even now I still didn't take the training seriously. I did just enough to get by, just like PE class.

I walked down to the basement, or training room, as it had been re-purposed. Various types of blades, bows, arrows, and other weaponry adorned two of the walls. Weights and workout machines were laid out on the right, and a large mat was placed in front of the wall-length mirrors on the left.

In the empty spot in the center of the room, Dad was fighting imaginary adversaries with a one-handed sword in each hand. He swung left and right, ducking, and blocking as he went, unbothered by the weight in his hands. I grimaced. I could barely lift one of those swords with two hands, and here he was carrying two as if they were nothing but steak knives. He noticed me after a minute and lowered his swords slightly.

"You know the drill. Warm up and get ready." I grumbled to myself as I stretched, wishing once again that I could have gone to watch a movie with Jess or be anywhere but here. Sighing heavily as I wrapped my hands, I wondered what it would be like to have a normal life like the rest of my friends.

We practiced hand-to-hand combat and using two-handed blades – typical for Tuesdays and Thursdays. I had yet to master using the twin blades like the ones upstairs. If I dared to admit it to myself, I kind of enjoyed the kickboxing lessons. Those we did on Mondays, Wednesdays, and Fridays. After a two-hour session, he finally let me go to my relief.

"Silivia," he stopped me as I went to hurry upstairs. I had already carelessly thrown my sword into the rack. His eyes seemed sad as he said, "I know this seems pointless now, but someday you will understand that all your mother and I wanted to do was protect you." Hiding my confusion and trying not to roll my eyes, I nodded and rushed upstairs, hearing his deep sigh as I went.□

***

The air felt...wrong. It was too dry and cloudy as if somehow fog had formed inside the house. My throat felt like sandpaper and my eyes blurred as they protested the burning. I sat up from my bed suddenly realizing why the bright red-orange color of my room looked off. I glanced under my door to see bright lights and smoke slithering into the room. Choking now, I jumped out of the bed and reached for the doorknob, only to snatch my hand back with a hiss. Clutching my hand to my chest, I raced for the window and glanced briefly down the two stories before jumping and rolling to lessen the impact. I sucked in a breath as I felt my ankle twist but ignored it as I stood back to see that the entire house glowed with red-orange light. I recoiled in fear but realizing that I had yet to see any of my family, I ran around to the front door. I paused long enough to realize how odd it was that the door just stood ajar, but I didn't have a chance to linger on the thought.

I went to run upstairs but something had me stopping at the wardrobe and reaching behind the coats. I drew out the twin blades. They felt yet foreign in my hands, but while I wasn't sure what had drawn me to them, they felt right.

The heat licked at my ankles as I ran upstairs to Daccy's room first, only to find it in disarray, and her gone. I turned then to my parents' room, but a loud crash sounded from downstairs, and I quickly raced towards it. I dodged a flaming beam with a yelp as it landed in my path and then turned the corner into our living room to see the back door lying on the floor several feet away as if discarded. Outside I could see some men dressed in all black with giant, dripping red B's on their backs carrying my unconscious sister towards the black trees.

"Daccy!" I tried to scream but the smoke choked my words and before I could so much as run outside, she was gone, disappearing into the forbidden forest. Tears filled my burning eyes as I looked around for my parents. My heart skipped a beat, then stopped completely as I noticed my mom's twisted body surrounded by the dancing flames. A few feet away my dad was dressed in blood. I ran to him, my knees barking as I fell on them despite the ash and crackling light around me. Tears and smoke blinded me as I reached for him.

□"Silivia," I heard my dad whisper as I leaned over him.

"Dad?" He met my stricken gaze, trying to speak through his gasping breaths.

"They...wanted...you...You...have...to...save...your...sister. The clan... clan...clan...." A choking cough ripped through him, causing his body to convulse for a second.

"Where Dad? How do I find her?" I asked as he stilled, tears streaming down my face. The fire roared louder, and more beams crashed nearby making me jump.

"Find.... Master.... Marcus...." The rasping breath barely caused his chest to rise.

"But Dad, where?"

"Find…. him…. And…Silivia?" I waited, unable to speak. "I…. love…." He fell silent and his eyes unfocused as the storm stilled forever.

"Dad? Dad? DADDY!?!?" I gasped in pain, and finally unable to endure the heat any longer, I dragged myself outside, the blades still in my hands. I limped into the woods as the sirens screamed their way to my house.

☐"Too late. Too late," I thought as I hid myself in a secret area that I had found when I was a kid, my dad's words echoing in my head

They wanted you.

I started to cough and cry uncontrollably. It wasn't until after the tears had subsided to the occasional sob, and the light had faded, did I realize my hands and knees were uninjured. My mind drifted unbidden to a time when I was five.

"Silivia! "I turned to my frantic mother, tears blinding me. She dropped to her knees beside me, grabbing my twisted wrist. "Oh, my poor, poor baby," she crooned, her eyes glistening as she straightened my wrist with a snap and kissed it. I screamed and she held me tightly as I cried.

☐"It broken mommy! "I cried in agony.

"No, no my dear. It isn't," she assured me, and I went to protest, but for some reason I felt no pain. I stopped crying in shock and held up my wrist.

"Mommy?" I asked surprised. There was blood on me and the grass, but when she wiped my wrist with a wet finger, there was no wound.

"See my dear, not broken." I looked up at her in wonder, at the tree I had fallen from in my daring adventure as a monkey, and back at my wrist."

"Mommy fix it!" I exclaimed happily. She gave me a sad smile that I didn't understand as she took my hand and led me inside to be cleaned up.

I shook myself out of my revelry and glanced back down at my hands. I examined my knees, and they too were clear of any injury despite my torn and burnt pajamas.

"What's wrong with me," I thought franticly, feeling tears beginning to clog my throat again.

They wanted you.

"But why Daddy? Why me!" I tried to breathe through my sobs as I watched the firefighters tackle the fire that roared and only spread its arms higher the more they battled, until finally, as if its tantrum was over, it began to calm and die. Our neighbors stood outside, probably worried that the fire would spread to their houses next.

"Why me?" I whispered to the night, as everything died down and I drifted to sleep.

***

Find Master Marcus.

I jerked awake. Dawn was just starting to peek over the horizon. I felt stiff and sore inside and out and hugged myself as I replayed my dad's words. The firefighters were still outside my house, as well as several police cars, but I knew they could not save my sister.

Find Master Marcus.

"But how and where Dad?" I yelled exasperated. Exhausted from all the crying and the ordeal despite falling asleep, I lay back against a tree, put my head onto my knees, and wrapped my arms around them. I closed my eyes wearily. After a while, I realized that I was in the forest that my parents had told us to avoid, and yet, this was the first place I had run to. Something about it had always drawn me in even as a child, and it had been my secret hiding spot until...

I stood to my feet, gripping the twin blades as I realized this was the area where I had supposedly seen the "bull man" appear.

"Was he real," I wondered, glancing around the patch of trees for some clue. I walked towards the one birch that seemed out of place among the other trees. Its twisted white and black branches seemed to wave me over, and I rested my hand against its bark. It felt weirdly warm to the touch like a mother's embrace, and I pressed harder against it only to have my hand disappear altogether. I gasped in shock and jerked my hand back. I glanced towards where our house used to be and back at the tree.

Find Master Marcus.

I took in a sharp breath, and I reached for the tree again. "There is nothing left for me here," I thought sadly, and with a deep breath, I stepped into the tree.

Curious to know what happens next? Follow Silivia as she fights to safe her sister, conquerors her father's world, and faces her heart's true desire in the <u>Fall of the Dragon King Trilogy!</u>

Afterthoughts

As I was working on the final book for Silivia and Ghost's story in the Fall of the Dragon King Trilogy, I started wondering what came next. It was a series a long time in the making, and there was sadness at the idea that it was coming to an end. But what would I write next?

I've always had a deep love for nature. I grew up with the forest in my backyard all my life, and if I was outside, there was a good chance I was within it exploring every part. Nature was, and is, my happy place. One of the things that always fascinated me was how balanced it was. Without fires, young plants never get a chance to grow. Water carves pathways through rock creating places like the Grand Canyon. Entire islands are often created by a volcanic eruption.

Then one day I thought, what if I built a story based on this needed balance? And with that, the Forces of Nature series was born. I hope you grow to appreciate the view of nature – all aspects of it – through their eyes as the series continues. Nothing in nature is inheritable good or bad, and honestly, there's a kind of magic in that alone.

Thank you to my Beta Readers for sharing their thoughts in those early days. You gave me the confidence to write the romance I enjoy reading so much. Shout out also to the Dragon Royals! Having a street team like you makes reaching readers easier and a lot more fun! Special shoutout to my Mom who manages to listen to me read every single one of my very long stories. You'll always be my number one cheerleader.

And of course, thank you to all the other readers out there who know there is no greater escape than the worlds found within a good book.

About the Author

Shaquilla M. Lunsford, better known as the "Dragon Queen", is known for writing fantasy worlds full of magic and majestic creatures. She enjoys the complexity and creativity required to develop an entirely new world with its own set of rules and characters. With her love of dragons, they usually make an appearance in her writing or daily life. She also draws inspiration from Greek and Roman mythology to create some creatures and characters, and sheer imagination for others.

Despite Shaquilla's passion for fantasy, poetry is her first love because it offers a freedom of open expression without judgement. It is where she first learned to create vivid imagery and metaphors of everyday experiences and emotions. This skill often leaks into her novels, and the poetry incorporated is usually her own.

Shaquilla developed her passion for both poetry and fantasy stories while growing up in North Carolina. She currently lives with her "mini zoo" (consisting of three types of reptiles, a cat, and a dog) as she continues to cultivate her love for writing.